The Girl
in the
Cottage
by the
Sea

BOOKS BY REBECCA ALEXANDER

Rebecca Alexander

The Girl
in the
Cottage
by the
Sea

bookouture

Published by Bookouture in 2024

An imprint of Storyfire Ltd.
Carmelite House
50 Victoria Embankment
London EC4Y 0DZ

www.bookouture.com

ISBN: 978-1-83790-736-6
eBook ISBN: 978-1-83790-735-9

To Léonie, my little lion, who taught me that life is measured in love, laughter and memories, not years.

PROLOGUE

PRESENT DAY, EIGHT MONTHS AGO

The pain shot down her arm like lightning, zapping up into her jaw and sparking and burning down her left side. Amber Marrak woke fully, wondering with some confusion if she'd dreamed the pain, or if something terrible had happened, like an earthquake. The sunlit bedroom looked the same as usual, but she couldn't move, pinned to the bed by the residue of that horrible agony.

This time she moved more cautiously, trying to sit up, but the pain was just as bad and her right arm didn't move with her left one. She was alone in the London apartment; Patrick had a commission overseas.

Her next thought was that she was going to be late for rehearsals with the orchestra. She needed to be there – tonight she would lead the strings at London's Royal Albert Hall.

What's going on? She tried lifting her head to squint down at her arm but the pain returned, making her scream involuntarily. *Where is my phone?*

It was set to sound an alarm at eight, but she often knocked it off the bedside table. By rolling her eyes and painfully turning her head a few inches, each move sending new flame into her head and body, she could just about see it. It was balancing on the edge but still there. Moving her right hand very slowly, setting off smaller aftershocks, she managed to grip it and bring it slowly back to her face.

Four minutes past eight, on one of the most significant days of her career: a televised concert attended by royalty. She held the phone so she could see it, her eyes blurry with tears from the pain. She dialled the number.

Three hours later, Amber was awaiting the results of a detailed MRI scan of her neck and arms. Words like 'life threatening' and 'life changing' had been thrown around, and her mother was on her way to London from the Atlantic Islands: three flights and a taxi across London that would take her most of the day. The painkillers she'd been given made her nauseous, and the drug for the nausea made her sleepy.

'What's happening?' The gentle voice was Kerry, her oldest friend and fellow musician in the orchestra. Amber opened her eyes to find herself in a hospital bed.

'We're just working that out,' came an older woman's voice. 'Amber?'

Amber tried to move her head but found she couldn't, her neck was clamped in some kind of painful contraption. An oxygen mask was fitted over her face. She struggled and the sharp pain flashed through her again, hardly muted by the drugs.

'Stay very still,' the woman said, and came into fuzzy focus. She looked kind, her smile genuine. 'Ah, there you are, you've been a bit out of it. What do you remember?'

'Pain,' Amber croaked before she realised her mouth was dry and she hadn't spoken for a while. She cleared her throat. 'I just felt this awful pain when I tried to move this morning.'

'We have to wait for a detailed examination of the scan you

had, but it looks like you have a bulging disc in your neck. We need to stop it completely slipping and damaging the nerves to your arms and body.'

'Will I...' Amber thought fast. 'Will I have to have physio or wear a collar?'

The woman laughed, but not unkindly. 'Both. But after the surgery. We can't leave it like that. Things could get much, much worse if we don't act now.'

'*Surgery*? And what do you mean, *worse*?'

What if I can't play? The idea shot through her as shocking and agonising as the pain. She tried to lift her arms a little, but nothing worked and the lightning returned, flashing down her whole body and making her cry out.

Tears were streaming down her face, wetting her ears and her neck under the collar, and Kerry was there, holding a tissue.

'Blow,' she said, with practical kindness, and mopped Amber up. 'Your mother's on her way. She should have landed by now; hopefully she'll get here in time.'

'In time?' Amber whispered.

'Before your emergency surgery,' Kerry said. 'They are assembling a team specially for you.'

'Will I' – the thought was almost too big to confront – 'play again?'

'Sweetheart, let's make sure you can walk again and pee by yourself first,' Kerry said, trying to sound teasing and light, but her eyes were filled with tears.

'I need to play,' Amber rasped. Nothing seemed more important.

Kerry's hazel eyes darkened with understanding. 'I know,' she said, her voice reverberating with that same passion she put into her own music. 'Don't worry, Amber, I won't let them forget how important it is to you.'

1

PRESENT DAY, 2 OCTOBER

Amber Marrak stood looking into the doorway of the smoke-blackened cottage. She was in a little side court behind a blue door, halfway up Warren Lane, which led from the cobbled quay. Within the side court, the burned cottage in the middle stood out from its three pastel-painted neighbours, all arranged around a yard full of pots of flowers. The cottages looked old, their walls sagging a little as if they were relaxed and about to sit down. Several windows were ajar, letting in the October sunshine and mild air.

Beehive Cottage's white paint had either flaked off or had bubbled off in the heat. The front windows were boarded up, the door stood open, and music drifted out. It wasn't even good music: there was some horrible drumbeat and a singer shouting over the top.

Amber stepped away from the bags she had dragged up the hill with the box of supplies. She put one hand on the door, thin and pale since her surgery, and leaned on the frame. Then, pushing her dark, straight hair out of her eyes, she shouted, 'Hello?'

The music was turned off, replaced with a silence that she

found unnerving. The black interior stank of the damage the fire had wreaked, and bare electrical wires hung down from the ceiling and walls. The floor was reduced to a charred wreckage of boards and joists, criss-crossed with a scaffolding plank path stretching to the back room.

'Oh. Hi,' said a man around her own age, mid twenties, balanced on one of the scaffold beams in the doorway to a back room. 'Can I help you?' He pushed back his hard hat to reveal a dirty face, dark red curls and a slim frame. The doorway just brushed the top of his head – he was a lot taller than her.

'I'm Amber Marrak,' she said, hoping he had received the messages her father had sent. 'I'm here to help with the restoration.'

'I know who you are,' he said with a wry smile. 'I'm Ben Kevell, the builder. I thought you were a musician.'

'I am,' she said, looking up at the ceiling. It had fallen down in places, bits of plaster dangling from what looked like horse-hair; the joists underneath looked solid, though blackened by the heat and smoke. 'I'm taking some time off,' she said shortly. Not wanting to explain about her injury, she stepped onto one of the planks. 'Can I come in?'

'It's your house,' he said, and disappeared into the back room. 'Watch yourself,' he shouted back. 'There's a hard hat on the windowsill.'

Once her eyes adapted to the low light sneaking around the panel over the window, she made out that the room was square. To her left, there was an enormous chimney breast taking up most of the wall, and the window on her right and the small door at the back of the room were charred. She jammed the hat on.

'It's my family's house, not mine,' she said, looking through into the back room.

It had recently been a kitchen; a melted fridge and a few burned kitchen units sat on a floor of peeling lino tiles. Looking at the old cooker, now sitting in the middle of the room, she could see the place had been old and rundown, which was probably why she'd never been here before. She remembered her mother saying they had had summer staff staying in it for a couple of years, but not recently. When she'd said she needed to get away for a while, her dad had suggested she could take on the project as a distraction. He thought it just needed a new kitchen and bathroom and a bit of decorating – maybe he hadn't seen it in person. At least it had been empty when something, perhaps lightning, started a fire.

'Why aren't we knocking it down and rebuilding?' she asked, gingerly ducking under the sagging back door. A spider's web hung from it, sprinkled with soot. There was a walled courtyard outside, now filled with bags of rubble.

'It's listed,' he said. 'And in a conservation area. And it's three hundred years old.'

'Is there a bathroom?'

'Loo and sink in the yard,' he said, inadvertently rubbing more soot onto his forehead, which made her laugh. 'No better, huh?' he said, with a reluctant smile. 'Basically, unless you're a plasterer or a carpenter, I can't see what you can do to help.' He looked down at her with a curled lip. 'You don't look as heavy as my rubble bags, which will need lugging down to the quay for the boat.'

'I'm stronger than I look,' she said, flexing her good arm. 'Anyway, my dad's happy for me to supervise and help where I can. I needed something to do.' She twisted her left wrist, feeling the ache already. She couldn't have stayed in the same place as Patrick, not after she'd called off the wedding. 'I'm going to get us a coffee, at least I can start with that,' she offered.

'Go to the Quay Café, then. Say Ben wants a refill,' he said, turning back to put his music on. 'It's on the seafront.'

She lifted a hand and almost asked him to turn it down, but she didn't want to antagonise him. She wrestled her bags and box across the front room and stacked them up at the bottom of the narrow stairs – charred threads of carpet clinging to them – before walking onto the cobbled street beyond the courtyard and down Warren Lane towards the quay.

The houses were all painted different colours, from bold to pastel, jumbled together from different eras and designs. The summer was having a last hurrah, light October winds following her down to the small row of shops and restaurants along the sea wall.

A few fishing boats were tied up, swaying on the high tide that she had just come in on. Beyond, maybe forty or fifty yachts bobbed on their mooring buoys for the last weeks of the holiday season. One end of the quay had a large, handsome pub called the Island Queen, with a picture of a fishing vessel on it. In front of it, a slipway was covered with dinghies and kayaks. Over the top of the pub, she could see the spire of the church. At the other end of the cobbled quay was a row of ancient cottages, crammed in a tight row, all different sizes and ages. In between them were scattered a deli, an art gallery, a gift shop and a café. She vaguely remembered having an ice cream there as a child, but it was painted in a smart green and white rather than the blue she recalled.

The door was full of posters for local events and groups. The largest was a shanty concert raising money for a child's medical treatment. The child was beautiful, maybe six or seven, smiling up at the photographer with big eyes and auburn hair. She recognised him as the same child who had been carried onto the small ferry by his parents, bags and a special wheel-chair with them, at St Brannock's. She had gathered from the pilot's conversation with the dad that their child had spent weeks away in London having surgery. It made the neuro-surgery scar on her own throat itch.

The Quay Café door was open, leading into an ancient-looking building, the internal walls gone to leave a cosy space with a dozen mismatched tables. A glass door led outside via steps, each one home to a different pot of late-blooming flowers. It was charming, and a relief to visit a place where she probably wasn't known.

She walked over to the counter, and a woman put her head around the kitchen door. 'Find a table and I'll take your order,' she said, swinging her ponytail. 'Inside or out? We've got some sunny tables up the garden.'

'I was just going to get takeaway coffees...' She hesitated. She had been dropped off on the morning tide, before she'd had breakfast. 'Actually, outside would be lovely. Could you hold a table for two? I just have to get someone... I'll be ten minutes.' She jogged back to the cottage.

Ben was banging on the back wall with a sledgehammer, and she had to time her shout to fit between his swings. He might be slim but he hefted the heavy tool effortlessly. 'Hey!' she shouted.

He turned to look at her, taking off his headphones and goggles. 'No coffee?'

'I thought I would buy you breakfast,' she said. 'And we could talk about the job. Since I *am* going to be helping you.'

He dusted his hands on his jeans, shook off his T-shirt and put down his tools. 'Only because I want one of the Quay Café's legendary bacon sandwiches,' he said, after a pause. 'And you're right. I do think we need to talk.'

As they walked down to the café, she realised just how dirty he was. There was soot on his face, plaster dust in his hair and handprints all over his clothes.

'I asked for a table in the garden,' she said, looking him up and down.

'Probably for the best,' he said, chuckling and looking down at his attire as they got to the café. 'But they're used to me dropping plaster everywhere.'

Amber walked through to the steps and up to the back.

As someone who had grown up in a mediaeval manor house with a world famous botanical garden, she appreciated the combination of formal planting and rambling wildness that created an idyllic space. When her grandparents had run West Island Manor, the gardens had been a wonderful playground for Amber as the only grandchild. But when she was nine, everything changed and her parents had moved to the estate to run its successful holiday cottages and try to make the manor hotel profitable after heavy inheritance tax. Amber was away at music schools much of the time, but the island always felt like home, although she often expected to bump into Grandpa with his secateurs at every turn. His loss added a quiet sadness to exploring the paths and looking out from the viewpoints, running her hands over the monkey puzzle trees he had loved.

The stone walls enclosing the café garden were covered with fruit espaliers, still heavy with late apples and passion fruits. Climbing roses dipped their heads and spread amazing scent and petals around the tables. One table had menus on it and a basket full of cutlery, the others were bare. A laminated flyer on the table had that cute kid on it.

'I saw this little boy this morning, on the ferry,' she said, picking it up. 'He looked very sleepy and sick, though.'

'Yeah, they're trying to raise money for a special course of radiotherapy. He's my cousin's boy, Kai.' He leaned the flyer against a pot of cutlery. 'So, what do you think of the café?'

'It's very pretty,' she said, breathing in the scent of recently trimmed lavender hedges and the musk roses.

'It's only just opened,' he said, looking around as he sat down. 'It will be packed in half an hour.' He smiled, his teeth very white against the dirt as he looked up at the woman Amber had met earlier. 'Hello, Lucy. Miss Marrak is treating the help to a bacon sandwich.'

Even while Lucy took down his order, Amber was furious at the way he'd just talked about her. And she would have preferred him not to trumpet her name all over the islands just now.

'Hi,' she said to Lucy. 'I'm Amber, I'll be here working with Ben for a few weeks.'

Lucy raised an eyebrow but said nothing. 'What can I get you?'

Amber went for scrambled eggs and a pot of tea, while Ben ordered a large coffee to go with his sandwich. As Lucy walked away, Amber turned to Ben, but he beat her to it.

'Let's get something straight,' he said, sitting back in his chair. 'You're not helping me, because I can't think of anything an untrained person could actually do. Your dad asked me to keep an eye on you.'

'What? B-but...'

'I know who you are, and I know what happened,' he said, looking back at her, light green eyes staring into her blue ones. He held his hands up. 'I'm not judging, I don't know why you called off your wedding and I don't want to know. But I built the semicircular wall in the sunken garden at the manor with Patrick. I know him. He's a good man. A friend.'

She couldn't answer, words stormed up but she couldn't say them. *Yes, he is.* She glanced down at the pale circle where her engagement ring had sat until recently. *And you are judging.*

'I must be able to do something useful at the cottage,' she said, her voice flat. 'And I expect you to let me help. I promise not to get in the way.'

He looked around the garden. 'Maybe you can help decorate, further down the line,' he said, finally.

'I'm sure you can teach me to do much more than that,' she said, firmly. 'I'm a quick learner.'

'Sir Michael said you had to rest your arm, though. Some sort of injury or something.'

'I damaged a disc in my neck, it was paralysing me. I had surgery on the nerves in my left arm too, and now I have to exercise. I can't play music as much as before, but I can't just keep still either,' she said through gritted teeth. 'My right arm is fine for the heavy stuff.'

He fell silent again, looking unconvinced. By the time their breakfasts had been delivered, she had fought back tears of anger and was ready to speak again.

'I don't know what you've heard about me and Patrick but that's our private business,' she said. 'I need something to do while I'm taking a break from my career as my wrist heals. My parents and I agreed it would be good for me to take some time away from West Island, make things a little easier for Patrick too. I think he's planning to stay on Westy for the time being. So, I came over here to help with the refurbishment of Beehive Cottage. That's it.'

He sipped his coffee, then blew on its patterned surface. 'It's not my job to make up little tasks for you to do that won't hurt your arm or upset you,' he said.

'I'm upset already,' she said, dashing away a stray tear. She couldn't find words for how hollow she felt inside. 'I will look after my wrist. Now, if you half fill those rubbish bags back at the cottage, I'll move them for you. I could do with the exercise.'

She had lost so much muscle while she'd had to rest. It would be good to feel like she was doing *something*.

He took a bite of his sandwich, and for a long time didn't say anything as she nibbled on her toast and the delicious eggs. She glanced over at the flyer about the child, wondered where to donate.

'Where are you staying?' he asked abruptly.

She poured her tea out and looked up at him. 'On the island, obviously.'

A slow smile lit up his face, as if he was amused. 'There won't be a hotel room or self-catering cottage available until after half-term,' he said. 'The whole island is booked up.'

Oh. She thought fast. 'Then I'll be staying at Beehive. I can rough it for a few weeks.'

He almost choked on his coffee. 'You can't... I can't make it ready – or even safe – in one day.'

'Well, you'll need my help then, won't you?' she improvised. 'If we're going to get it ready by tonight.'

'And – it's haunted,' he said. 'Honestly, everyone knows it is.'

She tossed her hair back, suppressing a little shiver at his intensity. 'One thing I am *not* afraid of is ghosts.'

2

OCTOBER 1943

Georgina Preston sat on the small boat with her children, surrounded by the few bags of belongings they had managed to salvage after a bomb went off next to their home in London. Fire had swept through their whole terrace, leaving very little of their lives from before the war.

She felt terribly alone, out here on the vast ocean, looking after two young children and starting afresh without her husband. Jim had been away at war for some time, but before the bomb she'd had the company of Lena, their elderly cook. Lena had been buried in the rubble while collecting their belongings, and had been rescued by firefighters and wardens, emerging battered but alive. She had decided to retire and stay with her sister while her broken shoulder healed, and while Georgie wished her well, she missed the banter of another adult, someone who had become a friend. Lena had also been an invaluable help with the children and a grandmother figure to them – Georgie's parents and Jim's parents were dead. After the bomb, while staying in a hostel room on the edge of Croydon, Georgina had reached out to Jim's great-aunt, Lady Alice, who lived in a large home in Cheltenham.

But Great-Aunt Alice didn't want them to stay. Her family owned a house on Morwen Island in the Atlantic Isles that Jim had loved as a child, and she had made it over to Jim and Tommy. Since the waiting list in London for rehousing was over two years, Georgie had no choice but to pack up what little was left and head for a place she had never been to. Jim had always described it as the 'perfect holiday cottage'. Two rooms downstairs, two up, no garden. At least it would be a roof over their heads.

Georgie fought back tears at the thought of Jim. He was missing; the ship he had been on had been sunk, and she could not stop worrying that something terrible had happened to him. She was all alone. She felt like one of those children waiting to be put on a train to be evacuated, with no idea where they were going. Of course, it was terribly generous of Jim's great-aunt to arrange for them to have the cottage, and she was grateful, but she didn't know anyone there and she needed a friend now more than ever. Thomas was ten, terribly sensitive to what had happened to his beloved Lena, and little Dolly was getting more demanding now she was five. She was full of questions, including the dreaded 'where *is* Daddy?'

The question of what 'missing' meant seemed to stretch across the world. Nobody had been able to tell her where Jim was for nearly six months. A few weeks ago, just before the bomb went off in the basement of number five, something must have changed, because the bank had written to say that Jim's wages had now stopped. Another plain envelope had arrived this morning; she had stuffed it in her coat as she left the hostel and couldn't bear to open it. She was terribly afraid that it was going to confirm his death.

After travelling all day by train and then ferry, they had another couple of miles to go on an open boat, optimistically called 'the Morwen ferry' by the harbourmaster. They were the only passengers.

'Can I help row?' Thomas asked the ferryman, Mr Ellis, who stank of tobacco burning in an ornate pipe, and had a grey beard halfway down his chest. 'I'm quite strong, sir.'

'Are ye?' he asked back, and moved over to let the boy squeeze in next to him and hold one of the oars. 'Mebbe ye can, mebbe ye can't,' he said, spitting over the side of the boat and letting Tommy try.

With a little help from the old man's left hand, Tommy started pulling the huge oar, and the boat began to move away from the shallows.

'You taking on Beehive Cottage, then, missus?' he asked her, his whole frame bent into the work of moving the boat. Tommy was already sweating and sliding on the seat.

'Yes. Do you know it?' She sat upright, holding down the fluttering hem of her dress, glad of her cardigan against the cool wind. It had been a waste of time to curl her shoulder-length dark hair over the gas stove this morning – the wind was pulling at her scarf already. Dolly squeezed close to her, keeping one side warm.

'I do. I was born two doors down from the court it's in,' he said, not missing a beat as Tommy's hand slipped off the oar and the little boy half fell back into the boat. 'You caught a crab,' he chuckled, but Tommy was soon back on the oar. 'One, two,' he said, encouraging him. 'That's it, lad, you've got the rhythm of it.'

'His father used to row,' she said, to encourage Tommy, but the memory of Jim rowing for Cambridge when they were both young caught in her throat, filling her eyes with tears. 'He won against Oxford in the coxed eights in 1931.' He was so tall; she had almost forgotten how small he made her feel.

'That's just one oar each, too, isn't it?' Tommy puffed.

The man let go of the end of the oar and let the boy pull a few strokes by himself. 'I reckon you'll make a good gig rower in your time,' he said, taking the end of the oar again as the boat veered slightly. 'Like your dad. Once you fill out.'

Dolly pressed closer to Georgie's side as the waves became choppier, mists of spray hitting them. Georgie was struggling with her tears now, gazing away from the two rowers, remembering Jim grinning up from the winning boat, jumping ashore to hug her off her feet. She'd give so much for him to hold her right now.

She cleared her throat. 'Is Morwen far?' she said, looking at the white sand of the approaching island.

'It's beyond this one. This is St Piran's island, nice for a picnic,' said Mr Ellis, smiling at little Dolly. 'Some of this beach is mined, but the other side isn't.'

The war had even followed them to these beautiful islands. 'That will be nice, won't it, Dolly?' she said, looking down at her subdued daughter. 'Sandcastles and paddling.'

The boat pulled along the tiny quay on St Piran's, and Georgie looked out at the cluster of houses and shops, and a small tower bearing a flag. 'We swing around the back of this island, then the currents will push us over to Morwen.' Mr Ellis was grunting with the effort of working against the tide. They were quite close to the shore, and Georgie could see minefield signs up on the corner of the island as they crept past.

On the other side of the next stretch of water were a few rock stacks covered with seabirds, and beyond them, a taller, dark island rising out of the sea. A small village with colourful houses lined the shore.

'Is that Morwen?'

It looked like a place from a story book, the streets and houses raking up the hill. It was tiny, with a grey church at one end. The land swept up behind the village to green fields and there was a large building on the very top of the island. A couple of boats were tied up to the quay, and a few more were working their way down to the open sea.

'Tide's good for fishing,' he mumbled around his pipe. 'Look at them seals,' he said, taking one hand off the oar to point to a few round black heads in the water.

'Dolly, look, seals!' As the boat swung into the racing water, they got closer. 'Look at their faces, like big puppies,' she said. Even Dolly leaned forward to look and smiled at their whiskery curiosity.

'Right. Now, lad, you've got to give it everything to get across this current. We call it the Sound,' he said, and they started heaving harder. The water was choppy enough to lift the open boat with each wave and slap it back onto the water, making Dolly scream the first time. Georgie fixed a smile on her face, telling her it was all an adventure, and wasn't it exciting. Thomas was spent, his thin chest heaving in his wet shirt, sea spray in his hair.

'You want to help, missus?' the old man said.

She waved at Tommy to swap with her, slid into place beside the old man and folded her coat beside her. The oar was ridiculously heavy, and as she pulled, her body slipped on the seat at first, but once she got going she found a movement which worked. She slipped off her low-heeled court shoes, let her bare feet grip the boards and pulled as hard as she could.

'One – two – one – two...' he counted and she realised she needed to keep her strokes short enough so she wouldn't fall backwards like Tommy had. *Catch a crab, indeed.*

Her hair started to fall out of her scarf and fly around her face but she focused on pulling again and again. 'That's it, missus,' he shouted over the wind, blowing strongly now. 'Just over the Sound, it will be better as we get near the island.'

'Well done, Mummy!' Tommy shouted, and hugged Dolly as she clapped.

Georgie was tired after a few minutes, but she closed her eyes and pulled, returned, pulled, thinking of Jim, what he would have said. *Good girl, Georgie...*

Her summer dress stretched and tore a few stitches at the armhole, which would mean more mending, but she put the thought aside.

'Ease up, missus,' the man said in her ear in a cloud of pipe smoke. When she opened her eyes, the water was flatter, little waves rolling up to the quay. It looked like it was made of solid rock.

'Oh, we're nearly there,' she said to the children. 'That's good.'

'Here, lad, take my oar,' he said to Tommy and threw a rope to a man waiting on a slipway. As they pulled alongside the slope, Georgie gathered up her shoes and bags and slipped her coat back on. The letter in her pocket rustled.

'Thank you, Mr Ellis,' she said primly as he handed her out of the boat, and she gave him a whole shilling,

'Thank *you*, missus,' he said, laughing, his eyes gleaming, as he passed her bags to the man on the quay. 'Seems your husband isn't the only rower in the family.' He leaned down to Dolly. 'We'll get you rowing when you're big enough. My granddaughters love going in the gig races. Patience can sail, too.'

'Are there other children here?' Dolly asked.

'Quite a classful. You'll meet them all at school,' he said. 'It's just up that hill, beyond Beehive Cottage.' He gave them precise directions, then whistled to a boy standing ready. 'Robbie, help this lady up the hill, lad.'

'You've been very kind,' Georgie said, on impulse.

'Well, you take care in that house.' He walked away before she could ask him more, but in his words, there was the hint of a warning.

3

PRESENT DAY, 2 OCTOBER

Back at Beehive Cottage, Amber looked around the second bedroom. Ben had already taken most of the plaster off, and the wooden framework of the wall between the two bedrooms was lined with stone, mud and horsehair. The window was intact but stuck half open, the sashes swollen and crumbling with rot. The top pane of glass had a crack right across it, secured with yellow hazard tape, and it looked over the small yard at the back and the fields beyond.

'People were really living in here, just a couple of years ago?' she said, finding it hard to believe. 'No wonder it's supposed to be haunted. By deathwatch beetle and dry rot.'

'That's what all old cottages are like when you take the wallpaper and paint off. This one's especially bad.'

The manor where she had grown up was even older, originally a twelfth century abbey. It had been taken over by her distant ancestors in the fifteen eighties. It had never looked like this, she was sure, not even when it was being renovated. The great building was stone through and through, castellated along its top ridge and with the original chapel now a tourist attraction. Amber's family still lived in the Tudor part of the abbey, which was extended into a hotel a hundred years before.

Ben was right; there wasn't a hotel or Airbnb available to rent on the island until after half-term. She searched through her suitcase. She had brought a blanket from home, and she had a long, padded jacket that could double as bedding, so she just needed something to lie on.

'Do you think the shop would have an airbed?' she asked, giving up on her search for something to use as a temporary mat and starting to bag up the grit and debris he had swept up. It raised plaster dust and made her cough.

'The campsite has a little shop, but it's probably closed at the moment,' he said. 'You could call them, though, see what they have in.' He nodded to the window. 'It's just along the lane. They do gas as well, maybe they have a little stove so you can make tea, and you could do with a battery lantern or a torch.' He frowned a warning at her. 'Don't set fire to the rest of the house, though.' He looked at his phone, and texted her the phone number of the campsite. 'They're lovely people, they won't let you suffer if they can help it.'

He disappeared onto the tiny landing and stomped down the stairs. She called the number, and despite the dodgy signal she managed a few words with a man who told her to walk down to the campsite to see what he had in store.

'Thank you for the suggestion,' she called to Ben. 'And for all your hard work. I'm just off to see what he has.'

'It's meant to go down to seven, eight degrees tonight,' he warned her as she went downstairs. 'If you get stuck, ask your neighbour for help. Betty gives me hot water for tea when I ask. Don't freeze to death. That wouldn't do my reputation with your father much good.'

'You can tell him it was all my idea.' She waved goodbye and headed up the hill, turning along the lane. Past a few holiday cottages looking over the town and out to sea, there was a field where a couple of tents were ranged in the lee of the wall facing the prevailing winds. She wrapped her jacket closer around her.

An older man met her at a reception hut. 'You're in luck,' he said, smiling. 'There were some tents and equipment left behind after the music festival in the summer. We sell them off for a donation to the lifeboat. This is our last few weeks – we close after half-term.'

She was able to choose a reasonable-looking airbed and even a sleeping bag. He added a camping cooking set with a couple of saucepans and a tiny kettle, and a brand-new portable stove with a few gas bottles.

'I'd get along to the village shop before it closes,' he warned. 'Get yourself something for breakfast and some milk, teabags and so on.'

'Thank you so much,' she said, almost as grateful for the kind smiles as the help. It had all been cool politeness back home on West Island once word had spread that she'd called off the wedding. A pang hit her stomach as she thought of Patrick, the prize-winning and much-loved garden designer of the manor. She had hoped islanders would have had more loyalty to her as a daughter of the islands, but no, the newcomer seemed to get all the sympathy. She couldn't really blame them, as she had almost left him at the altar, but she hoped the news hadn't reached *everyone* on nearby Morwen, too.

Down at the shop, she chose cereal and milk, tea bags and instant coffee, and at the gift shop next door she picked up a gorgeous enamel mug in sea colours. On impulse, she got a spare one, too, for guests or for Ben.

Back at Beehive Cottage, Amber set the stove up on a workbench Ben had left upstairs, filled the kettle from a half-full water bottle and rinsed out a cup. By the time the kettle was whistling and she had made a cup of tea, she was feeling rather proud of herself.

Ben had also left an electric lamp upstairs, and a battery pack he used for his radio. The single bright light made sharp shadows out of everything, and no amount of sweeping was going to make the floor clean, or free of spiders. The temperature, briefly warmed by the gas flame under the kettle, was sliding down as the light faded. Wind clattered the window in its frame, and whistled over the top sash around her ears. She could have sworn it was carrying a song – just whispers and snatches of melody.

As Amber sipped her tea and warmed her hands around the new mug, she felt lonely for the first time. The pressure of coming to the island, her shock at the state of Beehive Cottage, and even pretending to be bright and breezy with successive people from the boatman to Ben to the campsite owner... It had been difficult at times. Distractions gone, all she could think about was last week, when she had lain in Patrick's arms, sleepily talking about the wedding plans, feeling her nerves begin to twitch at the huge mistake they were making.

She had been going through something for a while, a slow realisation that the wedding was coming too soon and that she wasn't sure Patrick was the love of her life. Being vulnerable in hospital, he had been a huge support, and it seemed wonderful when he asked her to marry him, so they could get through this together. He was so funny and kind and warm – she ought to love him completely. But their whole relationship had been made up of intense episodes of stolen meetings and brief holidays where their work had taken them – with never enough time to really get to know each other. They had met originally when he was working on the manor gardens, and the attraction had been immediate. It was an absolute coup for her father to persuade him to make his base at the manor, and to house him in the gardener's cottage, now freshly renovated for them both.

The last few months, they had lived together out of necessity as she was diagnosed with nerve damage in her wrist and a bulging disc in her neck. It had been lovely to be surrounded by her family and Patrick while she was healing and feeling vulnerable, afraid she might never play at a high level again. But her gratitude wasn't enough to match his burning, all-encompassing passion for her.

She donned the long coat, made up a sort of bed corner with the airbed and sleeping bag, and draped her colourful blanket over the top. It had been on her bed this morning when she'd packed. It evoked the ghost of Patrick, his aftershave, that warm scent of his skin when he woke in the morning.

That brought the tears.

Amber woke the next morning, stiff and shivering, to the sound of people talking and laughing outside. Ben had a distinctive voice, low, quite musical, and the woman's voice was high and giggly. She struggled to her feet, piling up the layers of clothes she had used as blankets over the half-deflated airbed. Either her injured arm didn't ache so much, or the rest of her ached more, she couldn't decide. A blast of cold air up the stairs led her down to close the door. She squinted into the sun: Ben was standing with an old lady with a head of white curls and round blue eyes. They were both staring at her.

'Oops.' Ben waved at his own face. 'You might need to look in a mirror,' he said, smiling.

'Oh, hair,' she said, and swept it back off her face, the tangles catching in her fingers. 'I was more concerned about hypothermia,' she said, looking around. The adjoining house's door was standing open. 'Hello – are you my neighbour?' she said, trying a smile.

'I am, lovey,' the old lady said, extending a hand. 'I'm Betty. The other cottages are just holiday lets, they've both got couples in at the moment. Oh my, your hands are so cold! Do you want to come in for a cup of tea, maybe use the bathroom? The radiator in there is on, you can warm up.'

'Yes, please,' Amber said, unable to face the outside loo with its cold water and stained and spider-infested basin. 'That would be wonderful. I'll just grab my stuff.'

'Come on in too, Ben, I'll fill up your flask as well.'

Betty's cottage was like a doll's house, the front room so small Amber could almost have reached straight across it, then down a step – minding her head as the doorway was low – into a warm kitchen. It smelled like toast. A kettle was gleaming next to an old china sink, and a flowery tablecloth sat on a minute table.

'Bathroom's through there,' Betty said, waving at an open door to an old-fashioned but warm bathroom. Amber shut the door and looked at the mirrored cabinet. She looked like a ghost, with hollows for eyes where her mascara had smudged.

After a good wash with the most deliciously scented soap, she felt ready for the world. She couldn't do much about the rumpled clothes, but could at least take a couple of layers off and brush her bedraggled hair straight again before plaiting it and going out to face Betty and Ben.

A mug sat waiting for her, steaming lightly, along with a toast rack full of brown triangles.

'I've only got real butter,' Betty apologised. 'I know you young people like all sorts of nonsense, but I likes the real thing.'

'Me too. This is so kind,' Amber said, sitting on the spare chair. Her knees bumped against the table as she squeezed in, and she mused that people must have been shorter when the furniture was made.

'Do you take sugar? Benny Boy has sugar,' Betty said.

Benny Boy? She glanced at him; he had turned a little pink under his tan.

'Just with coffee, Bets,' he said, and took a huge bite of his toast. 'I have known Betty since I was tiny,' he added, as explanation.

'Your mam brought you round when you was three weeks old,' Betty said, sitting back and beaming at them both.

Amber scraped a little butter on her toast, noticing that the bread bag was empty, the butter dish almost finished. Betty probably hadn't been expecting visitors.

'This is lovely,' she said, around a bite of toast. She washed it down with the tea. 'I'm off to the shop in a minute if you need anything.'

'Perhaps you could get some marmalade if this is going to be a regular occurrence,' Betty said, her eyes twinkling. 'Benny says the house doesn't even have a proper kitchen yet. *Such* a shame.'

Amber lifted her eyebrows, revelling in the warmth of her cup. 'Shame?'

'Well, the fire! That was a lovely cottage once. I remember that house when Georgie had it, from back in the war. There was quite a scandal, back then. Of course, *he* had quite a story of his own, too. But the house was famous before that.'

'He?' Amber was mildly curious about the people who had lived in Beehive Cottage previously.

'Georgie had a friend, a Frenchman. People used to say he was a *spy*.' She got the impression Betty censored the next thing she was going to say, stumbling instead. 'It's got an interesting history even before that. There was a conscientious objector living there, back in the Great War, did time in prison, too. They say his mother nearly died of shame but he had his heroic moments, being an ambulance driver under fire in the trenches and all.'

Amber put her cup down. 'We know better, now,' she said, trying to be diplomatic.

'My father was sunk in the North Atlantic during the war,'

Betty said. 'Twice. But he came home in the end. Of course, I was just a babby.'

Amber smiled at the thought, as Betty lifted down a picture of a young man holding a fat baby in a christening gown. 'That was us, back then. And *this* one,' she said, turning to lift down another silver frame, 'was my mam with Georgie, from your cottage. Beautiful, she was.'

Amber took the picture from her. A tall young woman, probably in her thirties, with deep-coloured lipstick and curled dark hair, sat beside a fair-haired smiling woman she had no difficulty identifying as Betty's mother. 'They look lovely. Happy.'

'Happy to have their picture taken by my dad, I expect. He was a keen photographer. But them times were hard, with rationing and all. Money was tight, too, and men were dying. The island was full of widows and grieving mothers.'

Amber ate up and drank her tea, feeling more ready to tackle the day. 'Thank you so much. You've revived me,' she said, smiling at Betty and sensing Ben staring at her. 'I did get cold. I'm going to have to buy a warmer sleeping bag if I'm staying there.'

'I thought you might be going home at night,' Betty said, as curious as a robin, her head on one side. 'You know, at the manor, with your mum and dad. Especially after what happened with your wedding. Not sleeping in the old cottage, all alone.'

She did know about the cancelled wedding, then. Maybe everyone here did.

Amber managed a small smile. 'No. I'm staying on Morwen for the moment.'

4

OCTOBER 1943

Georgie led the way up the lane, following Jim's great-aunt's instructions, Tommy and Dolly trailing behind her like duck-lings, Robbie following with the bags. An open door led to a small courtyard with four houses, one at each end and two in front of her. The yard had half a dozen chickens scratching at the cobbled ground, which was liberally spattered with their droppings. The boy put the bags down, and she smiled and gave him a sixpence. She looked up and scrutinised the doors.

'That's the one,' she said, reading the lopsided sign. 'Beehive Cottage.'

'Mummy, it can't be,' Tommy said, in a little-boy voice. 'It's so small.'

'Well, Daddy grew up in that big house of Great-Aunt Alice's in Cheltenham.' She took a deep breath. 'That's why he loved coming here so much. We'll go in and find it will be big enough for the three of us.'

'Just until he comes back.' His voice was stronger now.

The official letter from the government still crackled unopened in her pocket, along with the polite note from Jim's bank asking when further funds would be deposited since his wages had stopped. His aunt had sent the keys, and ten pounds for travel and to settle in, but money was going to be tight and they would be isolated from their remaining family, a couple of distant cousins.

She'd give any amount of money to see Jim again. He could still be alive somewhere. The fantasy helped her sleep at night, although as the months went on it seemed less likely.

It could all change once she opened the letter.

She just couldn't face reading it yet, not until they were safe and warm.

'I'm sure there's plenty of room,' she said to Tommy. 'Here, darling. You should be the one to unlock the door.' She handed over the key. 'It's really your house.'

Aunt Alice had decided to pass ownership to Tommy and his father, rather than have to house them herself. She had never liked Georgie, she thought her too opinionated and modern, but she was very fond of Tommy.

Georgie leaned in to try to see through the small, square window, but ragged curtains were drawn across the glass.

Tommy fumbled the key into the door and turned until it clicked. He pushed; it creaked open and the smell of damp swept out.

The door opened into a single small room, with what looked like a tiled floor underfoot and not a stick of furniture. A door opposite was beside a steep set of stairs. Dolly, her thumb in her mouth, leaned around Tommy, and Georgie stared over their heads.

'See?' she managed, croaking a little on a suddenly dry mouth. 'It will keep us safe and warm. There's a fireplace, look.' She imagined Jim there, as a little boy with his nanny and his cousins, and the idea made her feel sad, and suddenly very cold. She should feel closer to him here, but instead she felt even further away.

There was a huge chimney breast with a tiny hole where a small fire had once been lit, and smoke stains had drifted up the plaster. Tommy walked in first.

'It's so small,' he said, subdued. 'It's like the pantry at home.'

'Nonsense.' The word hurt her throat, as if she'd swallowed a twig. She walked in and lifted the latch of the door at the back of the room. 'It's just right for the three of us until Daddy gets home.'

The door swung open into a kitchen, a step leading down. It had a wooden table and a chair, a large enamel sink and one tall cupboard beside an old range in a chimney. Shelves reached up to the low ceiling in an alcove, but were empty. Round marks in the dust showed where pots and crockery had lived previously. Everything smelled of damp and the sink was black with mould.

She pulled the cupboard door open but it was empty. 'I'm sure the pots and pans were put away for safekeeping,' she said, as she put her bag down on the table. 'And I've brought Dolly's Peter Rabbit beaker and my grandmother's teaspoon,' she said, pulling them out with her tea caddy. They had fortunately been in her bag in the shelter when the bombs fell. 'At least we can make tea.'

'We don't even have a kettle,' Tommy said, tears gathering on his eyelids. Dolly pressed against her. 'I really don't like it.'

'Mama, Mama,' Dolly said insistently. She only called her Mama now when she was very upset – or needed the lavatory.

'Let's find the bathroom,' she said, looking out the kitchen window onto a yard surrounded by rough stone walls that looked like they might fall down at any moment. A small outhouse in the corner suggested the horrible possibility of no indoor plumbing. 'It *is* upstairs, I suppose?'

Upstairs were just two bedrooms echoing the layout downstairs, one empty and one with a narrow bed with no mattress, rusting springs showing the bare boards underneath – and, thankfully, a chamber pot.

'Well, that's convenient, isn't it?' she said to Dolly. Tommy made himself scarce as she helped her daughter. 'I need to go now, too,' she tried to joke. 'Let's find the water closet. Do you think it's outside, like at school?'

She carried the pot downstairs, passing the back bedroom, and she noticed a wooden chair almost hidden behind the kitchen door, which she asked Tommy to put by the table. She was about to explore the outhouse to empty the pot when someone knocked on the door. She shoved the porcelain into the empty cupboard and walked over to answer it.

A woman about her own age stood there, fair curls escaping from a colourful headscarf, wearing a floury apron.

'I'm Clementine Brundle, I live next door,' she said, juggling a baby on her hip who looked about six months old. 'Call me Clemmie, everyone does. The Ellises told me you were coming over today. I've got a few bits to spare, if you need some bread and milk. Just until you sort out your coupons.'

'That is so kind, thank you,' Georgie said, a little over-whelmed. 'Can you tell me... I was told the house had furni-ture? Are there pots for the kitchen or another bed?'

Clemmie went a little pink. 'Well, people round here thought the house would be empty until after the war. The government wanted us all to donate a pot or two, bits of scrap metal, you know, for guns and bullets. Since no one had any spare...' Her voice faded away.

Oh. Her own neighbours had robbed the place to fulfil their quota of providing for the war effort. It was frustrating, but she took a deep breath as she realised it had been the sensible thing to do.

'There's a bunker out the back but no coal,' Tommy said, bursting into the room from the back yard. 'Oh, hello.'

Of course. 'It's rationed,' Clemmie explained, smiling at Tommy.

'This is my son, Tommy, and this is Dolly.' Georgie lifted

Dolly up and turned back to Clemmie. 'Is there a hotel open on the island?' Her last shillings jingled in her pocket. 'Or maybe a room to rent for the night? I'll have to buy some furniture before we can stay here.'

'My husband's mam rents out a room, she could take you for tonight. I'll put the word out about furniture,' Clemmie said quickly. 'At church, tomorrow morning. Are you a churchgoer?'

Her terror at what might have happened to Jim, and her memories of the devastation she'd seen in the London Blitz, filled her mind. 'Not any more.'

'I go,' Tommy said. 'With the scouts. And Dolly used to love Sunday school.'

Clemmie introduced eight-month-old Betty, balanced on her hip. 'My Nora is over at my mother's, on the quay,' she explained. 'She must be your daughter's age or thereabouts. She'll be glad to have someone to play with. Come next door, let me get you some tea, and I can make toast if you're hungry.'

The house was a mirror of Beehive Cottage. In the front room, the floor was swept and a long wooden seat was covered with blankets and a couple of embroidered box cushions. A small sideboard carried a row of books and a few knick-knacks. The door to the kitchen was open and the warmth oozed through it, along with the smell of baking bread.

Looking around, Georgina couldn't see any electrical lamps or outlets, nor even old-fashioned gas lamps. The cooking smell was mingled with smoke from an iron range embedded in the wall.

'Where do you get fuel for the stove?' she asked, putting her hands out to warm them.

'We collect driftwood off the beach or cut gorse,' Clemmie said, pulling out a chair for her and putting the baby in a metal cot with a few toys. 'And the ship brings some fuel from time to time. Here, Dolly, would you like to play with baby Betty?' She pulled a brown enamel teapot down from a shelf above the range. 'And we'll all have some tea.'

Georgie sat, suddenly exhausted by the long journey. 'Thank you,' she said, closing her eyes for a moment.

The letter rustled in her pocket and she flinched.

5

PRESENT DAY, 4 OCTOBER

Amber had picked up a bit of shopping for Betty and for her own dinner the previous day. It was a challenge without electricity, but she settled on a ready-meal risotto that could be defrosted and heated up in her one pan, and a bag of salad, ham and bread for lunch. She had also contacted the campsite owners and they offered to bring down a much better sleeping bag for her, and told her the showers would be working in the bathroom block until the end of half-term. That meant she had to think about buying a towel for the future, but she was looking forward to taking up Betty's kind offer of a bath when she needed it.

Which she would definitely need, as she was now filling rubble bags and loading them into a trailer outside on the lane. Her hair was gritty with plaster dust, her face was caked in it, it was inside her clothes, and she could even taste it. Without being asked, Ben had produced extra rolls of bags so she could fill them slightly less full than he had been doing, to spare her injured arm.

There was something so satisfying about the work. Sweep up, fill the bag, stack outside. No one asked her to fill a bag with more soul, or put more emphasis on the sweeping. The idea made her laugh; for decades, her playing technique had been scrutinised, every tiny movement commented upon. There was no perfectionism in bag filling.

Ben was a quiet companion, focused on getting the cracked plaster off without damaging the walls underneath. When it got too dusty to even see across the room, even with the windows open, she decamped outside to boil another kettle-full of water on her camping stove.

He followed, coughing. 'This is the worst bit, getting all the old stuff off.'

'I got some instant coffee for a change, if you want some,' she said, stirring hers with the teaspoon she had borrowed from Betty. 'Look at this spoon, it looks a hundred years old.'

He inspected the spoon and carefully stirred his coffee with it. 'I think she's lent you one from the set she has on the sideboard,' he said. 'Don't lose it. She's had that set since she got married. She must like you.'

She sat on the stone windowsill. 'You seem to know Betty very well.'

He leaned against his workbench. 'Betty is my great-aunt, or great-great aunt, I forget which. Or maybe my mother is her great-niece? It's too complicated. Don't you keep bumping into cousins on the islands?'

She sipped her coffee. 'I come from quite a small family. No siblings. My dad had a brother but my mother is an only child like me.'

'Your dad's family has been in charge of West Island since the beginning of time.'

'No, they were given the abbey in 1539 by Henry the Eighth.' She glanced across at him. He was strong, and moved neatly and sparingly when he worked. 'So, we're newcomers, really.' She smiled at him. 'How about you?'

He laughed at that, spilling coffee down his filthy T-shirt

and ripped jeans. 'My grandfather came here during the war, he's a northerner, he worked at the naval base on Westy. His family originally came from County Durham. He had a lovely accent – I swear he put it on to annoy the islanders. But my mum's family have been here for ever.'

Amber was cooling down now she had stopped working. The sky was a perfect blue, but the air was cold.

'What's next?'

'Mm, fireplace,' he mumbled around biscuit crumbs. 'You bought shortbread?'

'I know. If you were just a workman it would be cheap biscuits, but since we're colleagues...' She smiled at him.

'You should have a couple more, with all this hard work you're doing. You're skin and bone,' he said, looking at her with some concern.

'I had to rest for a long time,' she said. 'After an operation on my neck I couldn't face food for a while. Then they did my arm, I had nerve damage.' She flexed her fingers into a fist, making the scar stand out. 'I was very weak at first.' And the pain, she had never known pain like it. 'This has been a proper workout, and it's cheaper than a gym membership.'

'Was it an accident?'

'Slipped disc in my neck, it was bulging into my spinal canal,' she said shortly. 'Related to the way I was playing the violin.' She still felt like an idiot for not getting help sooner; she'd written it off as repetitive strain for a while.

'Do you feel like you're getting better?' he asked, brushing the crumbs off his hands.

They both must have eaten a sprinkling of plaster dust along the way. It had even fallen in her coffee from her hair even though she had tied it into a long plait. Ben had been carefully examining each layer of the wall to make certain there was no asbestos in it, but the cottage was so old, it was just crumbling lime.

'Slowly. I have a lot of exercises to do for my neck and arms.' Which she hadn't done for several days now, not since she left home.

The moment she had pulled away from her father's hug to get on the boat to Morwen came back to her. Her tears had blurred his expression. Caught between disappointment, confusion and sympathy after she broke off the engagement, he found it hard to talk to her for a while. But she knew he had been as worried about her as her mother was. She twisted her left hand without a twinge, maybe it was starting to heal.

Ben didn't probe further. 'Well, I'd better make a start on that chimney. I hate chimneys,' he said firmly as he went back inside.

'Why?' she called after him.

He showed her. It turned out people didn't sweep their chimneys before they blocked them up. Worse than that, great chunks of concrete-like lining fell down, covered with a tarry blackness that stank of burning. As he pushed an old garden rake up the flue, bits of plaster rattled down from inside.

'The problem is, the chimney is partly built inside the stone wall,' he said, straining with the handle, as if trying to grab something. 'There are all these little ledges. My home was like this when I grew up – we used to sweep our own chimney and it took ages.'

There was a crack then a whoosh as a pile of sticks and plaster fell out with a cloud of soot.

Amber just managed to catch her breath and close her eyes before the room went dark.

Ben caught her hand and dragged her towards the door, the pair of them stumbling over the damaged floor. Outside, they spluttered and gasped for air, and Amber tried to clear the stuff off her face. It wasn't until she sneaked a look at Ben, through soot-laden lashes, that she realised he was completely covered with the black dust.

'Are you OK?' she managed between coughs. She spat out the bitter-tasting dirt but the smell was caught in her throat.

'That big stone just missed my head,' he wheezed back. 'Are you OK?'

'I will be when I can see,' she said, her eyes watering.

He started laughing. 'Have you any idea what you look like...? Wait.' He dragged his phone out of his back pocket and before she could say anything snapped a picture then showed it to her.

'Ugh. I don't want to shock you, but you look just as bad. Let me get one of us both,' she said, holding out her hand for the phone. 'It's only fair. You're worse than me.'

He reached an arm around her shoulders, the warmth easing into her through her filthy top, and she lined up a selfie. They grinned, their teeth the only thing that looked clean.

'How am I going to get clean enough even to go into Betty's house for supper later?' she said, brushing herself down. 'I'm literally too dirty to go in her house to *have* a bath.'

'She'll be offended if you don't go,' he said, letting go of her, slightly reluctantly. Maybe he was cold too.

'Yes, but how?' The thought of traipsing through Betty's perfect little house was unthinkable. 'Do we have enough water even for a quick wash?'

'Most of the dust will come off as we work,' he said.

He was sort of right. As they cleaned up the chimney dirt, using masks he had in his toolkit, they covered some of the fallen soot with layers of plaster dust, but by the time she had to use the outdoor loo, she even found it inside her underwear.

She walked back into the kitchen. 'Are we done? I'm so filthy and gritty. I'd better go up to the campsite for a shower.'

He rubbed his face, the sweat and dirt making brown, tarry streaks across his forehead. 'I've got a better idea.'

She flexed her right shoulder muscles which were starting

to seize up now they had stopped. 'Does it involve a sauna, a massage and a hot bath?'

'Just come outside. We'll take the bags down to the boat and get them loaded on.'

The ride down the cobbled street was uncomfortable. Amber was wedged on the quad bike behind Ben; the weight of the trailer was pushing the quad bike's brakes hard, and they had to dodge plant pots and lobster pots outside the colourful cottages. She clung to the seat until they got to the broad quay, the sun just dipping over the houses and casting long shadows over the sea. Ben pulled up alongside the cargo boat, a rusty old vessel with an open hold full of boxes.

'Where's all this stuff going?'

'Under someone's extension, probably,' he said, lifting out the first bag.

Thirty bags later, with some help from one of the crew, the bags were stacked in a storage container at the front of the boat, and they were back on the quayside, overlooking the high tide lapping the top of the ladders.

'Now what?' She looked at him hopefully.

'Let's jump off the quay,' he said, catching her hand. 'There's a good spot by the slipway. You can ease in gently if you like.'

'I'm frozen already!' She tried to resist but he was strong and she was tired. 'And we don't even have a towel.'

'The water's at its warmest in autumn,' he said, grinning at her. He walked her halfway down the slipway. 'And we can go to my grandma's house to dry off. She lives just on the seafront, over there,' he said, pointing. He put his phone on the slipway, well away from the water, and slipped off his trainers. 'Come on, it will be fun.'

Later, she couldn't work out why she gave in so quickly.

She pulled her hand free, shed her shoes and put her phone and wallet inside one of them.

'I'm going to die of cold,' she warned, already shivering as she looked into the swirls of green off the side of the quay, peppered with bubbles. Flashes of fish lit up the water.

He grinned at her. 'You're a lot less posh than I expected,' he said, laughing.

It was easy to slam both hands into his midsection and watch his grin change to alarm as he cartwheeled off the slipway into the water. When he came up, at least his face was clean. 'You... you...' he spluttered as she took a deep breath and bombed him, landing right next to him in the water.

Ben's Grandma Kevell was a tall, grey-haired lady who lived in one of the smaller houses along the quay. She responded to their knock on the door with a sigh, told them to wait a second and returned with two old towels.

'Dry the worst off before you come in,' she said, struggling to keep a smile off her lips and failing. 'My goodness, how did you *both* manage to fall in?'

'She pushed me,' he said, vigorously towelling his hair then pulling it back to look at it. 'Is this the dog's towel?'

'It's clean,' she said, firmly. 'Come in the warmth, you can dry off properly indoors.'

She led them through a long, tiled hall to a sunny conservatory looking over a patio with a garden wall covered with ivy.

'I don't have anything dry with me,' Amber said, teeth chattering.

'Ben leaves a few bits here,' she said, rather curtly. 'He often goes kayaking and he *always* falls in.'

'I keep the kayak just along the quay,' he said. 'I'll get changed upstairs, Gran, thank you.' He dropped a kiss on her cheek as he passed.

'Throw something down for your friend,' she called after him, and a few seconds later she scooped up a few clothes from the bottom of the stairs. 'The bathroom is private,' she said, opening a door off the conservatory and barely looking at Amber. 'You can get changed in there, then come through to the kitchen. Have a shower if you like.'

'Thank you so much,' Amber breathed, suddenly feeling awkward at the woman's cool reception. 'I'm Amber Marrak, by the way.'

'I know who you are,' Mrs Kevell said, without smiling. 'There's a clean towel on the shelf over the bath.'

Amber stepped into the bathroom and shut the door, shaking not just from the cold.

I know who you are. Anyone would think she had killed someone.

6

OCTOBER 1943

Clemmie's mother-in-law, Mrs Brundle, kept a room she had let out to holidaymakers before the war. It had one enormous bed in it which would take all three of them and filled most of the room. She kindly slid a waterproof sheet over the mattress at one side for Dolly, having experience of young children. She also gave all of them a bowl of soup and a hunk of bread before they went to bed, which was a warming relief.

For an extra shilling, Mrs Brundle added a most unexpected and delicious breakfast. Herrings coated in oatmeal and fried, with chunky slices of toast and a thick apple jam that she called apple cheese to follow.

The children looked dubious at first but they ate every scrap, and Dolly even managed the fish when it was deboned for her.

'You'll find your feet, soon enough,' Mrs Brundle said. 'Clemmie said your neighbours have helped themselves to the cottage's contents, since they knew it was empty. Once old Mrs Stewart took over the tenancy in nineteen thirty, the landlords let it go a bit. She was a sweetheart, a lovely old lady, kind to everyone. She lost her only son in the last war, and her only grandchild in this one. Once her husband died, she faded away, died when the war started. But it's a shame if people took her belongings, even if their need was great.' She pressed her lips together tightly. 'It's been bad here, especially in the winter.'

'I don't blame people for taking her things,' Georgie said. 'I just wonder how I can buy more? A mattress, another bed, a few basic pieces of kitchen equipment. We have a few bits coming from London but no furniture...' One steamer trunk was coming as freight by train then ship, which contained almost everything that hadn't been broken or blown out in the blast, or burned in the fire that followed.

'I think there'll be a few red faces in the congregation,' Mrs Brundle said with satisfaction. 'I'm sure people will help out where they can. Especially for a mother with two children.'

'That would be kind,' Georgie said. 'It – it was where my husband used to come on holiday with his family, when he was little. He loved it here. His great-aunt has given it to him, shared with my son.'

Mrs Brundle shot a sharp glance at her but didn't ask more. 'Well, we always welcome people who love the islands. You were in London, before?'

'A bomb hit our neighbour's house,' Georgie said, the words coming out with the scratch of tears in her voice. She shook off the sadness. 'Our home collapsed the next day. So we were very grateful when my husband's great-aunt came up with this lovely idea.' The tears crowded faster then, cutting off her words, and she turned her face away.

'I'm sorry to hear about your house. I hope you'll settle down here,' Mrs Brundle said gently. 'Well, I'm off to church. You should expect a few visitors this afternoon.' She put her head back around the bedroom door before Georgie could swallow the tears back. 'There are a few bits I could spare, in a rush bag by the door. Just to get you started. Let yourself out, dear.'

'Thank you so much,' Georgie breathed, but Mrs Brundle had already started clattering down the stairs.

The rush bag was heavy with treasures. Two tea towels, a hand towel that was threadbare but smelled sweet, three odd plates and three cups without saucers. A few bits of old cutlery, a floor brush, a milk pan that looked well used, battered but serviceable. And a curtain that could at least meet the blackout requirements. A note recommended she call in at the shop, ringing the bell for the apartment overhead to let the shopkeeper know she needed a few things, even on a Sunday.

The shopkeeper opened the shop just for Georgie and the children and allowed them their rations without question although the address had not yet been changed. It did deplete further the few shillings in her purse but it was a relief to have a few essentials. She added a newspaper, just one page printed with tiny articles. A quarter page official poster warned of German spies and the importance of security.

She also bought a couple of ounces of tea. The precious half-pound sent by Lady Alice, in response to Georgie's asking if she could house them in her capacious home, would soon be gone.

They walked home with the goods, Dolly carrying an enamel pan and Georgie and Tommy taking a handle of the bag each. As Georgie pushed through into the court, she spotted a half-sack of wood by the door that looked like it had been taken from the sea, and another of cut gorse beside it.

Mrs Brundle was right. After church, people dropped by in ones and twos, introducing themselves and giving simple gifts, which she suspected might have come from the cottage originally. Someone brought a few children's books for Tommy and a small box of painted blocks for Dolly. There was a large mattress which would have to go on the bedroom floor and a smaller one just right for the bedstead upstairs.

Several children around Tommy's age also turned up, to awkwardly welcome him and invite him to join the scouting group. He would be ready to go to school the following day, and a couple of boys had brought a football to kick about in the field behind the cottage. They helped Georgie carry the heavy mattress upstairs first, laughing about it almost falling back down, which broke the ice. Tommy went off with them, and two little girls turned up to play with Dolly. They immediately started running around in the front yard.

Over the course of the afternoon, Georgie met the other occupants of their little court. In number one, Mrs Fry was very old and deaf but brought over a boiling kettle with a shaky hand to make tea in a donated pot. It was chipped and cracked earthenware but enough for several cups of tea in her new gifted china. Mrs Fry sat in the kitchen and wondered aloud – very loud – about which of the Ellises had the rest of the chairs.

The other inhabited cottage had a young, very pregnant girl staying in it. Barely eighteen, Maria Taylor said her husband was in the merchant navy, and she hadn't heard from him for ages. They had had just one month together since their wedding, she confided, and she missed him terribly. She stayed with her mother in the week, but liked to live in the marital home on Saturday and Sunday. Her baby was due in three months, and she was trying to knit and sew a layette but her mother wasn't very handy and they were trying to work out patterns.

'I can knit,' Georgina said, promising to help.

Everyone asked about Jim in a distant, polite way. Everyone seemed to accept her story that she didn't know where he was but was sure he was fine. They seemed to look around the house with some trepidation, though. Perhaps they hadn't liked the last occupant.

Later, Georgie was happy to close the door against the dusk, behind the last visitor. Someone had lit a small fire in the kitchen range, just ready for a few bits of the wood they had donated. Tommy and his new friends had filled the empty coal bunker with driftwood and covered over the gorse bags for dry kindling. It would be enough to cook a little food for a few days. They hadn't really eaten more than the breakfast all day. Georgie peeled and cut up a few small potatoes, and was able to wash them under the cloudy stream of water that trickled from the only tap.

'You remember to boil that water,' Clemmie had warned. 'The council says it's going to replace all the lavvies but at the moment they haven't got time.' The earth closet in the yard was one of many that might be contaminating the local wells. Clemmie had showed her where a natural aquifer ran into a stone basin up the hill, fresh and clean, but she didn't have a bucket to fetch any yet. One more thing to add to the list, but she could at least take the old kettle she'd been given up there.

A little salt and flour to coat the liver strips she had bought from the shop, hot lard to sizzle them in and a bit of sliced cabbage in the potato water to mash into a bubble and squeak. She fried patties of it in the liver pan and dished up something hot and savoury, feeling immensely pleased with herself.

In London she had always had someone who cleaned and cooked; all she'd had to do was the occasional breakfast or plan something special like a dinner party for their friends.

Poor Lena. Georgie missed her badly. They had become close over the many months of war, through gathering up the children to go to the shelter, through all the terrible stories of displaced people. They were the displaced people now. Lena had taken her badly broken shoulder and gone to live with her sister in Kent, and Georgie had ended up in this tiny, dirty house.

7

PRESENT DAY, 11 OCTOBER

After a week of heavy work, Amber and Ben had cleared most of the walls back to the stone, timber and cob they were built from. They had found everything from rat holes, cracks and bits of blanket to a whole dried bird in the cob. Amber ran her hands over the old walls, marvelling at their resilience to hundreds of years of use. She was looking forward to the electrician turning up to start the first fix for a new wiring system for the house, the beginning of the reconstruction. The remains of the rubber-coated cabling still survived where fragments of plaster clung to the wall.

'Grant, the electrician, will be here soon,' Ben said, as he walked in. He seemed refreshed, with wet hair flopping over his forehead, and he smelled of citrussy shower gel. 'Which means we can get on with some of the woodwork today. A nice change from all that plaster.'

'Woodwork?' she asked, feeling rumpled and grubby after a week sleeping in her nest on the floor. Amber was acutely aware of her greasy hair and the limits of a strip wash but didn't want to call on Betty or go to the campsite every day.

'Later. The timber's arriving on the tide,' he said. 'Along

with Grant, so we've got an hour to get a coffee at the café. My treat.'

'Give me a minute to brush my hair,' she said, energised at the thought of some coffee and maybe breakfast. She cleaned her teeth in the draughty outside bathroom and ran a brush through her hair. It hadn't yet recovered from the soot and plaster dust, tangles appeared out of nowhere. She jammed a soft knitted hat over it instead.

'Ready!' she said as she bounded out of the front door. As Betty's door was standing open, she leaned in. 'Want anything from the shop, Betty?'

'I have a friend coming up,' Betty shouted back, on the waft of baked goods. 'I'll have a few scones left over later if you bring your own cream and jam.'

'Definitely,' Amber said, feeling lighter than she had for weeks. The memory of the despair on Patrick's face when she called off the wedding was starting to soften and leave some relief behind. It had been the right thing to do.

They strode down the cobbled street, Amber amusing herself by matching her steps to Ben's much longer legs until he smiled down at her. 'Why are you so happy?'

'Sleeping on the floor in sub-zero conditions seems good for me,' she said, flexing her left hand. Still no pain. 'Isn't cold-water swimming supposed to be good for your mood? Maybe cold sleeping is, too.'

'I do have some good news for you on that front,' he said, turning along the quay. Despite the winds, the air was still quite warm for autumn. 'I'm having the glass delivered for all the windows. We – well, you – can sand down all the frames and I'll putty new glass in when it's ready. I suppose the heat from the fire blew out the front room windows.'

'What caused the fire?' she asked, following him into the café, even though the sign still said 'closed'.

'No one's certain, but something fried the electrics. Betty

thinks it was a lightning strike, she heard a huge bang. Obviously, with her house literally adjoining, she was afraid the fire would get into the roof and spread next door.' He glanced at her sideways and changed the subject. 'So, no ghosts at night? You must know the cottage has a reputation for being haunted.'

No ghosts, not exactly, although it seemed to her the draughts took on a musical quality once it was dark. 'Everyone says that about empty houses,' she said, dismissing the idea with a grin. 'I wouldn't know, anyway. I'm sleeping like a log once I'm warm enough.'

She didn't want to talk about the fragments of dreams that were creeping into her mind during the day.

A perfect day on the beach, hand in hand with someone, maybe Patrick.

Finding a boy floating in a foot of water, drifting in and out with the waves, a slight smile on his serene but frozen face.

It had disturbed her, yet she couldn't halt the sequences of notes – in a minor key – that seemed to attach themselves to these dream fragments, and made her think of sequences of notes, minor keys and slow songs.

'Betty must have been terrified when the fire started. It could so easily have spread,' she said, shaking the dreams from her mind.

'She says she heard the bang, then her electricity was knocked out and her phone with it. She had to get a neighbour to call the fire brigade.' He chuckled. 'She's still embarrassed about running about the town in her nightie to get help.'

A poster was stuck to the wall in the café. It was advertising a fundraiser at the Mermaid's Purse, a local pub.

Ben was watching her. 'Thinking of going? It's for Kai. There are some pretty good musicians on the islands, not at your level, though.'

'Actually, I love local pub music,' she said. 'I used to play folk and blues for fun. I'll try and get there.'

Amber thought about the little boy's face on the picture, snub nose with freckles, big blue eyes. Ben perused the autumn coffee menu and then called his drink order through to someone called Sophie in the kitchen.

She poked her head out of the doorway. 'We're not open yet, let us at least get the kettle on! Oh, hi Ben.'

She disappeared as Amber read the menu. 'Pumpkin spice latte?'

'Well, the Hallowe'en decorations are going up,' he said, pointing at webs and knitted spiders in the window. There were a few for sale at the cash register; some had little witchy hats on. She added one to her order once the waitress came back out, along with a large spiced latte and seasonal oatmeal for breakfast.

'What's seasonal about the porridge?' she asked.

Sophie smiled. 'Served with spicy vanilla and cinnamon sugar, and clotted cream.'

'Make that two,' Ben said, grinning at Sophie. 'Did I mention that we went to school together?'

Sophie thumped him on the arm.

'Ow! What was that for?'

'Putting seaweed down my neck on the boat,' she answered promptly. 'I've been waiting for years to get you back. Go and sit down, I'll put the lights on.'

They settled at a table by the window. Pale sunshine picked up white wavelets beyond the quay.

'What have we got coming, besides the glass?' she asked, wondering if the boat would be able to manage the rough water in the middle of the Sound.

'Hardwood for the window frames – we need to replace a few bits. Wood preservative and hardener, new sash cords, some softwood to build new door linings. Wood glue, screws and nails, that sort of thing. You'll be a carpenter in no time.'

She smiled at the idea. 'I've hung a few shelves in my time,' she boasted. 'Some of them even stayed up.'

Sophie brought over two large bowls of porridge and their coffees. 'There you go, sugar on the side, extra cream.'

They tucked in, watching as people came and went. The café wouldn't be open for a while yet, but many of the locals seemed to think it opened as soon as the door was unlocked. Eventually the owner, Lucy, turned the 'open' sign around at ten to the hour. 'Some days you just have to give in,' she said. 'How's the porridge? It's new on the menu.'

'Delicious,' mumbled Amber, aware of a smear of cream on her top lip. She licked it off.

'I hear you're in Beehive Cottage? That fire was awful.'

'Lucy's partner, Marcus, is with the volunteer fire brigade,' Ben said. 'I joined last year, too.'

Amber looked at him. 'You did? Were you there?'

'Yeah, I was there,' he said, looking down. 'It was horrible. You train to put out bonfires and the odd barbecue. Seeing a whole house go up is terrifying. I was mostly damping down from outside, Marcus was inside putting the flames out, trying to save the stairs.'

'And it worked,' Amber said. 'I mean, the stairs survived.'

Lucy nodded. 'Some people say the place had a bit of a reputation before, a bad atmosphere.' She hesitated. 'I honestly thought the owners would just strip out the inside, make it open-plan for a holiday let.'

'It's listed, so the owners are going to restore it,' Amber said, feeling a little blush creep into her cheeks. 'Actually, my family *are* the owners.'

'Of course. Sir Michael is the landlord, isn't he?' There was a tiny reserve in Lucy's manner.

'My grandfather bought it years ago,' Amber said, feeling a little defensive. 'He thought it was a bit small to be a home but it made a good holiday let.'

'Well,' Lucy said, 'it will be lovely to see it restored, rather than boarded up and smoky. Maybe someone will live in it long term.'

Amber finished her porridge in silence after Lucy left.

'You don't have to be defensive because your family are rich,' Ben said suddenly. 'Sir Michael is a good landlord – at least he is for properties on West Island from what I hear. I suppose the tenants mostly work for the manor,' he added.

'They do,' she said. 'No one likes landlords, but the idea that their poor tenants are making them rich is so far from the truth. Some years, with repairs and upgrading, my family makes a loss on the residential lets. The hotel, holiday cottages and the gardens are the only thing that makes money. Anyway, I have nothing to do with it.'

'Because you have your own career. A violinist.'

She felt the echo of the pain in her arm. 'Hopefully I still do,' she said lightly.

'What happens if you can't play any more?'

She looked up. 'You don't beat about the bush, do you? I don't know, I don't have a plan, and it's none of your business.'

He lifted his hands as he conceded. 'You're right, sorry. I just thought we were becoming, you know, friends.'

She immediately felt bad, tears crowding into her throat. 'We are. I'm sorry.' She managed a watery smile. 'Once you've jumped off the quay together, you're automatically friends. Isn't that how it goes? It does on Westy.'

He smiled back crookedly. 'I wouldn't say I *jumped* exactly...'

Ben kept the quad bike and trailer behind the church, so they drove it along the quay ready for the supplies. It took half an hour to load and secure everything, and Amber still had to walk behind it to stop lengths of wood sliding off as the lane grew steep. When they got to the cottage, the door was already open.

'Grant!' Ben said, greeting a tall, heavyset man with round, blue eyes. 'Come to bodge the electrics?'

'In the haunted house? I won't tell them if you don't,' Grant said. 'We'll just rig up a few lights and charge the Marraks double.'

Ben's eyes glittered with amusement and he stepped back, gesturing towards Amber. 'Grant, my friend, may I introduce you to Miss Amber Marrak, who will be overseeing our work?'

Amber fixed what she hoped was a sneering, snooty look on her face. 'How do you do?' she said, holding out a couple of fingers for him to shake. 'You were saying?' She couldn't keep the act up and started giggling at his expression.

Grant put his hand on his chest and feigned shock. 'You got me,' he said. 'I'll have to do a proper job now. Oh, Ben, we'll need the quad bike again for the boxes I brought over.'

They unloaded the quad bike and drove off to get the equipment, and Amber had a moment to look around the stripped-out kitchen. There were scraps of old wallpaper around the back window and where the broken sink had been. It was now stacked in the yard with a thousand other fragments of the house's many years. The wallpaper had tiny blue flowers on a grey background, the middles of each flower still a vivid yellow.

Wedged in the fallen plaster by the wall was something in the dirt. She bent down and dug it out of the dust. A tiny spoon, a silver hallmark just visible beneath the tarnish and grime.

She tucked it into her pocket and started looking around more carefully. A shape that looked almost like an animal was scratched into the windowsill, revealing layers of paint, from cream to shocking denture pink and garish green. The window was held up with an old piece of wood, which also had layers of paint on it. Beyond the dust, the window caught some light as the sun came around, and she suddenly imagined big pots of flowers, maybe a vine for some shade in the summer.

She thought about all the evenings she and Patrick had sketched out plans for the head gardener's cottage. Dad had been renovating the house for the two of them and it was almost finished. They would have received the keys in a couple of weeks' time, at the wedding reception. He'd also fenced off a larger garden for the two of them, as the original house barely had more than a large patio behind it. Presumably previous head gardeners didn't want to come home to mow and weed, but Patrick loved gardening for itself.

Patrick. She missed him – she *yearned* for him, as if she was instinctively leaning towards him. Every time a message pinged on her phone she hoped – dreaded – that it would be him. Instead, there were short, practical messages from her mother, checking in, making sure she was OK.

She felt guilty now about what she'd dropped her parents into. They had to cancel all the interwoven threads of the wedding, lost money on all the rooms they had reserved for friends and family. They had taken on explaining to everyone what was going on, and they saw Patrick every day. Thank goodness Mum didn't talk about him, but her father had sent her a long, savage message saying that he hoped she was using the time on Morwen to get her head together and stop hurting everyone who loved her.

She polished up the little spoon, revealing its bright silver under the black. It had been displaced, a bit like she had been, finding herself back in her childhood home being smothered with anxiety and kindness. Here, she felt like herself, her old self, carefree and adventurous, looking forward to seeing her new friends and immersing herself in saving the cottage. She wondered whether the music would haunt her dreams tonight.

8

OCTOBER 1943

Georgie had woken on their first morning at the cottage with a new sense of hopefulness after a rare good sleep. Sometimes in London she would dream that someone was calling for her, and she would wake with tears all over her face, still convulsed with sobs. *Jim.* But here, she was so tired she had slept through, and when she woke she couldn't remember her dreams.

The night before she had borrowed a bucket to get drinking water from up the hill. She had handwashed their dirty clothes during the evening in some tap water with plenty of soap, and hung them out over the single rope stretched across the back yard. By morning, the clothes just needed a final airing inside.

It was comforting to be surrounded by the scent of clean laundry and to have a few bits of food in the cupboard. Georgie noticed the absence of the overhead drone of aeroplanes. Although the worst of the Blitz had passed, so many buildings in the city had been damaged and new bombing raids seemed to come out of nowhere. It felt safer here, and they were better off in their own cottage, away from the worst dangers of the war.

She sat at the kitchen table, now scrubbed pale and the grain lifted up by a mixture of salt and soap. The beaten-earth floor was worn down by hundreds of years of use, and red wax had been applied over the top to keep the moisture down. Someone had carved wobbly lines suggesting tiles into the hard surface.

By leaning out of the front bedroom window, she could just catch a glimpse of the church clock. Half past seven. The sun was properly up and the chill in the air suggested another cool but sunny day.

She woke the children and started unpacking Dolly's school dress and clean underwear. 'Your socks are grey,' she observed. 'I don't suppose we'll be able to get new ones now. I'll have to bleach them. If I can get bleach,' she added.

Tommy had got up quickly when she had tapped on his door, and she suspected he'd been lying there worrying. Tommy was like his father and fretted about the small things. She still hadn't been able to bring herself to read the letter, but she needed to talk things over with Tommy first, especially if it was bad news. She wanted him to be prepared.

'We're taking you down to the school this morning,' she said, trying to get Dolly to balance on her right foot to put her sock on and failing, laughing with her. 'No, your *left*... This tickly one.'

'Is there anything for breakfast?' Tommy asked, putting his head around the door.

'I've lit a small fire for some porridge. Apparently, the local boys are going down to the beach after school – at low tide – to collect wood. Do you want to go, too?'

'I'd already planned to,' he said, his dark hair flopping into his eyes again. He pushed it back with a gesture that broke Georgie's heart. *Just like Jim.* 'Mum, I know you've got a letter in your bag. Is it about Dad?'

She took a deep breath, smiled at Dolly and kissed her forehead. 'I haven't read it yet. You and I can do that together later.' She looked down at the little girl, who was playing with her own dark curls. 'When you've had your breakfast we can plait your hair, Dolly. I have some new ribbons for you.'

What a change. Four years ago she would have been buying clothes for Dolly in Oxford Street and now she was reduced to buying a couple of knots of new ribbons, and bleaching and darning socks.

After she had boiled a kettle for tea for her and Tommy, and heated up a little milk for Dolly, she made a pot of oatmeal and cheered it up with a smidgeon of honey which had survived the bomb. Then she put Dolly into a cardigan, which was getting too tight to do up, and they walked out of the court onto the road and up the hill.

'I like honey,' Dolly announced. 'We should get some bees as pets and they could make some for us.'

Georgie exchanged glances with Tommy and smiled. 'Our garden is too small. Bees need a lot of flowers, darling.'

'We could grow flowers, too,' Dolly said, stopping to examine a white feather drifting down the cobbles on a light breeze.

'One of our neighbours keeps pigeons,' Tommy said. 'He sometimes has squabs for sale.'

Another source of meat. This war had made everyone obsessed with food. 'Can you find out more? I'll have a chat with him, see what he charges.'

The lane led to a tiny cottage with an arched doorway like a chapel, and beside it there was an old school building with 1815 carved into the stone lintel over the windows. A playground sat beside it with outside facilities, and a gate led onto a further field surrounded by hedges. Several small growing plots were filled with old potato plants, yellowing and falling over, and runner beans were now drying on their poles. A shed was surrounded by a couple of dozen chickens scratching in the grass in a small run.

A woman about Georgie's age walked out of the school. 'Ah,

Mrs Preston, how nice to meet you. The school board said Dorothy and Thomas would be starting with us today.' She smiled down at Dolly who was now clinging to Georgie's leg, and crouched down to her level. 'What smart ribbons. Are they new?'

Dolly put her finger in her mouth but managed a nod.

'My name is Mrs Pascoe,' she said, 'and I help the teacher. There's a little girl in the school who is waiting to play with you. Did you meet Florence yesterday, Dolly? She has a floppy dog called Barney and he sits on a shelf while she's at school. Do you want to see?'

The gentle voice seemed to do the trick, and Dolly transferred her grip to Mrs Pascoe and walked up the steps, just looking back to make sure Georgie was following. The teacher greeted them in a small hallway and introduced herself as Miss Cartwright.

'Mrs Preston, how nice to meet you. And this, I presume, is Thomas?'

'Yes, ma'am,' Tommy said, and looked over at Dolly, who had greeted her new friend Florence with a shy smile. 'Only, people call me Tommy.'

Miss Cartwright led the way to a single classroom as she continued talking.

'Of course. You'll be starting at the secondary school next year, as I understand it. We will be running the eleven-plus after the spring bank holiday, if you intend to attempt the grammar school entrance examination.'

She gestured towards a serious-looking girl who was handing out pots of crayons and pieces of paper. 'We often have older students working from their home islands when the weather is inclement. This is Patience Ellis. She's normally at the grammar school but she's staying another week on the island because she broke her arm.'

Patience held up a heavy plaster cast. 'One more week,' she

said, and smiled. 'I can show you the maths problems the class have been doing, if you like.'

Once the children were occupied, Miss Cartwright walked Georgie back towards the door, and back in the hall she lowered her voice and leaned towards her. 'May I ask, please, what the children's situation is? Are they evacuated?'

'No. Well, not formally. We came here because my husband was given Beehive Cottage. We... lost our London home in the bombings,' she said, choking a little. It was easier than the whole truth: that her husband's aunt didn't want to accommodate them in her large house, so had given them a small cottage in the middle of the Atlantic.

The woman took a tiny step back. 'Oh. Beehive Cottage? I'm afraid it's a bit basic.'

'Yes. It needs a bit of work but we should be comfortable there,' Georgie said, forcing the words a little.

'And may I enquire about *Mr* Preston... I assume he is fighting?'

Georgie took a deep breath.

'I'm afraid we don't know where he is. My husband – James – was in the Pacific. He's officially missing.'

Six months of not knowing.

Unless it was in *that* letter, the one she still hadn't been able to open. Until she read it, he was still just missing.

'I'm so sorry. We have a couple of mothers in similar positions with men away and, sadly, not all coming home. I'm sure as you make friends, you'll find a lot of support.'

Georgie nodded, fixed a smile on her face and answered the necessary questions about the children's education. An older girl with long blonde hair took Dolly out to the lavatories – at least, she hoped they were flushing toilets and not those awful earth closets. She suspected her own facilities were long overdue for digging out. The younger children had two low tables on one side of the classroom, the older ones had desks under a window. A small stove gave a scent of woodsmoke to the whole place.

'So, Tommy can join the older children. Patience will help him settle in, she's a good girl, very advanced for her age.'

'Thank you. I had better get home, I have some tidying up to do. The rest of our luggage is coming on the steamer today.'

'Have you much to come?' Miss Cartwright enquired, her head on one side.

'Not much, we lost almost everything, apart from a few clothes and books that were blown into the road. The house burned down and had to be demolished.'

'Well, Mr Ellis will be happy to bring it up, I'm sure. I just thought I should remind you that the steamer will bring the island's post too, you can collect it from the shop.'

Georgie nodded and then smiled at Tommy.

He came over to show her a mathematics textbook. 'I haven't started quadratic equations yet. I'll have to work to catch up.' He looked at the teacher. 'I was in boarding school before.'

'The curriculum isn't much different here,' she said. 'Most secondary pupils usually stay over at the hostel in the week and come home on Fridays. Grammar school students like Patience are full boarders in Truro during the term.'

'In certain circumstances,' Georgie said, carefully, 'my husband's regiment might pay for Tommy to attend his old school.'

Miss Cartwright stared into her eyes for a moment before dropping her gaze. 'Well, if that becomes an option, we can talk about preparing him. Let's assume he will be boarding somewhere for some time. Are you staying this morning, Tommy, or would you like to start properly tomorrow?'

'We have something important to do today,' Georgie said, looking down at her son and squeezing his hand. 'Don't we?'

They said their goodbyes to Dolly, who waved out of the

window, and walked back to the cottage. Tommy's hand gripped hers hard. She sat at the table. He leaned up against her as she fished the letter out of her bag.

'Ready?' she asked. Part of her screamed that he was too young for this, that she needed to soften the news herself. But that wouldn't have been her choice, at his age. She would have wanted to know, to be told it straight.

She tore the letter open and spread out the single sheet.

It was from the US navy. She already knew Jim had been on one of their ships, and it had been sunk in the Pacific.

Georgie felt a chill running through her body.

The letter confirmed Jim was missing, and that since he had not been rescued in several months... it was unlikely he would ever be found.

'But it doesn't say he's dead,' Tommy whispered, pushing into her arms.

'No. But I'm afraid it doesn't look good, Tommy. We need to face reality. He's been missing for so long...' And the War Office had stopped his wages. So they must be counting him as dead, surely?

If he was alive, they would have found him by now.

Tommy was crying now, and she hugged him tight, giving in to her own tears.

9

Amber found a new respect for tradespeople. Grant threaded sheaves of wires through the house as he designed the electrical system. He thought about the need for separate supplies to the electric shower, the cooker and outside lights, and added sockets for lamps and chargers and vacuum cleaners that she hadn't even thought about.

Amber and Ben were sent into the loft above the bedrooms to run the lighting circuit, and found it was a boarded space, abandoned decades ago. A primitive ladder had been pulled up along the floor.

'That ladder's mostly woodworm – it was probably the only way up once. But the floorboards are better, they just need treating,' Ben said, inspecting the floor with a lamp taken off his power bank. 'You could make a proper room up here.'

'This was a window,' she said, looking at a rectangular frame that was now covered with slates. 'It must have looked out the back, up the hill.'

'It's small but it should bring in a lot of light if you can restore it. There's decent headroom in the middle, too. You might get planning to extend up here properly.'

'Where would the stairs come up, though?' she wondered. 'That loft hatch is right over the stairs.'

'That airing cupboard off the hall probably had the ladder in originally, you see here, where the boards have been cut,' he said, running his finger around a dark line in the floor. 'You could put stairs in the cupboard but they would be very steep. I've seen houses like this elsewhere on the island. People had to squeeze their children in somewhere and extended up into the loft.'

A woman's voice called up the stairs. 'Ben?'

'Maggi? I'll come down.' He clambered onto the modern ladder to get down.

'I've got a parcel for an A. Marrak,' the voice added, and Amber followed him, as he steadied the ladder.

Downstairs, they found Grant filling up cups with hot water provided by Betty next door, who was chatting to Maggi, a sprightly-looking older lady with a large Royal Mail trolley. It turned out her grandson had played with Grant as a toddler. The islands were so small; Amber wondered what it would have been like to have truly grown up here, rather than be sent off to private schools and music colleges from an early age.

The box Maggi handed her was big but light. Amber knew instantly what it was.

'I'll open it later,' she said, trying not to let the bleak coldness leak into her voice. 'Is that tea, Grant?'

'I'll get another kettle and some mugs,' Betty said. 'You'll have a cup, won't you, Maggi?'

'I certainly will,' she said, 'but I think we'll have to sit out in the courtyard.'

Two wooden benches stood outside the houses; between them and one of Betty's chairs they could all sit down.

'So,' Maggi said, white hair dropping out of a bun into her eyes. 'We're all dying to know. What's in the box?' Her eyes twinkled so much it was hard to take offence.

'It's my violin,' Amber said. 'I've had some time off after an operation, but I have to start building my practice up at some point. I'm a musician. I play for an orchestra.'

'That's good,' Maggi said. 'If you're getting better.'

Amber flexed her left hand and lifted her shoulder. 'I *am* getting better. I didn't think labouring with Ben would be a problem, but it actually seems to have done my spine good. I had an operation on a disc in my neck, and another one on some nerves in my wrist. It was a repetitive strain injury, I had some bad playing habits.' Amber changed the subject. 'Anyway, I was wondering about the people who lived in the cottage before. Who had all the different layers of paint and wallpaper? One of them is really pretty, white and pink flowers and bright yellow dots.'

Betty nodded. 'Now, I do remember *that*. I recall Goldie covering it up – it must have been her mother's.'

'Goldie?'

'Her name was Marigold. She lived here back in the fifties with her husband. When the family on West Island bought the cottage, they let her stay in it until she died.'

'My family,' Amber reminded her.

'Yes, well. I'm afraid they weren't very good landlords, honestly. They didn't help Goldie, anyway. She got a bit confused and frail towards the end, used to talk to people who weren't even there.' Betty nodded. 'I kept an eye on her. Of course, the landlords lived so far away, they wouldn't know what was going on with her.'

Far away. Less than a mile and a few minutes by motorboat. But it was hard to see what help they could have given.

'I suppose they were waiting until the tenant left,' she said, as diplomatically as she could.

'She didn't leave,' Maggi said. 'She died. She was a funny old stick and she had early onset dementia. But the island looks after its own.'

'She wasn't even that old,' Betty said. 'Seventy-odd, younger than me. But she was happy here and we managed to help her stay until the end. Once it was empty, whoosh! It went up in flames.'

'Ben said you thought it was lightning?'

Grant, who had been munching his way through a packet of custard creams given to him by Betty, spoke up. '*I* thought it was lightning,' he said. 'It went through Goldie's wiring and started a fire in the consumer unit. There was a wooden ironing board up against it and it burned. I had to fix some of Betty's wiring next door, it got incinerated, too.' He took another biscuit. 'Mind you, the two cottages seem to share a supply. It's not as safe – you ought to get that seen to by the supplier.'

'It's funny, isn't it?' Maggi said, taking one of the biscuits. 'Marigold always said no one else would want to live in her home. She said it was haunted by some tragedy back after the First World War.'

'Well, *I've* never seen a ghost,' Amber said, looking over at Ben. 'We're fixing it up. People will be living there soon.'

'Just holiday people,' Betty said sniffing. 'Like the other two in the court.'

'We haven't decided.' Amber finished her tea. 'That was amazing, thank you, Betty. It's dusty work labouring for Ben and Grant while they draw wiring diagrams. They just gossip, while I clear up.'

Betty smiled. 'Come and help me with the cups and kettle, dear. Bye, Maggi.'

Maggi had already pushed the mail trolley, now considerably less full, to the gate.

'I hope you get better quickly, lovey,' she said to Amber.

Amber followed Betty into her cottage, stamping off the worst of the dust as she went across the cobbles. 'Oh, I need to return this,' she said, pulling out her teaspoon. 'I found one in the house.'

She showed Betty the now gleaming silver spoon she had found in the dirt.

Betty touched it, then pulled her hand back. 'That was Georgie's. It was one of the few things she rescued from her house in London. It was bombed, you know, during the war. You know, you remind me of her.'

Amber smiled. 'I'd love to know more about her.'

'She wrote a book – it might still be in the library some-where.' Betty looked at her curiously as she ran water into the sink. 'So, you are a violinist. What sort of music did you play?'

Amber put the cups beside the sink. 'I was a classical concert violinist,' she said, her voice coming out emotionless. 'Once you get to a certain level, you just can't take a year out. I don't know if I'll ever be able to play well enough again.'

The most recent letter from the orchestra had been kind but firm: they were letting her go, and would no longer be retaining her services. She couldn't blame them; they had been paying her a retainer for several months, and as time went on the chances of a complete recovery got further and further away. What on earth would she do?

'Go back to the boys,' Betty said, and patted her arm. 'No one knows what's going to happen. It's too early to give up on something you've worked so hard for.'

The rest of the day, apart from a brief respite with a pub lunch, was spent working hard to tidy up the walls, secure a spider's web of new cables and help Ben clear all the old wires. The four rooms would now have plenty of sockets and lights, and as the ceiling was being replaced downstairs, modern spotlights would cheer up the room which became dark the instant Ben turned off his work lamps.

As the afternoon wore on, he took his electric screwdriver outside and called to Amber. 'Come and hold this, will you?'

She stood outside and held the panel that covered up the front window as he unscrewed the fixings. It took both of them to lift it down, revealing the smoke-blackened glass and the two broken panes, one falling out as they moved it.

'We can replace these if I cut the panes properly,' he said. 'Get me a cloth and my safety goggles.'

She grabbed a tea towel and he carefully pushed each broken piece out into a rubble bag. The room was flooded with natural light.

Ben inspected the inside of the window frame. 'There's a bit of charring around here,' he said, brushing off bubbled paint with one finger. 'But it's hardwood, it should be fine. You start sanding – wear eye protection, goggles and a mask just in case some of this paint has lead in it. If we can clean up the frame, we can get the new glass in.'

Amber set to work sanding the intricate mouldings.

'The light makes such a difference,' Grant said, grinning at her as he came through. 'This is going to be a nice room.'

'Just tiny,' she said, brushing sweat off her forehead with a dusty and probably sooty hand.

'Perfect for one, even a couple,' he said. 'Me and my wife, we lived in a cottage like this when we first got married. Then we had our first kid and *boom!*' he said, waving his arms up. 'One million toys and bits of baby equipment. We've got three children now, and there isn't enough room in a four-bedroomed house.'

'Three children?' He had been outrageously flirty with her from the first time they met but there was something kind and safe about him, too. Married, that explained it.

'You ever got married?' he said casually, then his whole expression changed. 'Oh, I'm sorry, Ben told me...'

Everybody on the islands knows, she thought, cold settling into her again.

'Not married,' she said drily, turning back to sanding vigorously.

10

OCTOBER 1943

Georgie sat in the solicitor's office, ankles crossed, in a linen suit she had bought for a charity event. She had once been invited to the Lady Mayoress of London's appeal for refugees, all jewels and furs and rich donors. Now she was sitting in a shabby office on St Brannock's, the big island, in a tiny shop off the high street, hoping to scrape together enough money to live on.

Tommy was staying late at school, cramming for the grammar school entrance examination, and Dolly would be being picked up by one of her new friends' mothers. The solicitor's office was dusty and there were piles of papers and bound journals everywhere. Even on the windowsill, she noted, which ran with condensation.

Mr Seznec had remained sitting down since she had arrived, which irritated Georgie. It was common courtesy to stand up when someone entered the room. With a jolt, she remembered she wasn't very important any more. 'So, Mrs Preston,' he said, 'how can I help you?' His face was tanned, his hair almost black, just a few strands of grey. She looked away.

'My own solicitor is back in London,' she said. 'Or rather, my husband's. I think I need one of my own now.'

He lifted an eyebrow at that. 'Is this a – ah – separation? Are you seeking a divorce?'

'No. Nothing like that,' she said, choking back the sadness she always felt whenever she talked about Jim. 'My husband is...' She pushed the letter towards him. 'Please read this.'

She averted her eyes, not wanting to see – again – the line that said Jim had been missing so long it was unlikely he would be found. It had left Georgie and Tommy sobbing.

'It is a bit ambiguous,' he said. 'The Red Cross are not operating in large parts of the Pacific, and the Japanese have not released information about captured British combatants. They can't be certain he isn't a prisoner of war.'

'No,' she said. 'As you see, this information comes from the US navy, relating that all known survivors retrieved from the sinking of the *USS Porter* have been rescued and repatriated. But more than half of the crew are missing and one was found alive, washed ashore on the Solomon Islands. He says a few more men got off in small boats.' Her voice rose. 'He *could* still be alive.'

'May I ask what your husband was doing on an American ship?'

'He was in intelligence,' she explained, her voice bleak. 'That's all I know.'

Mr Seznec looked again at the sparse words, which she knew by heart. *While no remains have been found of the 146 men on board who are missing...*

'How can I help?' he asked, wire-rimmed spectacles slipping down his nose as he looked at her. She guessed that despite the odd grey hair, he was around thirty, not much younger than her. His eyes were somewhere between blue and green and his gaze was intense, unsettling.

'Why are you not—' *Fighting.* The words, the accusation, came out before she could stop it. 'I'm sorry, it's none of my business.'

'I'm a Breton,' he said, looking down at his notepad. 'I came here after being injured during the Nazi invasion of Brittany. My mother was half English, so I relocated here to recover. My law degree was gained at Cambridge.' He had very precise, English intonation but she could hear something underneath, the trace of an accent.

'I am sorry,' she said, her eyes filling up. Under his badly ironed shirt, his shoulders were rounded and powerful. He looked like he should be playing sports or working in the fields, not pushing papers around. 'I'm sorry if I was rude. This is all painful.'

'I understand. Other than this letter, have you received an official telegram upgrading your husband's status from – uh – missing?'

'No, just that his wages have been stopped as he is *presumed* dead. But I have only just moved here. Notifications would go to Jim's great-aunt – Lady Alice Preston – in Cheltenham. She will forward any correspondence to me here until my address is updated.'

'Missing but presumed dead makes it difficult to get a death notification, especially as the information comes from the Americans. You will need one to apply for a war widow's pension.'

'I know. I realised Jim's wages were stopped four weeks ago, just before we left London. His bank manager wrote a very nice letter asking when new funds would be deposited, as my account was running low.' She tried to keep her voice steady. 'Jim has a private income. Not a lot, but he put it away for our children's education. It won't stretch far, though, and I need to be able to get into his account. I also wondered if my son Tommy might be eligible for support from my husband's regiment since I can no longer afford his school fees.'

'I see.' He looked up, his eyes the same colour as the sea she could see out of the window, down the narrow lane onto the quay. 'Your first need, then, is to access your husband's bank account, and for that we normally need a death certificate. But in these difficult circumstances, we can often gain access just from the notification and a valid marriage certificate.'

'I have that. And the children's birth certificates.'

She handed over a paper detailing all the relevant information. 'Our home in London was destroyed by a bomb two months ago. We lost a lot of our belongings in the fire. Fortunately, I took our important papers into the air-raid shelter.'

'This Beehive Cottage on Morwen. Are you renting it?'

'Jim's great-aunt was fond of him, and of my son, Tommy. But she didn't approve of me at all. So instead of us going to live with her, she has made the cottage over to Jim and Tommy.'

'It would have been better in your name,' he said, looking at her, though his tone was sympathetic rather than judgemental.

'I know, but I'm not from Alice's world. She didn't approve of Jim's marriage to me. She had a young debutante lined up for him, not an independent secretary.'

When Georgie met Jim, a rakish young student, they fell in love almost immediately, not caring what either family thought.

'And your husband's private income?'

She looked down at her hands, scratched and roughened by scrubbing the house and doing laundry in cold water. 'Jim's allowance was cut off on our marriage. But his mother left him some stocks and shares. He saved the dividends up to pay for the children's education, as I said.'

'I'm afraid many investments have been frozen, or have fallen severely during the war – you must be prepared to find less in his account than you are expecting,' he said, his voice a gentle rumble.

'Yes, I understand.' The cold ran through her like a waterfall now. Could she really be running out of money? What would she do?

'I will speak to your husband's bank today,' he said. 'And I will write a summary of all known information. I will do what I can to press the War Office so you can get a death notification, which will help you apply for a war widow's pension and see about getting support from his regiment.'

War *widow*. The word settled heavily in the room.

'What else can I do?' she asked.

'Contact Lady Preston about any more correspondence she might have received, and let the War Office know of your new address.'

She stood. 'I'll do that, I can telegram her from the post office on Morwen. But I must go, I need to catch the boat back now. You look like you have a lot to do.' She looked around – some of the papers were water damaged, some a little scorched.

He waved a hand around the small room. 'These aren't my cases, I just took it over when the previous solicitor, uh – *retired* – suddenly, a few months ago.' He leaned forward to look out of the window. 'The tide's dropping. You'll have to be quick. I'll be in touch as soon as I can, Mrs Preston.'

He held out his hand, still seated, but when she took it she was shocked by his vibrant energy, his warmth. *He's alive.* The nightmare she kept having, of Jim's body rolling gently on a sandy beach thousands of miles away, intruded. She dropped his hand abruptly. 'Thank you, Mr Seznec,' she whispered.

His voice reached her even as she fumbled for the door. 'All that formality seems unnecessary, now, in a war. Please call me Hugo.'

Georgie stumbled outside and the tears fell as she lurched down the road, narrowly avoiding being hit by a boy on a bicycle, his bell jangling. She leaned over the top of the harbour wall to catch her breath, then ran for the sign that said 'Morwen'. Mr Ellis's boat was already lined up, his wrinkled face concerned.

'All's well, maid?'

'It will be,' she said, sniffing back tears. She was just glad to be out in the open air, on the sea that would take her back to the cottage.

11

PRESENT DAY, 14 OCTOBER

Amber waited until everyone had gone home before tackling the box she had propped up in the corner of the bedroom. She knew what it was, because she knew her father so well. She lit a couple of candles in jars to light the room. The arc lamps were too strong and she wasn't sure whether she could be seen undressing through the old curtains.

In the dark days of her recovery, when all the news was bad from the doctors and surgeons, Amber had drunk too much and stumbled, dropping one of her precious violins. Thankfully, it was not the loaned violin by Guarneri which was now in a storage vault, but her own, a Goulding 1801 instrument, worth several thousand pounds. It was the first violin she had bought after she had outgrown her practice instruments.

Having dropped it, she had screamed in frustration and pain and kicked it into the wall. Her father had found her sitting on the floor, her neck in a brace and her wrist bandaged, cradling it like a baby and sobbing.

'It can all be fixed,' he had said, sitting beside her and hugging her fiercely. 'Even you. We'll find the best doctors...'

It turned out that the best surgeon in the country for her

wrist injury was working within the National Health Service so she had had to wait several months to see him. His treatment had been methodical: physiotherapy, rest and then meticulous surgery, shaving off thickened structures which were compressing and damaging nerves.

But she had never been patient. Eight months of treatment and recovery felt impossible, and she couldn't imagine playing at the highest level ever again.

She opened the cardboard box, covered with tape marked 'Fragile'. Inside, the battered old case she kept the instrument in was enfolded in layers of tissue paper. She barely dared open the two clasps.

The violin glowed in the candlelight, like the dark honey produced in the manor gardens. The bridge had been replaced after it had been knocked off, and there was an extra scuff in the body's varnish to add to two hundred years of bumps and wear. She turned it over. She had put a couple of long scratches on it, but they had been revarnished and buffed in, now glowing deep gold rather than pale wounds.

Rather like Amber, it had healed, but wasn't really the same. She ran her fingers over the wounds. 'I'm so sorry,' she whispered. Turning it back over she noticed the chin rest, previously a modern addition in amberwood, which had been replaced by a carbon fibre one. She placed her chin on it tentatively, afraid of invoking the shooting pains she had grown used to, the numbness in her fingers that made them feel swollen. But the pain didn't return, and her fingers had free movement.

In the box there was a folded note. She recognised her father's large handwriting, scribbled hard enough to indent the paper:

> *Don't smash it up again, you're not a rock star. P.S. Chin rest prescribed by doctor.*

She smiled at that, and tried the instrument again. It meant leaning at a slightly different angle and she had already been told never – ever – to hold the violin just with her chin again. Now she supported the neck of the violin at the same time and it felt awkward.

Her father had also packed her favourite bow from her student days, which had been expertly restrung and had the scent of fresh rosin. She lifted the bow, trying not to grip it too tight. Her fingers and wrist found the shape automatically and she imagined the note – and hit a perfect G. The other strings needed a little tweak, and the pegs were perfectly lubricated with compound to make it easy to tune. She tried a little scale, gently, and nothing hurt.

Her heart jumped at the thought of playing again and she put it back down, holding the violin on her lap.

She reached for her phone, which she had charged from Ben's power bank. She was looking forward to having electricity in a couple of days. She had two bars, enough for a call.

'Hi Dad,' she said, when he answered.

'Have you smashed it up yet?' His voice was a bit growly, like he'd been serving in the hotel bar and had a few pints. She could hear the buzz of conversation in the background.

'You *know* I haven't. Thanks, Dad. It looks better than ever, beautiful. I never had time to give it a proper service with a luthier, we were always so busy. It's great.'

'How... how does it sound?' he said, and she could tell he wasn't sure whether he should be asking, whether it might be too soon.

'I didn't dare really *play* it yet, just tuned it and played a few gentle scales. It sounds so *rich*.'

'The repair place found a couple of small cracks, they've fixed those.'

She was instantly upset. 'Did I do that?'

'They reckoned there was about a hundred years of dust

inside the cracks, so you're all right. You just gave it a bit of cosmetic roughening up.'

'I'm so sorry, Dad.'

'I know, lovey.' He paused then and she wondered if he was trying to frame a question about Patrick. 'No plans to come home yet, then?'

'Not at the moment. Let me get past the twenty-first.' The wedding day. The day that should have been the beginning of a great new life with the man she still loved, just not the way she wanted to. 'How's Patrick?' she ventured, before he did.

'As you would expect. Very hurt, very confused at why you strung him along for so long.'

She sighed deeply, looking out the window at the setting sun on the horizon, over the garden wall and the fields beyond. 'Dad, I didn't string Patrick along. I fooled *myself*. You know I wouldn't deliberately hurt him, or you and Mum. I just woke up and knew I didn't love him. Not like that.'

'So your mother says.' There was another long silence. Dad didn't like talking about feelings at the best of times. 'I don't think I fell in love with your mother until after the wedding. Not really.'

The voices in the background had gone; he must have moved out to the terrace – she could hear the light wind.

'I'm sorry, Dad. I'm not going to change my mind. I am really sorry for hurting Patrick, for ruining all our plans.'

'I know that. I do, really. We're letting him stay in the gardener's house,' her father said abruptly. 'None of this is his fault.'

'He wants to stay on the island, then?' Her initial relief was followed by the realisation that she was going to bump into him every time she went to West Island, every time she visited her parents.

'For the moment, anyway. We've suggested he goes away for

a holiday, use up the honeymoon tickets since you two had already booked them.'

Weeks touring Bali, Thailand, Malaysia. That was a loss, too. She could do with swimming in warm seas, relaxing, sleeping in... She refused to think about what else they would be doing in the honeymoon cottages she had chosen. She missed being touched, hugged, even holding his hand.

'That's a good idea,' she said.

'You could go with him,' her father suggested. 'You know, scrap the wedding but talk things out, as friends. Separate rooms, even.'

The idea only warmed her for a moment. The stars were already out over the fields now. 'No, it wouldn't work. He wants me to adore him, love him like he loves me. But I just don't, not enough. It was lovely meeting up all over the world, for little honeymoons. But that's all our relationship ever was, snatched holidays. We hadn't even bought a home together, or had a pet.'

'You enjoyed staying with him at the manor.'

'I loved being home when I was so fragile after the surgery, with Mum and you. Patrick was so kind to me, too. He was lovely company when he wasn't working.' She sat down on her camping chair. 'I will always care about him, but I can't marry him.'

'So, you don't even miss him.'

Like crazy. 'Of course I do,' she said, her voice sad. 'I'm sorry, Dad. I don't want to talk about Patrick. I just phoned to say thank you for the violin, which is amazing. It must have cost you a fortune.'

'You can pay me back when you're working again,' he said, his voice rough.

She thought back to the letter. 'The orchestra let me go,' she said, tears making her eyes itch.

'How are you paying for your hotel room? You've never got

any savings and I know a lot of your money went on the wedding and honeymoon. It's not like I'm paying you anything.'

'Well, it was my idea, wasn't it?' She looked at the slowly deflating airbed and stack of sleeping bags and her new, comfortable pillow that Betty had lent her. 'I'm doing OK. I'll manage.'

'I'm afraid I haven't got much to spare at the moment, we lost a lot booking up the hotel for your wedding. I've also donated to an appeal for a local kid with a brain tumour. I can't do it all.' His voice was gruff, as it always was when he was thwarted. She could hear his sadness.

'I'm fine, Dad,' she said reassuringly. 'I'm looking after myself.'

'Well,' he said. 'You've always had someone looking after you. The orchestra, your agent, your manager, me and then Patrick...'

'I am fine,' she repeated. 'But thank you for the violin. I love you. Bye.'

She rang off before he could say any more.

12

NOVEMBER 1943

A week later, Georgina looked through the letter from Jim's bank, asking for more information before releasing any of her husband's money. She had enough for about five or six weeks' worth of food, maybe more if she was very careful. But she wouldn't be able to pay for other essentials like curtains, candles or coal, even when it was available from the cargo ship.

Grief was exhausting; she struggled to get to sleep without thinking, remembering, missing him. Missing Lena, too – any adult company, in fact. Before she had met Jim Georgie had enjoyed working in an office as a secretary, and rented a flat with two girls she met at her job. They had all got married in the same year and she had lost contact with them.

She needed to find work, and quickly. When the tide was right she could work in the day. Tommy could walk Dolly home from school now, but when he went away to grammar or boarding school she would need to get a babysitter.

Putting the letter aside, she walked down to Morwen's post office, a tiny space attached to the only food shop, and made enquiries about employment.

'Well,' the shop assistant said, looking her up and down,

'there are always jobs at the cannery but that won't suit you,' she said, hastily adding, 'because they won't fit with school hours.'

'Does anyone have any secretarial work?' she said, but the woman couldn't think of anyone.

'The best place to ask is on the big island,' she said. 'The boat will be here at lunchtime. You could nip across before the children come home.'

Georgie thanked the woman and rushed home to put the few groceries away in her bare kitchen, fretting about whether she'd be able to make it to the big island and back before school finished.

She shared her worries with Mr Ellis, who promised he would get her back, even if the wind did get up.

'The tides are all you can trust,' he said. 'I'm coming back at two fifteen, with or without you.' He smiled at her when she leaned back, nervous about stepping in the moving boat. 'And if you miss me, I'm sure your boy will look after your little girl until you get home on the steamer. It's calling at the quay, it's the last stop, about half past three.'

She managed a wry smile. 'It's not like this in London,' she explained, taking his gnarled, brown hand as he helped her into the boat. 'You can't just catch a bus or taxi here.'

'I'm sure it isn't, maid,' he said. 'What are you going over for?'

'I need to find a job,' she said. 'I was hoping there might be something over there.'

'Well, you might find something, but most people here work at the cannery, on the trawlers or on the land, and that won't fit in with school hours.'

'I'm strong, and a hard worker. I can clean and look after children, and I can type and take shorthand,' she said.

'I'll put the word about for you.' He pulled on the oars easily, and soon they were running with the racing water down the Sound. A few gulls chased after them, dipping into the water behind the boat.

She hung onto the gunwale, the surge of each wave under the boat making her feel weightless for a second. As they rounded the tall column of rock at the end of the opposite island – St Piran's – a pod of glossy dolphins arced out of the water, following the boat. She laughed as they leapt out and dived back in, spraying her with their tails until the boat curved around the corner. She could see St Brannock's harbour getting closer, dozens of small bobbing boats off the shore but none of the large ships against the quay wall.

'Are all the fishing boats out?'

'I expect so. Good weather in the forecast,' he said around his pipe. He only took it out to point out to sea. 'And the *Islander II* is coming in.'

She could see it ploughing towards them, still just a silhouette on the darker water out to sea. 'I'll be back in plenty of time,' she said, as she gathered up her bag and papers. She no longer felt she needed to carry her gas mask, as she always had in London.

She took a deep breath and walked down the tiny lane that led to Mr Seznec's office.

She peered through the dusty window, below a half-dropped blind, to see his chair empty. There was no sign up and the door was locked so she turned to go back into the town to put a card in the post office.

'Were you coming to see me?' a voice said behind her.

She turned to see Mr Seznec. He was much taller than she expected, and on two crutches. She remembered she hadn't seen him standing on the previous visit and her face warmed as she remembered how she had thought him rude.

'Yes. I was hoping you could spare just a few minutes,' she said.

He towered over her, inches taller than Jim, his frame

visible through a pale blue shirt. 'Come on in. I can make you a cup of tea, if you like.'

'I can't stay long, I have to catch the tide,' she said, twisting the handle of her handbag and following him into the shop. If anything, there were more papers in piles completely obscuring the desk. 'I've come over here to put an advertisement in the post office, for a job. I wondered if you might know of any secretarial or shop work?'

'I'll give it some thought,' he said, collapsing into his chair and standing the crutches up in the corner of a bookcase beside him. 'I'm glad you came in. I have a letter from your husband's bank. They need more information before they can release any of his funds. Like a valid will.'

'I do have a copy of his will.'

'I can check with your husband's original solicitor that it was his intention and, as far as is known, his most recent will. The bank may loosen their grip on the interest on his investments.' He made a little twisted face. 'It may not be much, but they can make an allowance for his wife and children.'

'He also had some sort of annuity.' She looked out of the window at the rushing sea. 'Just a small sum he inherited from his mother. A few hundred pounds a year.' It sounded like a fortune now.

'I'll do my best. Let me have any more documents you receive from the War Office, and the copy of the will. I'll keep trying for you.'

A horrible thought slid into her mind and made her catch her breath. 'You must let me know how much I owe you. Obviously, each letter must cost time and money.'

'I thought we had just agreed that you don't have any money right now?' he said gently, and she locked eyes with him. Sudden tears clouded her vision, blurring his face.

'Well, when we *do* get some money, then,' she said, looking down so quickly that a tear ran from each eye. 'I'm sorry, I'm rather tired.'

'Of course. I'll bill you when we win through,' he said, trying to stand up.

'No, stay there,' she said, putting a hand out to him. For a moment, her gloved fingers were held in a warm hand and she was filled with emotions. How sad it was that a young man was crippled, that Jim was probably dead and she was raising two children alone.

He slumped back in the chair. 'Tell me, Mrs Preston. Do *you* believe your husband is dead?'

'Most days I do,' she said, feeling faithless as she said the unfamiliar words. 'I feel like I would know if he was alive somewhere. I feel like he would have made his way back by now. I am just filled with sadness, all the time.'

'I'll proceed vigorously from the position that if the War Office have stopped paying his wages, they are acting as if he *is* deceased, so we might be able to apply for a death certificate. Then you can fill the form for the pension. I'll help you with it if they question it, which they may do.'

'Thank you, Mr Seznec,' she said, wiping her eyes.

'I told you, call me Hugo.'

She managed a watery smile. 'Hugo. Then you should call me Georgie.'

13

PRESENT DAY, 16 OCTOBER

Amber walked briskly up the hill with a small bag of supplies a couple of days later. As she reached the court, she saw that Betty's door was open.

'I've got your milk, Bets,' she called through.

'I've just put the kettle on,' Betty called back.

Amber put her own shopping on the windowsill of her now illuminated front room and realised it wouldn't keep as long in the morning sunshine. But the light was uplifting, lovely. She had propped the violin case in the shady corner, and a few phrases of melody in her mind made her fingers twitch as she caught sight of it.

She was hopeful that the electricity would go live today. It would be lovely to cook proper meals for herself, and although the café and shop had been great, she was running very short of money.

There were bags of plaster everywhere, and a thick stack of plasterboard. Thank goodness Dad was paying for all the materials and Ben's wages. It would be even better if he paid her some, too, but he probably didn't know the extent of what she had been doing. He had only allowed her to 'oversee' the project. He'd never have expected her to get her hands dirty as much as she had, to have thrown herself into the renovations.

Betty had made a pot of loose tea – she hated teabags in mugs if she could get away with a proper tray and nice cups. Amber put the pint of milk and a packet of biscuits on the table. Betty lived very frugally.

'How much, lovey?' Betty checked the receipt, as always, and carefully counted out the coins.

'I probably owe *you* for a lot of tea and biscuits,' Amber said.

'Nonsense. When are the boys getting here?' Betty said, patting the back of a chair in her tiny kitchen. It was almost a copy of Beehive Cottage's kitchen; Amber was starting to see where she could put units and a cooker. Only, Betty's room was a bit larger, and had a fireplace which housed an electric stove.

Most of the work in Beehive Cottage so far had been in the front room and the two bedrooms; they were leaving the kitchen and outside bathroom until last.

Betty opened the biscuits, put them in an ancient biscuit tin and offered it to Amber.

'Was there ever a fireplace in the kitchen next door?' Amber asked as she took a biscuit.

'Of course there was!' Betty scoffed. 'How do you think they cooked their food, back in the seventeen hundreds? The landlords covered it up and put some units beside it for Goldie. And a proper cooker. She didn't want the fireplace blocked off, but that old chimney was a liability.' She glanced over at Amber. 'Up until then I think she blamed the noises on the flue. You know, the ghostly noises at night.'

Amber shook her head, smiling. 'There really aren't any such things as ghosts, real life is stressful enough,' she said. A flicker of excitement ran through her as she looked at the fireplace. Now she thought about it, there were four chimney pots on the small, square chimney above the slates, to copy the four on Betty's side. 'I'd like to see if my chimney is still there,' she said, as Betty poured her a cup. 'It would be a good place for a cooker, like yours.'

'It probably would be.' The old woman leaned back in her chair. 'You must be getting cold at night, sleeping in that back bedroom.'

'It's better since Ben fixed up all the broken windows,' she said, savouring the warmth from the cup. 'And soon I'll have a heater! Dad sent an electric radiator over. I'll be able to plug it in soon. It seems like such a luxury now.'

'Well, if you ever get stuck, you come to me. You know I have a spare room for emergencies,' she said, carefully putting the lid back on the old tin. 'We'll save these for later, when the boys get here.'

'That sounds like them already,' Amber said, hearing the familiar clump of work boots. Having dropped a ladder on her foot – twice – she was yearning for some steel-capped work boots for herself.

She finished her tea, kissed Betty's cheek as a thank you and walked through to the court.

Grant and Ben were there, arguing over how to carry something rigid and made of spindles and barely fitting through the door. She rushed to help, and was astonished at what they were carrying.

'Is this a *bed*?' she said, registering an old mattress standing against the wall. 'For *me*?' It was the best present ever.

'It was knocking about in the spare room of my house,' Ben said, puffing a bit. 'My landlord said we could borrow it.'

They managed to wrangle the parts up the stairs and positioned them against the wall in the front bedroom, two pine ends and two long rails. A bundle of slats followed.

'It's a double, so it probably hasn't had generations of kids on it,' Ben said. 'Circa 1981, bought to accommodate relatives for a royal wedding, apparently. Our landlord thinks so, anyway.'

'It's amazing,' she said. 'It's been so cold on the floor. And the airbed goes down by the middle of the night.'

'Plumber's coming over this morning,' Grant said. 'From Westy. One of your estate staff. He'll start putting pipes in for the kitchen and bathroom.'

Oh. He'd certainly report back to her father that she'd been roughing it at the house. She decided not to worry about what anyone else thought, until one idea intruded.

Patrick. Patrick will know. He'll probably think it serves me right.

'Well,' she said, going for breezy but ending up squeaky, 'I'm off to do some washing at the campsite launderette before it closes for the season.'

'I'll start work in here,' Ben said, looking up at the ceiling, which was so low he could easily touch it. 'Perhaps we should put the bed up. Which room?'

'Thank you. I'd prefer it if you finish the back bedroom first, make it nice, then leave the front bedroom until last,' she said. 'There's a funny atmosphere in the front. I think it bore the brunt of the fire and it smells of smoke.' Besides, she made music in the back room, those snatches of imagination that were gradually weaving into a melody.

'You're the boss,' Ben said, then smiled crookedly. 'I just wanted to make it nice for you.'

'*Aww,*' floated up the stairs from Grant. 'Just help me with this mattress, I'm not sure it will go up the stairs.'

When they had delivered the rest of the bed and checked that all the fittings were in a bag and taped to one of the rails, Amber followed them downstairs.

'I was wondering,' she said to Ben, sidling around Grant, 'about the kitchen.' She tapped on the wall adjacent to Betty's kitchen. 'Betty has a chimney breast about here. I wondered if it was a mirror of this one?'

Ben tapped at it as well. 'I was hoping this was the

only wall that doesn't need completely rebuilding. Get me the big claw hammer, it's in the tool box.' She picked it up, heavy in her hand, and he stood back. 'Go on, then. I don't want to explain to your dad how I smashed his house up.'

She closed her eyes to guess where the opening would be, gripped the rubber handle in both hands and swung. The hammer bounced off the plaster with the first blow, but the second one – a little lower – crashed through with a fall of rubble behind it. She yanked at the handle with both hands and pulled out a large bit of the board, with layers of paint and old paper.

'Keep going,' Ben said, leaning against the opposite wall. 'I like to see a rich girl actually working.'

'That's harsh after I carried all your bags!' she said, laughing back at him.

Smashing holes in the wall was satisfying, and when he offered her gloves, she started pulling at the loose plasterboard. She stopped to peer into the hole she had made, and Ben handed her a torch.

'It's an old stove,' she said, amazed. 'A miniature cooking range, it looks Victorian. It's pretty rusty but it looks like it's in one piece.'

He leaned in close to look as well, their heads almost touching. She was strangely stirred by his proximity and immediately felt guilty.

'It will take a lot of work to clean it up,' he said, turning to look at her. 'But it's not like you're watching TV all evening.'

'No, I shall be watching videos on my phone from my glorious bed,' she quipped back, a little breathless from the exercise and her reaction to his closeness. 'When I can get a signal to download anything.'

He didn't move, but there was a curiosity to his raised eyebrows. 'Are you OK?'

'I'm fine,' she said, sliding further away. 'I'm going to tell Betty, and ask for some hot water.'

'Coffee!' bellowed Grant as she stepped around him.

'Tea for me,' Ben said, following her to the front door. 'Are you sure you're OK? You looked like you'd seen a ghost, you went all pale.'

'I'm fine.' She faked a smile and walked over to Betty's, who came in from her tiny yard carrying a basket of laundry. 'We found a fireplace like yours,' she called through the house. 'Only it's got an old range in it. It's really tiny.'

'Ooh, I remember that from when I was a little maid!' Betty said. 'Who'd ever have thought it was still there?'

Betty came over to inspect the stove. 'Look,' Ben said, pulling a little more plasterboard away. Beside the stove was a cupboard painted a lurid green. 'They covered up the whole thing. I don't know if it still opens, it looks like it was painted shut.'

'Georgie used to lock all her work in there,' Betty said. 'Official stuff.'

Amber pulled at it but the door didn't budge. 'I'll work at it with a blade, while I'm getting the rust off the stove,' she said.

'The flue looks OK,' he said. 'Not up to code, of course – if you lit it you'd probably suffocate with carbon monoxide.'

'I know a sweep,' Betty said. 'I'll give you his number.'

As she only got good signal down towards the quay, Amber thought it would be a great excuse to make the call on another evening walk. The sunsets were getting earlier each day as the autumn marched on. 'Thank you, that would be great.'

The idea of lighting the little stove was intoxicating, like bringing the cottage back to life after ripping it bare.

14

NOVEMBER 1943

Georgina walked along the sand at Seal Cove on a surprisingly warm, if windy, November Saturday. Tommy was racing ahead of her and Dolly, throwing a stick for a neighbour's dog, a chore he happily did every day before school for a few pence pocket money a week.

She had recently received a suggestion from Hugo Seznec that she apply to the local newspaper, the *Island Press*, to help write a few notices and advertisements. It contained little actual news, as bulletins were carefully worded and probably edited by government officials. Maybe they were worried about morale. The local articles and advertisements were haphazardly spelled and punctuated; she was sure she could do a better job.

Her mood had been low lately, but the cloud was lifting. Jim was gone; she could believe it now. Grieving was easier than speculating, than preparing herself endlessly for the bad news she was sure would come. Tommy seemed easier, too, although she sometimes heard him crying at night. That made her cry, too, both of them quietly sobbing in separate rooms, trying not to wake Dolly.

Dolly was just about to turn six, and was unflinchingly

certain Daddy was alive and would come home. She seemed to have latched on to the fantasy of him living on an island, playing in the sand just like her, collecting shells and surrounded by gulls screaming and fighting overhead.

Georgie shaded her eyes to look up – the gulls weren't fighting among themselves today – they were attacking a huge crow. It ignored them, looking down its heavy beak with disinterest as they just missed its wingtips. When he cawed, an answering cry made Georgie jump, then laugh as Dolly ran to her and hugged her legs.

'The bird noise is much better than London traffic,' she said, swinging Dolly into her arms. 'Oof! You've grown. You *must* be nearly six!'

Dolly gave a little smile. 'I don't like the black birds,' she said, looking up the beach at Tommy. 'They are the death birds.'

Georgie put her down, reeling from her words. Although Dolly wouldn't consider that Jim might be gone, she talked about death all the time. You couldn't shield children from the reality of war when they grew up with gas masks and bomb shelters.

The dog charged along the beach and Tommy whistled for it to come back. Tag seemed to know the way off the beach to the path that ran along the edge of the island all the way to the big house at the end. The stink of seaweed filled the air, and Georgie called to Tommy.

'You get Tag, we'll stay here,' she shouted as Dolly came back to her, covering her face against the smell.

Right on the shoreline was a small platform, like a grave marker, covered with weed, barnacles and limpets. She could just make out two initials, J and C, covered with plants. She wondered who it was for. Someone who had drowned, perhaps, or someone who loved this place? She wondered if Jim would like a memorial stone somewhere, even if they never found his body. Maybe where they spent their first week together in Norfolk, before they were even married.

'Pooh, smelly weed,' Dolly said, skipping to the high-tide line to look for more shells. By the time she had collected some, along with a long white feather and two pieces of pale blue sea glass, Tommy had returned with the dog.

'I need to call at the shop, to see if we have any letters,' Georgie said, as Tag and Tommy started playing tug-of-war with a thick piece of rope.

'The post won't be until this afternoon,' he said, then laughed as the collie pulled him almost off his feet. 'The tide's too low. Come on, Tag!'

Of course, the tide. She still hadn't adjusted to the way the whole island organised itself each side of high tide. She jammed her hands into her jacket pocket, walking behind the children along the quay. A stab of grief hit her again. She would have given anything to put her hand in Jim's warm fingers and enjoy their little family together.

She sniffed back the onset of tears and walked towards the end of the town, in front of the church.

'Mrs Preston!' A middle-aged woman in tweed was half jogging towards her, waving. *Oh, Lord, the vicar's wife.*

'Good morning, Mrs Anstruther,' she called back as they approached the slipway at the end of the quay. 'We were just walking the dog.'

'Good morning, Thomas, Dolly. How are you all settling in?'

Dolly pressed against Georgie's skirt and Tommy nodded. 'I'll just take Tag home,' he said as he put the leash back on and ran along the quay.

'It's going very well,' Georgie said. 'The children are settling at school.'

'And you're quite comfortable in the house? It's a funny little place.'

The stare that came with the question was probing, intrusive. Georgie decided not to take offence, the woman was probably trying to be kind. 'It's a little draughty and smaller than we're used to, but we're glad to have a home. So many families don't.'

'Indeed.' Mrs Anstruther looked over the sea. 'We've all had to make sacrifices.'

Georgie's heart lurched in her chest as she remembered Jim. *Some more than others.*

'Our son will be home for Christmas,' Mrs Anstruther continued. 'He's at Calke Oak School, of course. You probably know of it.'

'Tommy was at Wycliffe Prep, before the war. His father went there. He came from a military family,' she explained.

'It's so important to continue their education as best we can. Will Thomas be resuming his studies there when... your situation becomes clearer?'

For a moment, Georgie wondered who had been tattling but it hadn't taken her long to learn that news spread fast on a small island.

'I hope so. At some point,' she said. 'But at the moment I think some time off, away from London, would be good for him. And probably much safer.' She had no idea if Wycliffe Prep would consider having him back, and she couldn't apply for the full scholarship until her pension had been secured and Jim's situation clarified.

'You know, we have a ladies' circle, for war work. If you would like to join us, you'd be very welcome. We do all sorts of useful mending, knitting and correspondence. You could be most helpful.'

'That is very kind,' Georgie said. 'But I think I should be with the children. At the moment.'

'Perhaps when they are busy at school?'

'Ah,' Georgie said, sidling past Mrs Anstruther. 'Perhaps I

can, I'll try. I have been looking for a job, though, and I don't know how much time I will have spare. Excuse me, I need to get back.'

'A *job*?' She made a little face. 'Surely you want to concentrate on the little ones?' Her eyes were narrowed with curiosity; in one instant, Georgie decided she didn't like her.

'I am used to occupation,' Georgie said, taking Dolly's hand. 'I am sorry. I think Dolly needs to go home, she's getting cold. I'll certainly be in touch if I find I do have time to help such an important cause.' She smiled as she marched them both along the quay and up the hill to the tiny court.

The door to number four was open, and young Maria was sweeping out the front step of her honeymoon cottage. She was noticeably larger now.

'My goodness, you've grown,' she said. 'How is that matinee jacket coming on for the layette?'

'I'm struggling with finishing off the neck. But it looks lovely. I wish I'd done it in blue, now. Mam is convinced it's a boy.' She rubbed the small of her back. 'She swung my wedding ring over my tummy, a circle means a girl and a straight swing means a boy.' She didn't look convinced.

'That never worked for me,' Georgie said. 'Go and get the jacket, I'll put the kettle on and see where you've got to with it. Pregnancy gets tiring at the end, doesn't it?'

She welcomed Maria in, blew the embers of the morning fire and added some driftwood on the top. She had a small sack of coal, and she added a couple of pieces carefully, right under the kettle. 'The tea won't be long.'

'I've run out of tea,' Maria said, sighing as she sat at the table. 'Mam's got my ration. But I like being in our own house, I'm making it nice for when my husband comes home.'

'How's he doing?' Georgie could see where she was going wrong with the neck and showed her. 'See, you need to decrease here...'

'I see. Thank you.' The girl bit her lip and looked down at the wool, making a loose stitch. 'I don't really know how Peter's doing. No one tells me anything. Is this right?'

'That's it, and then the next one.'

Maria looked up, her expression remorseful. 'I mean, I know Pete's all right, it's just that he doesn't write much. I think he's in Scotland, they are based up in the north.'

'That's good news.' Georgie tried to make her voice confident. No one knew when bad news would arrive, and merchant seamen were dying too. 'Would it be easier to stay with your parents full-time? Until the baby comes, anyway.'

'Well,' Maria said, resting her hands on her bump, 'I'm second-eldest of nine, and Pete doesn't get on well with my dad. I got this way,' she said, waving apologetically at the baby, 'before we was married.'

'Me too,' Georgie said spontaneously. 'It happens.'

Maria's eyes had opened wide. 'I didn't think it happened to people like you,' she said.

'Like me?' Georgie turned to warm the pot with a splash of water. 'People are all the same, really. When they are in love.' She and Jim had been bowled over by each other. There had been no shame when they fell in love, no hesitation. She took a cottage on the edge of the sea in Norfolk, and they had had a wonderful week together, and conceived Tommy. The fact simply accelerated the wedding. 'No,' she said cheerlessly, looking over the ivy-clad back yard, still buzzing with the last of the bees on the tiny late-autumn flowers. 'Love always wins.'

15

PRESENT DAY, 20 OCTOBER

Amber walked down to the Mermaid's Purse pub, just around the corner, after the week's work on the cottage. It was the evening of the open mic fundraiser for Kai; it sounded like fun, and she wanted a glass of something before she got into bed.

Night-time temperatures were falling even though the days had been dry and sunny. The stars twinkled like frost, and the clocks would go back in a week or so. She was hoping to have lighting and heating by then.

A young man not much older than her was behind the bar. At one end of the long, thin room was a cluster of people holding instruments and glasses, laughing and chattering together. An older man, formidably tall and heavy, looked over at her and narrowed his eyes. She knew a bit about him: he'd been a member of a band back in the nineties. She remembered seeing articles about his band in the *Island Press*.

She perched on a bar stool and ordered a pint of a local beer. The chatter stopped and she turned around to watch as a single fiddle player walked forward and played the intro to 'Inisheer', an Irish folk song. It had been one of her favourites to play when she was about six or seven.

The band joined in, with the pub slowly starting to stamp and nod in time to the music, smiles all around. By the time the rest of an odd collection of instrumentalists had joined in – two guitarists, a whistle player who looked like she was still at school and an older man on a melodeon – she was tapping her foot, too. It got fast towards the end, with a big finish; a few people were dancing along. Her fingers twitched.

The big man walked over, brushing his long hair off his face, and took a standing pint of something dark off the bar. 'You're Amber Marrak.'

She leaned back and smiled at him as he drank deeply. 'I am. You're Mitch Tate.'

He reached out a large hand. 'Everyone calls me Elk.'

She shook it. 'You played at the music festival a couple of months ago. I saw you.'

He nodded, drank again, made a face. 'Ugh. Diet drinks.'

'Not beer?'

He shook his head. 'I've given up beer until Christmas. Are you still playing? Last time I saw you, you were in a neck brace.'

She couldn't speak for a moment as too many words crowded forward. *Yes, I still want to play. But maybe I can't play ever again.* 'I had an injury,' she said. 'I'm supposed to be building myself back up.'

'Come and play with us, see what happens.' It wasn't an offer, it sounded like an order. 'Just borrow my fiddle. It's not like you're playing a concerto, just a bit of gentle busking along.'

'I haven't brought – I don't know the music,' she stammered, although she looked at his old instrument, propped up in its open case.

'"Niel Gow's Lament". You must know it?'

She'd heard it played a hundred times. She could hear the melody in her head, almost feel her fingers on the strings, the pressure on the bow.

'Without the music I could only bodge it,' she said, her voice thickened with unexpected emotion.

'That's what we do,' he said, and laughed. 'I've got the dots on my tablet, it will get you started. Come on, girl. You give it a go, and if you're any good I'll join in.'

He was a brilliant guitarist. She wasn't sure she could do his playing justice, but hesitantly walked into the circle and took the proffered fiddle. She glanced at the music on the screen, let the first few notes play in her mind.

The fiddle was light, beautifully balanced, and in tune. She lifted it up, feeling the weight, put it under her chin. Dad was right, the chin rest was a bit low and she could feel the stretch in her neck, the slight pull on the scar. There was shushing, several of the other players were sitting back as she faced the audience, unable to make eye contact with Elk.

She touched the bow to the strings, just to feel her way, playing a few notes that were lost in the pub. The lament began to grow in her head, her fingers connected more firmly with the instrument, and somehow, the music streamed from her bow, filling the tiny pub.

She shut her eyes, letting the slow march soar, finding each moment as she breathed in time with the music, her whole body resonating with the sound. She heard the guitar join in, the notes plaintive and powerful, and she opened her eyes.

The audience were spellbound; a few had their mouths open, and she realised she was playing too loud for the small space. She took it down a notch, letting her body follow the music, releasing energy that had been cramped up in her neck and shoulder. As Elk picked up the pace, she matched him, laughing as he took her into a faster tempo.

The young girl beside her stood up and started playing the whistle over the top, and she could feel they were heading towards a jig. She turned a little to watch Elk as he launched into it, and joined in.

By the end, she was hot, her hands starting to slip on the strings with the effort. She laughed again as they went into a coda, and the pub erupted with applause, stamping, clapping and banging on tables. It was nothing like the polite classical world she had trained for. A bucket was being passed around, and was filling up with coins and quite a few notes.

She swung the fiddle down, her shoulder cramped, her neck aching. 'Thank you. I've missed that,' she said, over the noise, to Elk, who had managed a smile. 'It's a lovely instrument.'

'I rescued it from a charity shop in Bath,' he said. 'And did it up.'

'You're a luthier, aren't you?'

'I worked on your instrument,' he said. 'Your dad brought me your violin.'

Her mouth fell open. '*You* did it?'

'He had it X-rayed in London in case it had more serious damage. It had historical cracks, which needed repairing. It's a good instrument, you'd just messed up its face. Didn't you notice the sound getting a bit dull?' He nodded to the bar.

'It's always been like that,' she said, returning to her drink, handed to her by the barman. 'I had to work a bit harder to get a good sound out. But it was worth it, it has a lovely tone.'

That extra work might have contributed to her repetitive strain injury. Maybe it wasn't all down to some inherent weakness in her body, or in her technique. Amber felt something like relief, hope. She sipped her beer.

'We've doubled our takings,' he said. 'We should get you in for all our fundraisers.' He smiled as he turned back to the barman. 'A pint of Pirates for the lady, Sam. I think we should celebrate her return to music.'

Everyone wanted to talk to her, even when she laughingly refused to play again and sat in the corner to listen to the other musicians. She started her second ale.

'Wow,' came a familiar voice at her elbow. 'If you didn't already have a beer, I'd get you one.'

'Ben!' She was suddenly awkward, embarrassed. 'I didn't know it very well. I just busked through it, really. It was good that Elk knew it and could join in.'

Ben squeezed into a chair in the corner beside her and beckoned to someone behind him. 'Come on, Lizzie. Meet Amber.'

A girl with blue hair, a narrow, pixie-like face and rainbow-coloured glasses joined him. 'Nice to meet you, Amber,' she said, putting her own glass of dark beer beside Amber's. 'I was going to play, but I can't follow that.'

'What do you play?' Amber asked, seeing a narrow case beside her on the floor.

'Flute. *Folk* flute, if you know what I mean. I'm not exactly trained.'

'That's brilliant,' Amber said sincerely. Music was the thread that had run through her brain constantly, until she had woken up from the anaesthetic a few months ago. Then it was all mixed up with the anxiety that she would never play again. But she could feel it there again now, rolling and dipping through the lament as it transformed into a jig. 'Playing anything is magic. How about you, Ben? Have you got a secret cello parked somewhere? Bassoon?'

He laughed. 'Not me.' He took a draught of his beer. 'No, I'm just a carpenter who does a bit of plastering.'

'He's *totally* lying,' said Lizzie. 'He sings. He sings in the church choir, and he's a shanty singer, too.'

'But I only sing the rude ones,' he said, and drained his glass.

Lizzie watched him walk back to bar. Amber could see she was interested in him.

'Have you known each other long?'

Lizzie jumped. 'No! I mean, it's not like that, we're not a couple. We share a house. No one can afford a place by themselves on the islands.' She glanced over her glasses at Amber. 'Well, most of us can't, anyway.'

'Ben must have told you I'm living in a building site with no kitchen and no heating?'

Lizzie nodded. 'It sounded like it was your choice, though?'

'I don't mind roughing it,' Amber said. 'It serves me right, really. I could be packing for my honeymoon right now.'

'And your wedding. When was it?' Her wide eyes were curious, and Amber felt safe talking about it to a stranger, in a dark corner of a pub, bathed in music.

'Tomorrow.' She finished her beer and wiped her mouth with the back of her hand, like a child. Then she noticed the tickle of moisture at the corner of each eye. 'But I'm sure I did the right thing. It's got to be right, hasn't it? You have to be really sure, to commit for life.'

'I like Patrick,' Lizzie said. 'But I understand. I can't imagine getting married myself, I'd have to be head over heels, absolutely certain.' Her gaze travelled around and settled on Ben.

Amber wiped her eyes discreetly. 'I think you're right, marriage should be to *the one*.' She looked into the glass. 'I may be a little drunk, I knocked that back too quickly.' *Intoxicated by the music, too.*

Elk was standing, calling for quiet, and Lizzie shushed her.

'So, to finish off the evening, since we're all tired, I'm going to ask Amber Marrak, world-famous classical violinist, to come back and play us something in her usual style of music.' He beckoned to her and her heart raced. 'Come on, you must remember something else.'

'No, no. I've been injured, I'm supposed to rest...' she said, as Ben reached for her hands and pulled her upright. The contact startled her.

'Come on,' he said into her ear over the cheering. 'Just play us something easy. We won't know any different.'

She was shaking suddenly, even as his hands warmed her. 'I don't know if I can,' she said to him, even as she stepped closer. When Elk held out the instrument, she let go of Ben and reached for it.

'I don't know what to play,' she said, turning to the crowd, who had calmed down. 'OK, OK, I have an idea. This is by John Williams, it's the theme from *Schindler's List*. It's not too much of a stretch. But you have to forgive me if it's really rusty, I've been out of action for eight months...'

Her mind recreated it, and her fingers somehow translated the notes on to the unfamiliar instrument. She bowed hesitantly at first; then, she lost herself in the melancholic melody. By the time she had finished, just a few minutes later, she was sweating, her heart was thumping in her throat and she couldn't speak.

I love doing this. I love this more than anything.

After several seconds of breathless silence, the pub erupted into laughs and whoops and clapping, the release she had been craving.

16

NOVEMBER 1943

Georgie had dressed smartly in a dark heather tweed suit she had worn years before when working in an office, ready for her first job in eleven years. The middle section was a bit snug, but she felt professional-looking – as long as nobody saw her getting off Mr Ellis's ferry. She still hadn't worked out how to get into or out of the small boats with any dignity.

Mr Alden, the editor of the local paper, had just a few hours' work for her, each week until the spring. He was short and heavyset, about ten years older than her, with horn-rimmed spectacles that he was constantly looking for. He explained the role.

She would be writing up adverts and notices, and proof-reading his articles and the news they were required to place on the front pages from the Ministry of Information. He had offered her four hours' work a week, within school hours where possible, and she had been introduced to the office. She would have to write every word by hand as they didn't have a functioning typewriter, the old Hammond needing repairs.

'If you can take shorthand, you can work on it at home, as long as you send it back to me by Wednesday lunchtime. Then my brother and I typeset the whole thing on the old press, and run off the sheets.' She had seen the newspaper: a single broadsheet printed small on both sides. 'Paper's rationed,' he said, unnecessarily. 'I can pay you ten shillings a week, until my wife comes back to work.' He handed her a pile of scraps with scruffy writing on. 'And see if you can make any sense of these.'

The first piece was a death notice – of a local sailor lost at sea, barely eighteen years old. Just eight years older than Tommy. Her heart jumped and she looked down at the papers, pretending to sort them, although she could barely see through the tears.

'Ready to take dictation?' Mr Alden said, sitting on the edge of a table by the back-office window, blocking out the light. She made a fuss of getting out some pencils, her notebook and sitting ready. She managed to sniff back a stray tear.

'Yes, Mr Alden.'

He made a face. 'None of that, lovey. I'm Bob, and I'm going to call you Georgina. If that's all right with you?' he added, a little snappily, as if worried she would insist on the formalities.

'That would be lovely, Bob. If you will call me Georgie.'

As the time wore on, she took dictation and became bolder at offering suggestions as he tried to edit his features down by a few words to fit on the page. At the end of her shift, he walked her down to the boat, introducing her to his wife, who had walked down to the quay to meet him. She was pushing a baby in a perambulator, even though it was drizzling. Georgie suspected Mrs Alden wanted to check that her temporary replacement wasn't too glamorous or too young, but the two women soon found a connection in the baby. By the time Mr Ellis had pulled the boat alongside, Georgie and Rachel Alden were exchanging birth stories and Bob had vanished back to the office.

In her pocket was now a crisp ten-shilling note, wrapped in an old receipt. It was such a relief, even if the job would only last a few months while Rachel was on leave. She planned to ask her mother to mind the child by the spring, once she would take a bottle.

'So, you had a good morning at your new job?' Mr Ellis asked, as he coaxed a smoky rattle out of a tiny engine. 'Tide's too fast to row easily,' he explained, as he waved at the oars, lying ranged each side of them. 'Mind you, if the engine chokes across the Sound, you and me, maid, we'll have to row, both of us, or we'll end up in France.'

'It was good to be working again,' she said, waving a wisp of exhaust away from her face and fitting her scarf over her artfully curled hair. She wouldn't need to dress up so much next time; Bob Alden smoked and spread ash everywhere – she'd be brushing it out of the tweed for the rest of the week – and her fingers were covered with ink.

The water was a strange colour, almost yellowy green, the sky overhead a dirty grey. Rolled up in her bag was a mackintosh, and she barely had time to unroll it and slip it over her suit before the rain came down.

Mr Ellis ignored it; the large drops beaded on his thick jersey and in his luxuriant beard. He pulled out a waterproof hat and put it on, the wind getting stronger. He fastened it under his chin, and in that moment, the water swung the boat around in right angles.

'Don't like the look of that,' he said, clamping his unlit pipe between his teeth. The engine coughed but managed to catch a new rhythm as he guided it between streams of water slipping over themselves, swirling into little pools. 'That's over a submerged rock called Peryllus Ledge,' he said. 'At certain depths it creates this rough water.'

'Is it dangerous?' She peered into the turbulence.

He grinned around the stem of his pipe. 'Well, maid, that's why they called it *perilous*. We'll be fine.'

The rain was coming faster as they left the shelter of the

coast and headed straight across the water between St Bran-nock's and St Piran's. She pulled her scarf forward over her eyes to shade her face.

'We'll go right over the Sound,' he shouted to her, staring ahead with concentration. The oncoming waves were lifting and thumping the boat around. 'You'd better hold on. It gets a bit tricky around Kettle Rock.'

She tucked her bag under the seat and held the sides; it was frightening but exhilarating, and she breathed deep. She felt safe in his confidence, in his grim smile as he shot the boat past the end of the island, past the mined beach, and curved around the stack the locals called Kettle Rock. None of her neighbours and new friends could tell her why it was called that, but it soared overhead, monolithic.

'We'd better get carried down to the south slipway,' he shouted over the wind, guiding the boat head-on into the choppy waves. 'It's safer than getting capsized.' He grinned at her.

Georgie couldn't agree more, clinging to the gunwale. For the first time, she felt Jim's loss like a missing tooth in childhood: sore but meant to be there. Out on the water, at least, she could accept his death without feeling the terrible grief and guilt that he had died while she was comfortably at home. She'd looked up the exact time the ship had gone down: she had been reading *Little Red Riding Hood* to the children at that moment. There hadn't been a sudden foreboding or shiver down her spine. Just a girl, a grandmother and a wolf, coming to life through words and pictures.

The engine whined when the front of the boat was lifted out of the water, and groaned when the back was forced deeper. The rain gathered on her face, ran down like tears. She had never felt more alive.

17

PRESENT DAY, 21 OCTOBER

Amber woke early to the cries of gulls flying overhead. She hadn't slept well, and had spent part of the night crying. Tears welled up out of nowhere, poured out of her in a tide of pain. Maybe they had been triggered by the music; the last time she had played that last piece had been for Patrick. And today was *the* day. She got up, pulled the thin curtains back and stared out of the window at the dark hill.

My wedding day.

She had, with her mother, planned everything from flowers and centrepieces to the dessert wine. They had handcrafted the invitations and the place cards. The dining room wall had the table plan pinned to it when she left. The tickets and their passports for the honeymoon were in her bedside table. She wondered if Patrick had still been sleeping there.

The sky was clear, a pink echo from the east touching the edges of clouds. She tried to remember if that meant good or bad weather. Red sky in the morning, shepherd's warning...

It didn't matter any more. She wasn't going to be photographed in the sunken garden in her 1920s-style gown, holding Patrick's arm in his silk suit. She wasn't going to listen to speeches and toasts and smile and kiss and dance. She wasn't going to listen to beautiful music played by her talented friends in a haze of late roses and hothouse orange blossom.

She was going to get into dirty, ripped jeans and scrape rust off an old stove. She wondered, as the tears welled up again, whether she would cry all day.

Her phone pinged. She saw that a couple of messages had come in overnight on the intermittent signal, but the last one was from Patrick.

Last chance if you want to talk? No pressure.

She rocked herself through the pain of another bout of sobs. By the time they subsided, she was numb, all emotion squeezed out of her.

Amber picked clean clothes out of her bag, added her thickest jumper, and fumbled with jeans, socks and trainers. As she walked out the front, Betty's door opened, but she couldn't bear to stop to talk. She headed up the hill towards the lane that led all around the island, past the school, houses and the campsite, in front of the coastguards' cottages. The path curved around the end of the island, rising as it went.

She gasped at the view from the cliffs. The water was steel grey in the early light. When she turned to look at St Piran's she could see the red sunrise, and the wind was picking up. The clouds were the same colour as the sea, and a few white birds swept over it, crying mournfully.

Walking briskly up the path, she came to the top of the steps. There was a warning about the tide attached to the signpost: Seal Cove. She could see the tide was going out, so she started down to the semicircular bay.

She didn't remember having been here before, the steps led into the middle of a curved sandy beach with lines of shells and a few pebbles. Seaweed rolled at the edge of the water, woven into strands, and the cliff behind was full of gorse and undergrowth.

Right now she should be getting ready with her two best friends. Kerry, her oldest friend from music summer camps, was going to play the cello as Amber walked in. She was an amazing musician. Her best friend from college, Chloe, had just got engaged. They had all been looking forward to a few days of wedding chatter before the actual event.

More messages pinged through to her phone. Both told her they still loved her, and both wanted to hear from her to make sure she was OK.

She couldn't answer them just yet. Instead, she huddled on a bench at the bottom of the steps and breathed in the air, the salt tickling her throat.

She closed her eyes and pictured Patrick's face, his smile, his enthusiasm about planting their own plot. The family were lucky to have an award-winning designer living on the island and working for the manor garden. She wondered if he'd be off soon, looking for another world-class site to call his own, maybe a world-class woman to fall in love with.

No, she wasn't ready for that just yet. She didn't want him herself, but she definitely didn't want him in the arms of someone else so soon.

She folded her arms and leaned back. Why didn't she want the fairy tale wedding to the perfect guy?

The answer came on the wind creeping down the neck of her jacket. Because she wasn't that kind of woman. She had spent most of her childhood pushing away from home, forging her career around the globe with youth orchestras, building up to her own world-class career. Second violin, first violin – she was just beginning to get offers of soloist parts when the tingle she would feel in her fingers at the end of a long concert became burning needles through her shoulder, then numbness.

Now she flexed her hand without pain, moved her shoulders up and down. A few black and white birds cried to each other down the beach, their red beaks and legs glowing in the autumn sun. She stood up and walked to the edge of the water, which was just creeping in and out a few inches, almost still.

She had loved Patrick, of course she had, but she had never postponed a gig for him, her music always came first. *He* had been known to delay a flight or postpone a job to spend a few more hours with her. He was generous and kind, thoughtful, happy to follow her as she blazed her trail around the world.

It had been her time to shine. She had paid her dues playing endless popular classics, operas and recordings. She had been ready to have her name leading the bill.

A lot of her grief was tied up in the moment the doctors told her she might never reach the previous heights of virtuosity, that her dreams might be over. She would need to find something that excited her as much as playing. Would she be the same person if she was based at home, maybe teaching a few classes or doing a few ensemble recordings? They had argued over having children. For him it was pretty important, but she couldn't imagine it. Could they really have been getting married before they had sorted out all the important questions? It had all felt too urgent, too rushed.

A line of melody crept through her grief, the same fragment that had bothered her last night, just a handful of notes.

She hummed the line, listened to her soft voice in the sharp air. As a child she'd always written songs down, played made-up music, sang along as words came to her. Sometimes she had played her own songs at college but had been put down by the lecturers who were teaching composition. *Too easy, too simple.*

All her lines seemed to end with 'I miss you,' which made her stop. An unruly wavelet splashed her trainers, making her jump from the icy water onto a flat stone just at the tideline. She almost slipped on the weed covering it.

Do I miss him?

She missed the company, the affection, the physical comfort. Now she was cold and one foot was wet.

Amber jumped as someone spoke behind her.

'You aren't going to walk in, are you?'

She turned to see a slight blonde woman holding a toddler's hand.

'No! Nothing like that.'

'You just looked so... sad.'

The toddler scampered over the sand, stopping to pick something up to show her mother.

'I'm having a bit of a bad day.' She tried a smile but it slid off her face when she realised the woman was looking at her with sympathy. 'I imagine you already know why. Everyone seems to.'

'Well, there are only a few people on the island. If we hadn't been away visiting my father in London, we probably would have bumped into each other before now. You're Amber Marrak, Sir Michael's daughter. You just called off your wedding.'

'Would you believe me if I told you I tried to slow down the train months before, but no one was listening?'

The woman smiled. 'I believe you. I'm Ellie Roberts. I know what you mean. My partner is keen to get married, but I'm not so sure.' She took another shell from the toddler, who swung around to stare at Amber with dark, intelligent eyes. 'This is Zillah. Look, would you like to come back for a coffee? She's tired after all those steps and we've walked right around the island this morning.'

Amber almost said no, but instead nodded, tears blocking her words again.

'Look, Zillah, this lady is going to come home with us!'

'Cuppa tea?' the child asked, cocking her head on one side as if sceptical. Amber hadn't much experience of small children and couldn't work out how old she was. 'Biscuit?'

'Well, yes, that would be lovely,' she managed to say, and was rewarded by a frown.

'Up steps,' the child said, pointing. She walked over and handed Amber her treasures: a handful of pebbles, shells and, after a careful transfer, a precious empty crab leg. At least, Amber hoped it was empty. 'In your pocket,' Zillah explained imperiously, then smiled under her bouncy dark curls. Amber was lost; she stuffed the smelly treasures into her pocket and took the hand that was held out. 'I got new boots,' Zillah elaborated as Amber followed her to the stairs and Ellie took her other hand.

'She can be a little bossy,' she said, trying not to laugh.

Zillah's hand was gritty and damp, and clung tight.

'That's OK,' Amber said, 'so can I. It's lovely that she's so confident.' It warmed Amber that Zillah seemed to trust her immediately.

'Confident, yes. But now she's going to expect us to swing her all the way to the top.'

Which proved to be quite a workout, with a few funny moments along the way. Ellie lifted her daughter onto her hip at the top. 'We're just along here, past the coastguard cottages,' she said, leading the way. A pale green cottage was set back from the lane.

Amber looked from the gate over the slope to the quay and the misty islands beyond. 'What a fantastic view!'

'I don't suppose you get one from Beehive Cottage,' Ellie said, pushing open the door.

'A bit out the back.' Beside the porch was a drive leading to what looked like a garage. 'You can't have a car, surely?' There really were no roads on the island.

'It's Bran's studio,' Amber explained. 'Zillah's dad is an artist. Come on in, if you can get past the toys in the hall. I think they were building towers this morning so they could knock them down.'

'Castles,' said Zillah, snuggling her head onto Ellie's collarbone.

'I definitely think it's nap time,' Ellie said, putting her lips to Zillah's curls. 'Since we've been up since *five*.'

While Ellie took the toddler upstairs, Amber walked into the living room and looked over the island from the bay window.

'Best view on the island,' a deep, masculine voice said. 'I'm Branok Shore. I'm guessing you're Amber Marrak?' Her eyes filled with tears even as she took in the tall stranger. He was good-looking, and she could see where his daughter got her dark curls from. He shrugged. 'I know Patrick,' he said, his voice neutral.

'Oh.' She could feel her muscles tensing as she waited for the judgement, the criticism.

'I saw him a couple of days ago, when we got back. He was devastated. But I only know his side of the story. I'm sure you had your reasons.' He waved at a comfortable-looking overstuffed couch. 'Do you want to sit down? I'll put the kettle on.'

'Would you listen?' she blurted out. 'I mean, to my side of the story?'

'I would,' he said, his expression calm and still, then he smiled a little.

He disappeared, and she found tears streaming down her face again. Today was going to be one of those days, she reasoned. By the time he returned with three mugs of tea, her tears had eased off. She sat opposite him and warmed her hands on the handcrafted mug. Its glazed surface rippled in her hand like a piece of sea glass, pale green.

Amber sipped it, unable to start talking. He waited, perhaps for Ellie to join them, and before long she came and sat beside him on the other sofa.

'You must be feeling very emotional today,' Ellie ventured,

not difficult to guess given Amber's swollen eyes and probably pink nose.

'It was supposed to be our wedding day,' she started before the tears caught her again. She put the cup down on the coffee table and gratefully took a handful of tissues from Ellie.

'I should have had second thoughts right at the beginning,' she continued. 'When we got engaged,' she managed to say, hoarsely. 'Look, I'm so sorry to be doing this to you. I should go.'

'No,' said Ellie firmly. 'Settle down and I'll get the biscuits.' She smiled sympathetically. 'Zillah promised,' she said, as she disappeared.

'So this has hit you *both* really hard,' Bran said as Ellie returned with the biscuits. 'I know it's not my business, but why...?'

'I made a mistake. I was going through this horrible time, and when he proposed – well, it was just the nicest bit of good news at the time. I didn't really stop and think about actually getting *married*. For *ever*.'

Bran looked up at Ellie before he spoke. He cleared his throat. 'I was commissioned to make a sculpture for the garden,' he said. 'As a wedding present from your parents. That's how I got to know Patrick so well when he came to live at the manor.'

'Oh,' she said blankly.

'So, he talked to me after you left. He couldn't understand it – not at first. But I think some of your arguments must have got through. That it was rushed, it was too quick, you weren't certain.' He shrugged. 'No one wants to go into a marriage knowing it could change things.' He managed a twisted smile up at Ellie. 'Which is Ellie's argument.'

'Owning a house together and making a baby – that seems like a bigger commitment nowadays,' Ellie said, smiling fondly down at her partner. 'And life is *perfect*.'

'We weren't doing either of those,' Amber said. 'We were going to live in the gardener's house courtesy of my parents, and

I wasn't sure about children. It doesn't really fit with my work.'
She took a sip of the hot tea. 'That was before I met Zillah, of
course,' she said with a crooked smile.

'Having a child is the biggest responsibility,' Ellie said softly.
'I would die for her.'

The room was silent, then Bran took her hand. 'Which is
how I feel about you,' he said.

She smiled back but let go, reaching for her own cup. 'But
today we're talking about *Amber's* wedding. Or *not* wedding.'

They were virtually strangers, but it was somehow easy to
look into Ellie's understanding face and talk.

'We never properly lived together...' she started. Bran took
his tea and vanished but Ellie slid into his space, curled up in
the corner of the sofa, and really listened.

'So, your affair was all about the romance, the chemistry,'
Ellie said, at the end of the story.

'Exactly.'

'What made you think it wouldn't have been just as
wonderful to live together?'

Amber tried to remember when her doubts had first started.
'He was desperate to settle down,' she explained. 'Patrick's six
years older than me. He's not someone who enjoys travelling, he
just does it for work. He's ready to settle into his thirties.'

'And you were...?'

'Twenty-six and loving the life, flying all over the world,
playing with some extraordinary musicians, recording new
music...' She looked down at her fingers. 'When I thought I was
going to lose all of that – the truth is Patrick would have been
second best to that life. We would have ended up unhappy—'
She couldn't finish the thought.

'Because you would have lost your music.'

Amber jumped up to look at the sea again. 'He couldn't
replace the thing I've been working towards since I was four
years old. I missed an education on the islands because I had to

go to a school with a good music programme. Tutors, coaches, mentors – I was playing professionally from the age of nine in youth orchestras.'

A little rain misted the view over the sea, rattled onto the window.

'It was your whole life.' Ellie's voice was soft. 'But Patrick was comfort and kindness and love and a future?'

'But not *my* future.' Here it was, the ugly selfish truth: 'I would have swapped Patrick for my arm and neck to be healed. I wanted to go back to our old life – me travelling the world and meeting up with Patrick for magical holidays.'

'Do you think you might be able to play for work again one day?'

Amber's mind went back to the dark pub, the people swaying, almost as mesmerised as she had been. 'Maybe,' was the closest answer she could manage. 'I hope so...'

'What if you can't...'

What if I can't play? That was the question that had been haunting her when she woke from nightmares of not being able to play, not even being able to hold an instrument. 'I don't know. But marriage with Patrick isn't the answer, and it wouldn't be fair to him.' She turned to look at Ellie. 'You said you would die for Zillah. That's the love I want. That's the love I feel playing music, but I've never felt it for Patrick. Not wild and dangerous, burning with passion.'

'There are different kinds of love,' Ellie said. 'Bran and I didn't have an easy journey. But we found it.'

'But you won't commit to marriage yourself?' Ellie looked awkward and Amber corrected herself. 'Oh, I'm sorry, it's none of my business! Your situation is completely different, I'm sure.'

'No,' Ellie said slowly, 'it's not that different. I adore Bran, I couldn't bear to lose him. But *marriage* feels so constricting. I've been confined by conventions all my life, until I moved here and fell in love with the island, and the cottage, and reconnected with my memories of my mother. Bran is my adventure.'

'And marriage would change that?'

Ellie laughed and shrugged. 'I have no idea. All I know is I have a lovely life and I don't want to rock the boat.'

'And my experience hasn't helped,' Amber said.

'It's certainly given me something to think about.' Ellie put her cup down. 'Bran's very fond of Patrick. They've been working on that piece for the garden for a few months. Patrick is really shaken up.'

Amber shut her eyes. 'I know. And I don't think I can make that better.'

When she looked back, Ellie was nodding. 'Maybe you can't. But you might be able to help him understand.'

18

NOVEMBER 1943

Before work, Georgina waited in the queue for the greengrocer on the big island to open. There was a little more choice here than in the tiny shop on Morwen. It was a small bonus for the ferry fare and the hours of editing.

She was able to take a lot of work off Bob Alden's hands. The newspaper's revenue was tiny, less than ten pounds a week for putting in national news from the ministry. A few national companies paid for small adverts for baby milk and biscuits, but the rest was local advertising. A tutor doing examination preparation for the grammar school caught her eye, but at two shillings a session it was beyond her reach.

She wondered – again – whether to ask Great-Aunt Alice as she seemed so interested in Tommy's future. Two shillings a week might make a huge difference to the entrance examination coming up in a few months.

She purchased a large swede and some battered carrots, cheap because they had been damaged when they were dug up, and a couple of onions almost too large to hold. A few pounds of potatoes wrapped in paper at the bottom of her bag and she was set. The local butcher usually had a bit of offal, and she could

get some shin of beef on their rations back on Morwen. It was
satisfying to be able to feed her family, even if the cookbook she
had received as a wedding present had gone up in flames with
the house. She had shadowed Lena enough to have learned a
bit, and the local library had some recipes, too. Kidney ragout
with half the ingredients missing had been a complete disaster,
but she had mastered batter, and one egg and some apples made
a whole plate of fruit fritters that the children had loved. A bag
of chestnuts for a few pence was irresistible, and when she
asked the shopkeeper how to cook them, several helpful
suggestions came from the waiting queue. Having broken the
ice, the women felt empowered to unleash their curiosity.

'How are you getting on in Morwen? Funny folk over there
on the rocky isle.'

'My mother was from Morwen, Ena,' an older lady
interjected.

Ena grinned at her. 'Exactly, Ethel,' and everyone laughed.

'Everyone's been very kind,' Georgina said.

'And your children are settling in?' an old lady who didn't
come up to Georgina's shoulder asked. 'The school's nice, I've
visited it a few times. My great-nieces used to go there.'

The feeling of connection grew. 'What are their names?'

'Patience and Susie Ellis. Susie isn't well, she's in a hospital.
Patsy is the clever one, she goes to the grammar now.'

That was the dream she carried for Tommy, although she
couldn't imagine how she would manage without him to bring
Dolly home when her work ran a little late or the boat was slow.
'I had better go,' she said smiling at them all. 'I'm just off to help
with the newspaper.'

'Well, Bob Alden's got his hands full with the new baby and
his young wife,' one said, eyes twinkling. 'Maybe you'll make
him smarten up a little.'

'It's just to help them over the first few months,' she
explained as she escaped.

There was something speculative in the woman's eyes, as if there was something clandestine going on.

She half ran up the high street and into the office.

'Mr Alden,' she said, panting, 'sorry I'm late, I was queuing for vegetables.'

'Bob, remember. You look bonny this morning. Ready to take some notes?'

'Yes, but – I wondered if we could stay out here, in the shop?' she said in a rush, putting her shopping and handbag down. 'The office is so cramped and – the light is nowhere near as good as in there. I'll be faster taking dictation out here.'

'We'll get interrupted,' he said, looking at the glass door.

'I'll make a notice to say we're closed and to post advertisements through the letterbox, as usual.'

'Folks will think we're being very rude,' he said, still looking doubtful.

'They will be able to see how industrious you are, and how hard you work to put the paper out every week,' she said, sitting at the desk. *And no one will suspect anything untoward.*

The morning went fast, and when Rachel Alden came in, carrying the baby, she looked around with approval. 'It's much lighter in here.' Then she smiled, jiggling the baby. 'And people won't warn me about letting that glamorous Mrs Preston work with my husband all day.'

'Psh,' he said, kissing her cheek, then the baby's head for good measure. 'Whoever would think that?'

The women's eyes met. 'Probably no one,' Georgina said, 'but I wouldn't want anyone to think ill of you.' *Or me.*

'How are you getting on with your pension? I hear people are struggling to get them,' Rachel said, sitting down with her back to the window. 'Oh, this pesky child, do you mind if I feed him here in this corner?'

'Not at all,' Georgie said, getting back to her notes. 'No news on the pension yet.' She sorted through the scraps of paper laid out in the shape of the page. 'So, we have one too many personal ads and a space in the corner.'

'Let's choose one to make bigger,' Bob said, looking through the scraps of paper she had mocked up. One of her innovations on the first day had been to cut papers to the size of the most common advertisements and features to make it easier for them to visualise the whole page. Previously he'd kept it all in his head. 'There's a notice for the island council of churches here. A monthly tea to raise funds to support widows of our boys overseas, and their families. What do you think, Rachel?'

Rachel glanced over the baby's head to Georgina. 'How much *is* the widow's pension?'

'The basic pension is ten shillings a week,' she managed to say, although the words came hard. 'And eight shillings extra for both children. But Jim was on a higher rate of pay because of his commission, so it might be more.'

'That would hardly pay for rent and basic foods,' Rachel said, frowning. 'Everything has gone up so much, even when we can get the ration. Butter has almost doubled in price this year.'

'Fortunately, I don't have to pay rent,' Georgina said, changing a line to cut a word out. 'My husband and son own Beehive Cottage. It will be in Tommy's name soon.'

'That's good,' Rachel said, looking down lovingly at the top of the baby's head.

With a dragging pain, Georgina remembered she would never feel that sensation again, the tugging, the scratching of little nails on her skin, that intense gaze of a baby staring up at her. It was like another bereavement.

She put down her pencil and found a handkerchief to discreetly dab her eyes. Not that discreet, as Bob cleared his throat vigorously and Rachel reached out a hand to touch hers.

. . .

As Georgie walked back to the ferry, she was startled to hear her name called. 'Mrs Preston! Georgina!'

Uncomfortable with her name being shouted up and down the quay, she was ready to frown at whoever was calling her, and was surprised to see Hugo Seznec hobbling towards her on his crutches. 'Can I speak to you?' he asked.

'Of course.' She looked around; there were a dozen people nearby, from fishermen unloading boxes to a couple of old, white-bearded men on a bench outside the pub, all of whom appeared to be listening. 'Is it confidential?'

'Oh, I don't think so. But maybe. Would you mind walking a little way up the quay?'

Further up, the road was clear of people.

'Yes?' she asked, looking over the water to see if the ferry was coming.

'May I make a proposal of a few hours' work that might assist your finances?'

She was surprised, thinking of the tiny shop, steamed-up widows and ramshackle files. 'I didn't think you would need a secretary.'

'Well, I didn't, and all my earnings, such as they were, went on rent. But now I've done a few wills and sorted out a couple of marital issues, I have a little money in the kitty. I will be paid for organising all the previous solicitor's paperwork. His executor has promised me twenty pounds for archiving it all. We could do it together.'

'Twenty pounds?' The amount she would have spent on a pretty dress before the war now seemed like a fortune. 'I didn't know he had died.'

Hugo hesitated for a second. 'The problem is that I no longer have the time – or the skills – to archive thirty years' worth of paperwork. Not to mention drying it out from the damp running down the walls and windows, then deciphering and filing it.'

'You are really offering me a job?' She was astonished.

'A few hours, at the most basic wage, I'm afraid. You would still need to work a few hours for the paper, I expect. But you could do a lot of work for me at home to fit in around your children.'

Those two-shilling lessons for Tommy started to seem more manageable. 'I was just wondering,' she said, her voice choked, 'how I was going to afford to get a tutor for Tommy, for his entrance examinations for boarding school.'

He smiled crookedly. 'I can do better than that. I am happy to exchange a couple of extra hours' work for tutoring Tommy, if you like. I *was* educated at Cambridge, you know.'

She stared at him, his mop of dark hair and the broad shoulders, and then at the twisted legs. 'Are you good at mathematics?'

'I aced mathematics and science at school,' he said. 'Not to boast, but I learned them in three languages. French, Breton and English. And passed exams in all of them.'

'I can help him with English, although my grammar is a bit rusty,' she admitted. 'And I've only been able to teach him a bit of basic French, so your help would be much appreciated.'

'Then it's a deal,' he said, wobbling a bit and leaning his hip on the sea wall. 'There's your boat. Come and see me on Monday. The tide's about ten so you should be able to get over after you take the children to school. We'll have a chat, and I'll show you what has to be done.'

'So, I can take papers with me to work on at home?' she asked, starting slowly towards the quay again.

'As long as you keep them strictly confidential,' he said, catching her up. 'You'll be doing me a huge favour.'

'Why haven't you asked one of the local people—' The answer came into her head immediately. 'Oh. Confidentiality.'

He stared out to sea for a moment. 'It's even more than that,' he said. 'The locals think I'm a spy. They are suspicious of me because I'm a foreigner. But – and you mustn't tell anyone about this – there is real intelligence work to do here. There may be spies on the islands.'

The words hit her hard. Jim's work – Jim's passion – had been for national security. He had died for the cause.

'Because of the garrison at the airport and the submarine base?' She looked back at his intense gaze. 'Of course I'll help.'

19

PRESENT DAY, 22 OCTOBER

Amber started the next day, the one after her planned wedding day, with a bit of yoga, stretching her neck and shoulders, flexing all her muscles. She'd picked up a rug on social media, the island having a very active second-hand marketplace. Using two of the camping mats on top, she worked at centring herself, ignoring the guilt about the wrecked wedding and her grief at losing Patrick.

She had the window open, the shouts of squabbling jackdaws and gulls replacing the music in her head. The clocks were going to go back soon, the days were becoming shorter. Now she just wanted somewhere warm to stay.

Having wriggled and awakened every part of herself, down to her restless fingers, she picked up the violin, ready to play scales she had been playing since she started school. Instead, she paused, frozen in position, unable to take that first breath and sound the first note.

Rapidly, she mentally scanned herself. Was there some imbalance, some injury or stiffness she hadn't noticed? Then the realisation grew that her wayward fingers had framed not the beginning of the scale, but the beginning of the song that had been whispering in her head. In fact, there were several phrases now, some whole melodies, even.

She closed her eyes, pulled her attention back to her body, and played the first note of the song, gliding with her breath into playing it. As she played, she riffed on it, embellished, played with it until it became a younger sister to the mournful lament she had imagined. By the time she put the instrument down, she was vibrating; the light in the room seemed suddenly brighter. She wished she'd recorded it.

As she lifted the instrument again, ready to do those annoying but essential scales and exercises, she heard a knock at the door. She glanced at her phone. Half past nine on a Sunday morning?

The tide must be well out; like everyone on the islands, she'd become expert at remembering where they were. Maybe it was Betty, who wouldn't mind seeing her in her old sweatpants and plastering T-shirt.

It was Ben, instead, looking quite different in clean jeans and jacket, holding up a bag of something that smelled like buttery baked goods.

'Hello,' she said, leaning against the door frame. 'I didn't expect to see you today.'

'I was bringing you some rust remover for the stove,' he said. 'Then I thought...' He held up a cardboard tray with two large cups. 'Breakfast. Do you want to eat it on the quay?'

She was astonished. He'd always been kind but joked about a lot, kept things impersonal. This was different. His eyes had sparks of something in them. Maybe concern.

'You go on ahead,' she said, almost before she had thought about it. She realised she was still carrying the violin.

'That's beautiful,' he said, pointing at the violin. 'It sounds amazing.'

'You heard? This is my favourite instrument in the world.' She smiled. 'I'd better get changed.'

'I'll meet you down there,' he said, unsmiling. 'We need to talk.'

We need to talk? Her heart beat a little faster at the words. She went upstairs and laid the instrument carefully in its case. She brushed her hair, cleaned her teeth in the outhouse and splash-washed while swearing under her breath at the coldness of the water.

In the suitcase, abandoned under heaps of clothes ready to be run through the campsite launderette before it closed for the winter, were a few clean, nice clothes. She selected a pair of black jeans that she couldn't normally wear in the dusty house to go with a velvet top. It had been a Christmas present from her mother. She missed her almost as much as Patrick, but Amber still hadn't made contact. *I should call her.*

She pulled on some suede ankle boots, also a no-go amid the plaster dust, and sidled through the door to go down to the quay.

'I heard you playing,' came Betty's voice from her doorway.

'Hi Betty. Did you? I hope it wasn't too early. I'm just off down the quay.'

'With Ben.' There was something quiet and unsmiling about her. 'Ben's a nice lad.'

'He's very nice. A good collaborator and a great carpenter.' She put her head on one side. 'Is everything all right?'

'I'm fine.' Betty stared at her, pale blue eyes boring into her until she felt uncomfortable. 'People are talking,' she said, finally. 'You wouldn't want to add to the gossip.'

Amber shook her head. 'There shouldn't be any gossip. We're just friends.'

'Well then,' Betty said, opening the door to her cottage a bit wider. 'Enjoy your breakfast.'

Whatever was all that about? Betty hadn't looked her usual bubbly self for a few days.

Amber walked down the steep street to the quay, and

headed over to a bench where Ben was sitting, looking over the mudflats and sand bars that had been revealed by the low tide.

'This is a nice surprise,' she said, taking the cup from him and a pain au chocolat in a bag. 'And thank you for the rust... stuff.'

'I thought I should clear the air,' he said, and sipped from his cup. 'People are talking about us, they're getting the wrong idea.'

The smell coming from her favourite coffee was lovely, spicy and sweet. 'I don't care what anyone thinks. Anyway, what people?'

'You know what the islands are like. I don't want to upset anyone.'

She stared out at the water. 'Do you know, I don't know what the islands are like, not really. I know my parents live here, but they were in London when I was born and I spent so much time away at school...'

'Or in your ivory tower.' He turned to look at her. 'You didn't mix with the other kids on the island, did you?'

'Most of our houses were full of staff working the summer season. There weren't that many children. I played with the visitors' kids, though.'

He stretched out his legs and crossed his ankles and shrugged his shoulders. 'I went to school with every child on the island. When I was eleven, we all went up to the same high school. We even boarded there. We all knew about the princess up at the big house.'

She looked away for a moment, tears stinging. 'Is that how you saw me?'

'I saw you in the paper more than I ever saw you in real life. Maybe once or twice on the ferry or at the manor, when I was working as a carpentry apprentice.'

She had been feted on the islands as her musical career developed, as she competed in international competitions or performed for the local TV news. 'OK,' she said, slowly. 'Where is this going?'

'So people are saying you've moved on without a care in the world, while Patrick nurses his broken heart.'

'Brutal,' she said, the tears turning to stone in her chest. 'And really not true. I still love Patrick but I can't marry him.'

'And you couldn't just postpone the wedding, or let him down more gently?'

'I tried.' She turned to look at him. 'Why are you taking this so seriously?'

He turned away, his jaw tense. 'People think *we're* flirting, that maybe we're even together.'

She exploded with indignation. 'That's ridiculous! I'm broken-hearted about Patrick. I may not talk about it all the time, I don't sob on the quay about it, but he's on my mind every day! We were together for three years, he's the only man I've ever loved.' She dashed a tear off her cheek. 'Anyway, why should I worry about what people think?'

'Because the people here care about what we do. And when Patrick reached out to me—'

'What?'

'—and asked me what's going on, I realised that we are getting a bit close, that he has every reason to ask hard questions.'

'No, he doesn't,' she said, seething, putting the cup down with exaggerated care so she didn't throw it. 'How dare he? If he has any questions, he should ask *me*.'

Ben scowled at her. 'You must be joking! You broke his heart, how can he just phone you up casually and ask, "Are you shagging someone else?"?'

'Is that the question he asked you? I hope you reassured him,' she snapped.

'It wasn't quite how he put the question – I paraphrased. What I'm saying is, while I appreciate the work, I'm getting

Lewis Bolitho from St Brannock's to finish the job. He's happily married so hopefully there won't be too much gossip.'

'You'd give up a job because of a bit of gossip?' she said, incredulous, though there was a wrench somewhere in the pit of her stomach at the thought of not seeing him every day.

'I was hoping you would understand, that you would realise it's hurting *Patrick*. Even if he's got it wrong.'

'He's on our – his – holiday. Honeymoon,' she said bleakly.

'No, he didn't want to do that. Your parents used the tickets. As far as I know, *they* are on holiday. Patrick is back at work, at the manor. And you did break his heart, by the sound of it. I'm going over for a drink with him one night this week. Honestly, he was desperate for news of you, how you were.' He stared at her. 'He wouldn't say a word against you. He just needed to know if you had moved on.'

'Has Dad agreed to this *Lewis* coming to finish the job?'

'I told you, Sir Michael is away. Patrick authorised it with the manager of the hotel when I asked. I'm going over there to sort out a bit of storm damage, which Lewis was working on but now it's mostly carpentry.'

She wrapped her arms around herself 'So, this is all being done behind my back?'

'Wasn't what you did to Patrick behind his back? You didn't give him any warning.'

'I did! I told him about my doubts every day, he just thought I was upset over my neck and arm.' But he was partly right. She had known Patrick wasn't listening, so expressed most of her doubts to her father, who brushed them off as wedding nerves. Tears were rolling down her cheeks now. 'When I was ill—'

She couldn't explain the terrible feeling of vulnerability that had enveloped her when she learned she needed neuro-surgery on the disc in her neck. She knew she might not play again, but she'd also had to accept there was a risk she might lose so much more – her ability to walk, to breathe, even. The whole experience was terrifying, and she had clung to her family, and Patrick. Lovely, undemanding, kind Patrick. She hadn't deserved him, and she should never had agreed to get married.

'I made a mistake,' she said bleakly. 'I mistook comfort and affection for love when I was really terrified I would lose my music. It wasn't real love, you know, the love that poets write about.' The way music made her feel. Her dreams invaded her thoughts of the walk on the beach, the floating boy, and the melody, notes echoing in her mind right now.

'Well, I think I should step back. And, honestly, Lewis is a great builder.'

The tears had given way to sobs. She looked up to find him holding out a tissue. 'OK. But you really don't need to. I mean, there was never anything romantic going on between us, was there? You could tell Patrick that.' Although she had started to rely on his good-natured banter, his friendliness.

Ben looked out over the water. 'That wasn't what he asked me,' he said, finally. 'He asked me if I liked you. Fancied you, was attracted to you,' he explained.

Oh. Her stomach dropped.

'And when he asked, I realised I do. A bit. Fancy you.' He looked upset and angry at the same time.

Hot tears tickled her eyes. 'You're all talking behind my back,' she said slowly. 'I know I did the right thing. How about poor Lewis, will people gossip about him and me?'

'Lewis and George have been married since gay marriages were allowed,' Ben explained, a little smile sneaking in, crinkling the skin around his eyes. 'Lewis has been a sounding board for Patrick for the last few weeks, along with the other staff at the manor.'

They had all loved him, as far as she could see; while some of the staff were a bit ambivalent about her. *Princess.*

'You should look around for somewhere else to stay, so

Lewis and his guys can get in and properly plaster. There will be a few holiday lets available by the end of the week.'

That tugged at her even more. 'I don't want to leave,' she said in a small voice. 'I really like the cottage.'

There was a long silence. 'I am sorry. I've enjoyed working with you,' he said finally, lifting his cup and tucking it into a bin a few yards away. A gull screeched his disappointment. 'Maybe a bit too much.'

She watched him walk away and a strange idea rang in her head like the church clock. *I sort of liked you, too.*

20

NOVEMBER 1943

Georgie read the letter over again, scanning the pages of information. She had been told she *could* be eligible for a basic war widow's pension subject to further enquiries, but even if she qualified, she would have to abide by the conditions. There was no money yet and the restrictions were confusing.

Hugo had managed to make a strong case to Jim's bank for more funds but the news was disappointing. There was little money available: as Hugo had suspected, most of the investments were frozen. He had added a little note in the envelope. 'Will you be able to manage for a bit longer?'

There wasn't an alternative. Georgie slipped her boots on and climbed the hill to the school to collect the children. There was no money to purchase new furniture from the mainland, and there was little for sale in the islands. She needed to buy some wool to make Dolly a new jumper, she was growing so fast. And if Tommy did get into the grammar school, she would have to find the money for the uniform, ferries and train tickets. The idea of him going back to his private boarding school slipped further and further away.

She turned over the letter from the pension authority, with

the conditions in tiny print. There were requirements that she had to be a good mother, housewife and a moral person. To remarry or even meet someone could lose Georgie her pittance.

Working outside the home might invalidate her claim, too, even though the war widow's pension was barely enough to live on. How on earth could one be a full-time housewife and mother, and still keep one's children in clothes and shoes? It all seemed irrelevant, anyway, as without a death certificate it wasn't certain she'd get the pension. The War Office had just listed Jim's situation as 'obscure'.

Not that obscure, she thought. The ship had certainly been sunk.

She walked through the snicket gate onto the school play-ground, looking up at the tired growing plots and the chickens scratching about miserably in the mud of their run.

Clemmie came up to her. 'Poor little things,' she said. 'The school asks for scraps for them but they don't get much. Now they've stopped laying, they will probably end up as soup.'

Georgie salivated at the thought of proper chicken soup. 'But,' she said, thinking aloud, 'all these grasses and plants in the rest of the field must be full of seeds. Don't chickens eat grass, too?'

'The children feed them through the wire, so I suppose so.'

Georgie turned to her. 'We could turn the school field around, if we tried. Make it into a tiny farm.'

'Well, the children still need somewhere to play,' Clemmie said doubtfully, hitching baby Betty on her hip. 'But they could do with fresh vegetables, too.'

'I'll ask at the school, to see if we can do better than those little plots.'

'The children planted them,' Clemmie said. 'I know one of the land girls, she might have some ideas.'

Georgie was getting excited. 'Do you think they could help us plant it up?'

Clemmie shrugged. 'I think all the food they grow goes to the war effort. They might have a few plants for the winter, kale and so on.'

'Some of it ends up in the grocers in St Brannock's,' Georgie said. 'I asked where their huge onions came from.'

An older woman came over. 'Are you thinking of growing some food?'

'If the school will let us,' Clemmie said. 'Oh, Georgina, this is Eve – she's little Robbie's grandmother.'

'We've got a bit of a garden,' she said. 'My husband's got a few cabbage plants left over, maybe a couple of leeks and onions. You could put in some greens for the spring.'

After the children had all come out, Georgina and Clemmie went to talk to the teacher.

'I can't cope with the field,' she admitted immediately. 'The man who used to cut the grass is away, and we don't know what to do with the poor hens.'

Georgina outlined the idea of building some sort of moveable ark for the birds, where they could be put out to eat the grass and seeds and probably scratch for worms, then be put back in at the end of school each day.

'It's such a good idea,' Miss Cartwright said. 'We were offered ducklings this spring, but we couldn't look after them. Ducks lay well, too.' She smiled, looking around at the group of women, the children running on the small playground. 'If you coordinate it, I'll help where I can. I can certainly look after the fowl over the weekends, but we'll need a rota over the holidays.'

Georgie walked home with Clemmie, feeling so much more connected with Morwen, with the islands. She felt more positive, even if the pension would be a while coming. It was going to be a struggle, but she would make things work.

· · ·

By the time she reached home, Tommy was rubbing his stomach. 'I hope there's something nice for tea,' he said. 'I'm starving. We went on a beach clean and picked up wood for the school at break time. And lunch was soup and bread again.'

Tommy was shooting out of his clothes; Georgie would only be able to take his hems down another inch on his shorts, and maybe his jacket cuffs.

'I have some tinned fish on toast today,' she said. 'From the cannery. And I managed to get some apples, too, so maybe fritters again?'

'That would be good,' he said, looking up at her. Not very much up, she noticed – he was already up to her chin. Of course, Jim was tall, she thought with a jolt. 'Did you hear about the pension?' he asked.

She smiled at his maturity; he'd really grown up since they came to the island. 'They haven't decided yet.'

'Good,' he said softly.

'Well, darling, we could really do with the money.'

He shook his head. 'But that would mean he was definitely – you know, gone.'

'No,' she explained again. 'Whether he has passed away or not it would stay exactly the same, we'd just have a bit more money.' She took a deep breath. 'But if I am going to do some work for Mr Seznec, and for Mr Alden at the newspaper, we will have enough to get you some extra tuition. Mr Seznec says he can tutor you in mathematics and science once a week. And he speaks wonderful French.'

Tommy scuffed his shoe in the mud as they walked down the road towards the court. 'He's a foreigner, isn't he?'

'He's from Brittany. Goodness, news travels fast here, doesn't it? He escaped the Nazis but got badly hurt.'

Tommy pushed open the door into their court. 'The boys at school say he could be a German spy. Or a Jew.'

'Well, he's unlikely to be both,' she said, trying to smile. 'No, he's just trying to live out the war until his legs get better. He has no reason to love the Germans, they were the ones who shot him.'

Tommy shrugged one shoulder as she opened the door. It never seemed necessary to lock the door here. He mumbled something as he passed her.

'Tommy? What did you say?'

He walked back, his cheeks pink. 'I just mean – I wish you didn't have to spend time with him.'

'He's my employer. I'm his secretary.'

Tommy didn't answer but she could see his eyes were full of tears. 'Thomas? What's bothering you?'

'They might say you're his girlfriend.'

She wrapped her arms around him. 'My dearest boy, I can't have a boyfriend, I'm still married. Just because Daddy might – or might not – be gone, doesn't mean I want anyone else.' She pulled back a little, smoothed the tears off his cheeks. 'Anyway. You are the man in my life, and that's enough for me.'

21

PRESENT DAY, 23 OCTOBER

Amber didn't feel as welcome to help out at the cottage with the new builders. Lewis was a tall, heavily built man with grey hair, who was polite but not friendly. Jake, his gangly teenaged assistant, had hair that flopped over his eyes and was a bit too friendly.

They arrived when she was scampering in from the outside bathroom in her pyjamas and layers of sweaters.

'Late night?' Lewis said, raising an eyebrow, and Jake laughed.

'No, I—' *Don't have to explain anything to you.* She stalked up to the bedroom and scrambled into her clothes.

Downstairs, she found Lewis measuring up the walls in the kitchen. The radio was blaring.

'Ben hasn't done a bad job,' he said, marking something on the walls. 'For a carpenter. We can get this stove thing out today, get back to the original wall for replastering, but it will cost more. You might be better just to board the fireplace back up.'

She shook her head. 'No, no, I want to keep the stove.'

'*And* the cupboard?' he asked, tapping the painted-shut

door with his pencil. 'It's probably full of damp, there's no ventilation.'

She stood as tall as she could in dirty jeans and scuffed trainers. 'I'm restoring it, not taking anything original out.'

'Except that woodworm, in the back yard.' The remains of the attic ladder were crumbling out there.

'I was going to burn that.'

'The only thing that didn't burn down in the fire and you're going to incinerate it,' he said, but she could see something like a smile around his eyes. 'Well, you're the boss. In the meantime, we need to prep for replastering now Grant has done the first fix of the electrics.'

'I'm still living here, at the moment.' At his astonished look, she added, 'While I can.'

'Well, that's not going to work, lovey. The walls are going to be soaking wet, you won't have electricity a lot of the time and we're going to raise even more dust. You don't want to be breathing in a houseful of fresh lime.'

She looked back through to the lounge, where Jake was grinning at her. 'I haven't found anywhere else yet,' she said. 'You know what half-term's like, everything's booked up. Can't you put off plastering until all the preparation is done?'

He shook his head. 'I can give you a few days. By next Saturday there should be a few hotel rooms and cottages opening up. Ben said there was an attic in reasonable condition? Maybe we can look at that first, get on with the work up there.'

The attic was the most exciting discovery so far. Amber had found scuff marks where a bed had once sat; the window had lost its glass under the slates but seemed intact. The frame had survived the woodworm, probably because it was solid oak.

'You'll need a new ladder,' she warned.

'We'll bring one tomorrow. If you don't mind us working on the downstairs today, we'll score and treat the walls as we go. The prep includes a fungicide, so you'd better sleep with the windows open.' He grinned slyly. 'Don't want Sir Michael's only child to glow in the dark.'

'Oh, shut up,' she said, weary of the jibes. 'That's such an inverted snob thing to say. What *can* I do?'

'I suppose you can help get the wallpaper off upstairs. How much is there?' She led him up and he looked around, his lip curling. 'Ratty little place, isn't it? I suppose it would do for a holiday let. Someone was living here before, full-time?'

'The tenant. Her family sold it to my grandparents but she was allowed to stay for her lifetime. For a peppercorn rent.'

'That was big of them,' he said, knocking on the kitchen ceiling. 'This is damp, this brown patch. The winter storms probably lifted some of the slates and blew the water in – it probably trickled all the way through the cottage.' He brushed aside yet more of the interminable supply of dust with a boot. 'There's a water stain down there, too. She probably had to put buckets down.'

'Ben thought it was historical,' she said dubiously.

'Maybe they fixed the roof at some point.' He walked through to the bedroom she was using. 'Yep, this has all got to be prepped. You'll have to move all your stuff out, it will get damp.'

'Where am I supposed to store the bed and my other stuff?' she said, looking around.

'If you rent a cottage, you could put the mattress and frame in there,' he said.

Disheartened, Amber wandered next door when she saw Betty come back from the shops with a heavy bag.

'I would have carried that,' Amber said, following Betty inside and noticing the house was colder than usual. 'What have you got there?'

'Just a bag of kindling,' Betty said, but she looked pale. 'Goodness, that hill gets me every time.'

'Sit down, I'll put the kettle on and put those sticks away. Seriously, Bets, I'm just next door. What are neighbours for?'

'Thanks, lovey. I'll just catch my breath here for a moment.' She sat back, eyes shut, her muddy boots uncharacteristically left on her feet, resting on the edge of her spotless rug.

Amber bent down and eased them off one at a time. 'I'll make some tea, shall I?'

'In a pot,' Betty said, without opening her eyes, but Amber was reassured.

'Of course. What sort of heathen do you think I am?' she scoffed as she went through to the kitchen and prepared one of Betty's comedy pots, most of them in the shape of animals. They were usually spotless, but today there was a film of dust on them. She cleaned and filled the pot shaped like a chicken, fetched the tray from the tiny dresser and two cups and saucers. As she reached into the fridge for the milk, she saw it was almost empty again.

'Thank you,' Betty said as she returned with the tea tray, and Amber was glad to see she looked better. 'I wouldn't have gone out but I needed the sticks to light the fire tonight.'

'I'm going down to the shop in a minute,' Amber improvised. 'If you make a list, I'll pick up some bits for you, save you another trip. I don't mind.'

'I can't,' Betty whispered, and dabbed her handkerchief at her eyes.

'Betty? What on earth is wrong?'

Betty folded the hankie and tucked it into her cardigan.

'You can't tell anybody,' she murmured. 'But I have to say something.'

Amber crossed her chest. 'Cross my heart and hope to die,' she said. 'I promise. What's going on?'

Betty waved a hand at Amber to pour the tea, and it wasn't until she had taken a few tiny sips that she could speak.

'I got a phone call, a few weeks ago.'

Amber nodded, holding her own cup in her cold fingers. 'OK.'

'It was from someone I didn't know, he sounded so official. He said he was from the police, the fraud squad, trying to help me.' Tears welled up in her eyes. 'But it wasn't. It was all a scam. He sounded so nice, too. I panicked, and did what he said.'

'Oh, Betty.' Amber put down her tea and took Betty's hands. The old woman's face was a mass of wrinkles, her hands twisted and knobbly. 'How much did they get?'

Betty said something under her breath, then swallowed hard. 'All of it, more or less,' she said. 'I can't afford to buy much food in the shop.'

'We should contact the police and the bank, immediately,' Amber said, anxiety clawing at her chest. 'We must get it back.'

'I did all that,' Betty said, detaching her hand and reaching shakily for her cup. 'I went to the bank. They say that since I moved the money into the so-called *safe* account, they can't help me.'

'How much was it?' Amber asked, shocked to see that Betty was shaking.

'Almost eighteen thousand pounds,' she said, before Amber gently took her cup and sat beside her to hug her.

'We'll get a lawyer on it,' she said. 'Straight away.'

'I can't afford a lawyer,' said Betty, emerging from Amber's embrace to wipe her eyes and blow her nose. 'It's all gone, it's all I had. I'm afraid they're going to take my pension out of the bank, too.'

'But it is going in all right?' Amber asked.

'I don't know. I think I closed my account over the phone, the man told me to. I don't know where my money's going now.'

'Look, I have a friend who is a solicitor. I'll get him to look into it, liaise with the police for you. He won't charge – I'm sure he'll be outraged at what's happened.' All it would take was a quick call to the manor lawyer. If necessary, she would pay him, but she knew he hated this kind of injustice and was sure he would help.

'Could you?' Betty looked so small and fragile. 'I've had to break open the jar of change I keep for my grandchildren, just to pay for the kindling. And I don't know how I will pay all my bills when they come in.'

'Let me make some calls. Then perhaps we should go over to the bank and talk to someone in person. Would you come, if I arranged an appointment?'

'I don't know if it will help,' Betty said. 'But yes, all right. Let's give it a go. I've just about got enough for a boat.'

Amber almost interrupted to offer to pay for the boat, but she decided it was best to leave Betty with her last shred of independence.

'I'll walk down to the quay to get a decent signal, and phone up for an appointment,' she said firmly. 'Let's get this sorted out. And I'll pick up a few bits for your tea.' When Betty opened her mouth to argue, she shook her head. 'We'll call it a loan. You can pay me back when we get this sorted out.'

Amber called the bank and made an appointment that would fit with the tide. The manor's solicitor confirmed that if Betty had been persuaded to empty her account, she was unlikely to get any of her money back. He got more excited when she mentioned the pension, though. 'So this could be an *ongoing* fraud?' he said, his voice crisp.

'She thinks it might be. She was told to close her account and set up a new one.'

'You'd better call the police. They might be able to help track her pension payments. I'll have a look at the situation once you've sent me all the details, including the crime number. Let's have a go.'

They finished the call, and Amber let out a long sigh, angry with herself that in the middle of her own troubles, she hadn't seen anyone else's. Betty had been suffering so much these last few weeks, right next door to her.

It was time to reconnect with the world.

22

NOVEMBER 1943

Each night, Georgie laid the papers out in piles and had managed to complete a few files, in reused folders with summaries on the front.

She pulled the next packet of files towards her and almost immediately a name jumped out at her. Beehive Cottage.

She ran her hand over the paper to flatten it. It had suffered water damage, stuck on a windowsill that ran with condensation in cold weather. It didn't make sense at first.

It seemed to be the second page of a complaint made by the family of Jago Carney, a nine-year-old boy.

There was some complaint about someone at Beehive Cottage? She couldn't make head nor tail of it. At the bottom was a name she recognised. Great-Aunt Alice's solicitor? She supposed if there was a grievance against someone at the cottage, it must go through him.

She put it aside, wondering if she should write to ask for more details. But it was an old issue, none of her business really – it was dated 1919.

She knew that the village was like a library of local knowledge and gossip; surely someone would know. She could ask Clemmie.

She repurposed an old folder that looked a hundred years old, with beautiful copperplate writing faded to brown, and glued a new label on it. She wasn't sure what it was about and couldn't find the previous page, so lightly inscribed in pencil: *Jago Carney, Beehive Cottage?*

Clemmie knocked on the door early the next morning, to ask if she should take Dolly to school. 'I thought you'd be busy with all your paperwork,' she said, looking over at the towering piles of neat folders and bags of shuffled papers. 'It all looks like homework from school,' she said, giggling. 'I'm glad I'm past all that!'

'It's getting organised, but it was in a bit of a mess,' Georgie said. 'I'll just get my coat, I fancy a walk with you. Tommy went out early for a bit of football.'

They rounded up the girls, and for the hundredth time, Georgie thought how lovely it was not to have cars on every road, busy on official business or delivering goods. Instead, here a whiskery old pony called Samson delivered coal and logs from the cargo ship, vegetables when they could get them, and returned scrap metal from the villagers. Georgie waved at the driver as they started down the hill at the lane, and the children stopped to pat Samson's nose.

Once they were past the old pony, Georgie found a way to frame the question that had kept her awake last night. 'I don't think this is breaking a confidence. Who lived in the cottage before I did?'

'Old Mrs Moore and her granddaughter. She was a tenant of the Prestons for a while, I think she was a retired servant. But before that, every summer, your family came down, Easter to

October, they used the place for their holidays for at least a decade.'

'My husband remembered coming here for several summers. But I'm looking for a boy called Jago. Maybe he lived in Beehive Cottage at some time?' Something in Clemmie's expression froze as they approached the school gate. 'What is it?'

'I'll tell you later,' she hissed. 'Hello, Mary, Gwen. How's little Arthur's cough? You should let that new lady doctor see him.'

Standing back watching Clemmie, Georgie could see there was a distance between herself and the island women. They were very polite. They were also fiercely independent, some were bringing up their children alone, widowed or abandoned or divorced.

No one excluded her – they just spoke in code, using a word of dialect here and there, or speaking of some event she knew nothing about. She listened to the school bell, saw Dolly line up, wave and grin over her shoulder with one gap tooth, and walk in with her new best friend. The island had done her good, and Tommy smiled, too, when he ran in from the field.

As the other women walked away, Clemmie turned to her. 'I didn't want to say anything in front of Gwennol,' she murmured.

'Say what?'

'About Jago,' she whispered, as they reached the court gate, where the pony was still parked. They both gave him a pat, and Clemmie called out to their elderly neighbour who was sitting outside in the October sun before walking into her own kitchen. The fire was just embers but the kettle was still warm on top. 'Gwen is his sister.'

'Is there some sort of secret about Jago?' Georgie asked.

'It's not a secret exactly,' Clemmie said, the back of her neck

pink as she leaned over the kettle and warmed the teapot. 'Just
from – you.'

'A secret from *me*? Why on earth would it be... no one even
knew me before I got here.'

'Well, not strictly speaking *you*. Your family. It's not something people around here would want to talk to them about.'
Clemmie poured the water and turned to put the pot on the
table, her face flushed and her eyes brimming. 'The Prestons. I
haven't thought of Jago for years. He was a friend of my
brother's.'

She must have known him personally, then. 'Did he live
here, on the island?'

'He did. Not at Beehive Cottage, though. He was such a
lovely boy, so friendly. He was a champion swimmer in all the
junior competitions.'

Georgie sat quietly, waiting while emotions flashed across
Clemmie's face: sadness, grief, confusion, anger.

'What happened?' Georgie asked. 'If it's not too upsetting to
talk about.'

As Clemmie poured the tea, her fingers shook. 'I can't
believe it still gets to me,' she said. 'After all these years. I
suppose, with our men away at sea, and your... Jago got caught
in a current off Seal Cove. He was only nine.'

'Oh, how dreadful,' Georgie said. 'Poor boy.' Even younger
than Tommy, who she knew had waded into the sea a few times
with friends, coming back soaked and shivering. *Just rescuing a
dog... getting the ball back... helping Harry get out.* She would
have to warn Tommy to stay out of the water. She still dreamed
about Jim, lost somewhere at sea.

'Did they find out what happened? I assume he just fell in?'

'He was out on the beach with a friend, a summer visitor to
the island. They were fishing, we think. But at some point the
other boy wanted to swim. He was a little older than Jago –
eleven, I think. He took off his shoes and shirt and went into

the water. I remember seeing the clothes still with the fishing tackle, leather sandals and a pale blue short-sleeved shirt. It had been nicely folded, not like the local boys who always just throw theirs on the sand.' Clemmie's voice was dreamy now. 'I had just been playing with a friend at the top of the cliff when we heard the calls and shouts about someone in the water. Half the island was there by then, they lit a fire on the beach so he'd know where we were as the light went.'

Clemmie paused, and Georgie held her breath for a moment. 'So, what happened?' she prompted.

'One of the old lifeboatmen, Albert Ellis, he heard the screaming. He could see the boy struggling. He knew at once there was a vicious current sweeping across the bay which would drag him out, so he ran back to get the lifeboat. Jago just kicked his shoes off and dived in.'

Georgie shivered at the tone in Clemmie's voice. 'So, now both boys needed to be rescued?'

'Exactly. The currents can pull you under, drag you out into whirlpools. When Albert looked back, he could see the boys clinging to each other, Jago shouting at the other boy. It looked like the older boy thought he was drowning so he clung to poor Jago. But Jago wasn't strong enough for two, and his head was being dragged under the water.'

Georgie's tears were dripping onto Clemmie's tablecloth, and she dabbed her cheeks with a handkerchief. *Those poor children, one mad with fear, the other being drowned by his friend.*

'Did the gig find them in time?'

'Just in time for the older boy, who was floating on his back. He was taken to the hospital by the coastguard. He got pneumonia, he was terribly ill for a while but he survived.'

'But what about Jago?' Georgie's throat was dry.

Clemmie shook her head. 'We were told to go back to our homes while they searched for him. He washed up a couple of days later. He was covered with scratches from the other boy clinging on to him, his neck was black with bruises. They both must have been mad with fear.'

Georgie sipped the tea put in front of her. In the edges of her mind was a question she was suddenly afraid to ask.

She pulled her shoulders back, looked up at Clemmie. 'Why was there a letter about someone at Beehive Cottage, about Jago Carney?'

Clemmie looked away. 'The boy who drowned Jago was staying at Beehive Cottage.'

23

PRESENT DAY, 27 OCTOBER

While Grant was inside starting work on the loft room, Amber was outside talking to Rowena, the owner of Shambles Cottage, one of the two holiday cottages in the court. Rowena was cleaning and generally sprucing up the place before moth-balling it for the winter.

Amber asked if she could rent it for a couple of weeks; Rowena agreed but the best deal she could do was half price – still eye-wateringly expensive. But Amber would have space to store her stuff, including the bed, until she was ready to move back into Beehive Cottage.

'One of our visitors was asking about that beautiful song you keep playing? I think they would like to buy the CD,' Rowena said, broom in hand.

'What song...?' She blushed with the realisation that strangers had heard it. 'Oh, it's just a little tune I've been devel-oping.' That was one word for it; darker shades had attached themselves to the plaintive melody, and she had found herself jotting down orchestration, humming along with the violas and cellos, maybe a piano part... 'It's just something I'm writing.' Something that was playing in the back of her mind when she tried to sleep, or concentrate on scales and exercises or practise yoga. 'I'm working on it.'

'That's lovely. Hello, Betty, everything all right?'

'Lovely, dear. Are you going to let this talented girl stay in your house?'

Rowena sighed. 'We are. Half price, too, and it means we have to bump up the insurance and services for another month.' She smiled at Amber. 'Give me a few hours to at least sweep out all the sand and change the beds, and it's yours.'

'Thank you. I'll only need one of the bedrooms. But at least I'll still be here in the court.'

Betty looked brighter today. Although there was no resolution to the fraud case yet, investigations were in hand. She had been able to open a new account for her pension, and she had been able to get on top of her bills.

'How have you been getting on with the ghost?' Rowena said chattily, shaking out a doormat onto the cobbles.

Amber spun around. 'People keep telling me the place is haunted.'

'By *the* ghost. Tapping and groaning, strange lights at the window. Beehive Cottage is supposed to be one of the most haunted places on the islands.' She frowned. 'It's even on our annual ghost walk from the pub. You know, it has a history of catching fire, too.'

Betty stepped forward. 'Don't worry about all that. These old houses creak all the time, mine feels like it whispers to me sometimes.'

'There's nothing like that,' Amber said firmly. 'Mine just hums to me sometimes, the wind sounds like music. I'm sure that's what has inspired the new composition I've been working on – the draughts coming in the windows and down the chimney. Can I have a quick look around?' she asked Rowena. 'I have to store a bed, but it collapses down. I just want to see if there's enough room.'

Shambles Cottage layout was similar to Beehive Cottage, but it had been updated, with a tiny shower room squeezed between the bedrooms. There would be just enough room for the bed and her camping supplies. Each room had an electric heater, and she could almost feel the warmth even though they weren't on. There was also a tiny wood burner in the living room fireplace and what looked like an electric range in the kitchen, which oozed heat. 'Is this like an Aga?' she asked, running her finger over the nameplate on the oven door. It was warm.

'Similar, but cheaper to run. It's on all the time – most of the year it's all the heat you need,' Rowena said. 'It's affordable and works well with the solar panels on the roof. We have to be self-sufficient over here as we're usually the last area to have our electricity restored if a storm knocks the power out.'

She showed Amber how the stove worked, and gave her the instructions and recipe book before she returned to cleaning up a summer's worth of salt and sand tracked in by the summer visitors. Amber couldn't wait to actually cook real food; living off one pan on a gas ring was getting tedious. It would have been nice to have enough cash to eat out occasionally, but now the rent would stretch her resources even thinner.

'It says here you can use it as a slow cooker. Can I use the pans on the shelf?'

'Of course,' Rowena said. 'That's what they are for.'

Even the simplest comforts seemed like luxuries now.

By the time Amber had walked down to the shop for the ingredients for a tomato sauce and some pasta, and a few bits of basic shopping for Betty – despite her arguments – Rowena had finished and gone. Amber took a closer look around. No nest of coats to sleep under, and that stupid airbed could be thrown away. She started the sauce in a pan, which made the house smell fruity and garlicky. While it cooked, she had a long shower and dressed up a bit, in the few clothes not ruined by building work.

The stove had brought the temperature up in the cottage, she could pad around in socks and in indoor clothes. There was also Wi-Fi, and as she ate her dinner, she caught up with emails from friends that she'd been avoiding from around the wedding. Most could be read then discarded – a few of Patrick's friends had said things that ranged from questioning to downright harsh. But most of her own friends had been kind and under-standing. Fellow musicians knew the life of a player was one of relentless commitment, it was clear they thought losing that would have thrown her decision-making out of kilter. 'We understand' became a common theme, along with 'call me!'

She sat at the table playing around on the internet, looking for any history she could find about Beehive Cottage. Mostly articles about the 'mystery fire' came up. It did seem possible that the house had been hit by lightning, even though there had been no storm at the time.

An article about the last tenant, Goldie, also turned up. Her full name was Marigold Lippett, and she had been in conflict with the local history group ten years ago. Apparently, the pub had organised a ghost walk back then, and wanted to include Beehive Cottage on the tour. She was angry and didn't want them in the court, even though it was a public space.

The writer had included a ghoulish, probably exaggerated tale of the drowning of the young boy who lived nearby. Why he would haunt the cottage wasn't explained, but he was called Jago, itself an interesting local name.

She looked up the reference and found an article about a Jago Carney who had been drowned in a tragic accident in 1919. A memorial stone had been placed in Seal Cove. She thought back to her walk there, maybe that had been the strangely flat stone around the high tide mark? But she couldn't see the connection to Beehive Cottage. She thought about her dreams of a drowning child. Maybe she *had* heard the tale as a girl, and being here brought it back to her.

A wider search for the boy's name led to a flurry of articles, many written recently.

Jago was a local hero: he had gone to the aid of a holiday-maker who had got into trouble in a rip tide. Jago had drowned, but the boy, aged eleven and not named, had been rescued by a local boat. The surviving boy was open about Jago's heroic actions, and said Jago had kept him afloat long enough to be rescued but sank below the waves before the boat arrived.

The official police report from the time was different to the coroner's verdict of accidental drowning for Jago. The police report suggested that the older boy, who was not a good swim-mer, might have panicked and overwhelmed Jago, whose body had scratches and contusions indicating that he had been grabbed around the neck. The contemporary account pointed out that because local reports were so different to the police report, the spectre had been raised that the eleven-year-old's family had paid to have the story sanitised somehow, and remove all suggestion that the older boy drowned the younger in his panic.

It was hardly his fault. He must have been mad with terror.

Jago's mother was reported to have died of grief after losing her youngest child, although another article in the *Island Press* pointed out that she also had tuberculosis. Amber supposed it couldn't have done her any good to be grieving and speculating about her son's last moments.

A collection provided enough money to buy a flat stone of granite and the islands' stonemason carved it for free.

JAGO CARNEY
GAVE HIS LIFE FOR ANOTHER
11 AUGUST 1919
RIP

The story made her sad, but she still couldn't see how Beehive Cottage was involved.

Amber turned off the heating in Shambles Cottage and went up to bed. It was luxury to lie under a duvet on a good bed – the free bed had a ratty mattress that twanged every time she turned over. She had managed the two weeks' rent but even at half price it was still nearly a thousand a week, it would eat into her remaining savings. Savings she'd been planning to spend on decorating and furnishing the new house that Patrick would now have to himself, she thought with a jolt.

She lay listening to the silent house. She no longer heard snatches of song, humming or wordless singing. There was no creaking of floors and stairs, or the attic overhead, nor draughts whistling around the front door.

Somehow she still felt cold, and she drew the quilt around her shoulders before she fell into a broken sleep.

24

NOVEMBER 1943

Georgie used the excuse of returning neat, archived folders back to the office to ask Hugo if he knew any more about the other half of the letter about Jago, the drowned child. She hoped that the other pages were in one of the piles of records she had to sort through. She took the sheet she had found to show him, but he didn't have any idea.

'I know who might be able to help,' he said, then sneezed. 'You should go home. I'm not fit for company. I seem to have picked up a cold; my landlady is making me stay here overnight. Her husband's an invalid, she doesn't want him to get it. I'll box up some more work for you.'

'There must be somewhere else you can stay,' Georgie said indignantly, once she saw the pile of newspapers and blankets he was sleeping on, in the tiny back room.

'A sickly foreigner?' he asked, half smiling before sneezing again. 'I doubt it. And I'm broke, even the few shillings I pay my hosts wouldn't get me a proper room in the town. Let me put a kettle on the paraffin stove.'

She stood by the door, listening to him cough. 'You might get worse,' she said dubiously.

'I might get better. It's just a cold.' He looked ivory pale, so she stepped forward and felt his forehead. He shut his eyes, like a child. He was hot, too hot. She snatched her hand back at the odd feeling the contact gave her.

'I have a better idea,' she said. This would all have been so much easier in London when they always kept a spare room for visitors. 'Come home with me, and I'll look after you. No one could think anything odd about it, you're really ill. You need plenty of liquids and rest.'

He managed a tired smile. 'No one in London would think anything of it, but here the locals will be deeply suspicious of my motives.'

She watched him struggle to his feet, then fall back into his chair. He swore – she assumed it was an oath – in Breton. 'My husband would be the first to say, look after the poor man,' she said. 'We had refugees in London all the time.' They had mostly welcomed Jewish refugees but also fleeing Dutch and French families, until the authorities had found them places to stay in the early months of the war. 'I will explain to my neighbours.'

'Very well, but don't blame me if they decide you are harbouring a spy,' he said, looking too tired to argue. 'When's the boat?'

'Mr Ellis is already here. I think he went straight in the pub when I arrived. I'll ask when he's able to take us back. Why don't you pack your things?'

While he filled a small rucksack, she packed another box with loose papers, her eyes catching something unexpected.

On the edge of one of the carefully typed documents from the 1930s she noticed a word and date written in pencil just along one edge. *München 1/11/41*. First of November? And surely that was the way the Germans wrote Munich?

She tucked the paper in the box under an old will, and headed down to get Mr Ellis from the pub.

Georgie walked along to the entrance, feeling awkward

about stepping inside, and the conversation died as she pushed the door open. She clutched her bag more tightly, lifted her chin and walked up to Mr Ellis.

'I forgot to ask you,' she said, in what she thought of as her 'London' voice, 'when you are next returning to Morwen?'

He looked up at a clock behind the bar. 'I'm taking three ladies back at about quarter past two.'

'Do you have room for me and another passenger? The solicitor Mr Seznec has nowhere to stay and he's very unwell.'

He looked at his drinking companions. 'Where will he stay?'

She shrugged. 'I suppose, in my son's room. It will only be for a few days. We must help where we can. The poor man is sleeping on an unheated shop floor.'

''E's a furriner,' one of the older men said.

'He certainly is,' she answered firmly, pushing down her own doubts. 'Driven out of his homeland by the Nazis. We must do what we can.' She was surprised at the apathy they seemed to have developed about the war. Out of sight, out of mind. 'As I would hope that somewhere, kind people have taken my husband in,' she said, tears starting to roughen her voice. 'Well? Do you have room, Mr Ellis?'

He tipped his hat back. 'Yes'm,' he said, and nodded. 'Ten minutes or so, if that suits you.'

'That will be perfect,' she said, and sailed out of the pub, head high but eyes prickling with tears.

She couldn't stop thinking about it. *München.* Was Hugo some sort of spy, like the locals suspected? No, she told herself, he would never do that. Anyway, it didn't look like his large, energetic hand, and he wasn't even on the island then.

Hugo was looking even paler, standing next to his kitbag and the box of documents, just outside the shop.

'This is very kind of you,' he said, his voice rasping. 'I'm sure it's just a nasty cold... I wouldn't want your family to catch it.'

'Nonsense,' she said briskly, lifting the box, his bag and her handbag as he put his crutches under each arm. 'How are your legs? Are they getting better?'

'The German bullets shattered the bones in both legs. They have talked about rebreaking them and setting them straight, once they heal more. I was lucky they didn't amputate both of them.'

As he hobbled down to the quay, she steadied his arm a couple of times. 'Will you be able to manage the stairs at my house? They are rather steep, I'm afraid.'

'I'm sure I will. I live upstairs at the boarding house, and I often go up backwards. Good afternoon, Mr Ellis.'

Georgie handed down all her packages to the other passengers, then she and Mr Ellis helped Hugo aboard. He wrapped his scarf over his mouth. 'No point spreading this cold,' he said, looking even paler as he closed his eyes and leaned back against the side of the boat.

'I'm sure the fresh air will keep us all safe,' she asserted, but the odd coughing fit kept the three middle-aged women pressed together at the front of the boat.

They stopped at St Petroc's, West Island and St Piran's, dropping one lady off at each, then finally they had the boat to themselves. Mr Ellis stood at the engine, guiding it across the rough water.

'I hope you know what you're doing,' he said to Georgie. 'There are a few old tabbies who will say you shouldn't have a man in your house. They won't think it respectable.'

'Well, let them come and talk to my face,' Georgie said, already tired of the conversation. 'I've taken in French Jews, injured Polish airmen and even German refugees. I don't think a Frenchman should be any problem.'

Perhaps she would be able to find out more about the pencilled note as well. She trusted him, but she did want an explanation.

'Breton,' Hugo said, his words muffled by the scarf, before coughing again.

She laughed a little.

Mr Ellis brought the boat in and tied it up. 'I'd better help you with your charity case,' he said. Although he was probably in his seventies, he was stocky and strong, and had no trouble helping Hugo up the slippery cobbles to the court.

By the time they got to the house and pushed the door open, Hugo was shaking. Georgie got him to slump in the chair by the warm hearth in the kitchen, although the fire had gone out.

'I'll stay to help you get him upstairs,' Mr Ellis said. 'Go and make a bed for him.'

She had no choice but to pull back the sheets on Tommy's narrow bed. Together, they got Hugo up the stairs and settled him into bed, where he fell asleep immediately.

'I'll get Martha, my daughter-in-law, to come around,' Mr Ellis said. 'She's a good woman and a capital nurse. She worked through the Spanish flu as well. She'll also be able to tell the local gossips that the Frenchman is no threat to your virtue.' His smile was accompanied by such twinkly eyes she couldn't help but laugh.

'Breton, Mr Ellis,' she said, smiling. 'And I can look after my own virtue.'

25

PRESENT DAY, 28 OCTOBER

Amber woke up in the silent house and enjoyed the luxury of a hot shower, refrigerated milk on her cereal, and a proper coffee maker. There was nothing she could really do back at Beehive Cottage for now, but she was determined to get the cupboard open and salvage the antique doors if she could, and protect the old stove. She knew the builders would rather rip it all out and start again. She said as much to Ellie, who had invited herself in for a coffee.

'I'd love to see inside that cupboard, I'm nosy as anything! Bran will look after Zillah,' Ellie had replied.

When she arrived, Amber pushed open the door to Beehive and walked in. The atmosphere felt thick and welcoming, and at the very edge of her hearing was the melody that had been driving her nuts. She hummed a few bars into the voice recorder on her phone.

'That's nice,' Ellie said. 'Wow, I thought our house was small!'

'It will be a bit bigger when we get this chimney sorted out.

Look, they boarded the chimney in along with the alcoves each side, and plastered over the lot.'

Ellie ran her hand down the heavily painted cupboard door. 'It looks like it's just painted shut.'

'The men are saying the door will fall to bits if they force it open. I thought I might try a craft knife.'

'Oh, don't listen to them. You can chip away at the paint. I bet there's only one or two layers. I had something similar in my house.'

Amber rummaged through the tool boxes and found a knife with a newish blade. She gave it to Ellie. 'Have a try.'

Ellie scraped away at it. 'Look, it's easy. You have a go.'

Amber started tentatively at first, but soon a shower of paint chips flaked onto her hand and she could start to see the gap. 'It doesn't have a handle, I don't know how to... Oh!'

The corner of the door was sticking out just enough to grab it and pull. With a little more scraping and pulling, the door creaked open.

Inside, the shelves were stacked with papers spilling out of old boxes and folders, almost reduced to dust by bugs and mice. On the lowest shelf, directly on the floor, were odds and ends from probably a century ago. Broken crockery, what looked like a wooden box chewed around its metal clasp, and what looked like the celluloid head of a doll, gazing eerily up at them.

'That's – horrible,' Ellie said, wrinkling her nose and stepping back.

The worst of the smells came from the decomposing body of a mouse by the door, but mostly it just stank of age and dust.

'These are useful shelves, though,' Amber said, peering up and down them. 'And not much woodworm, just a bit here on this one.'

'It's probably pine,' Ellie said. 'Look, the cupboard door is heavier, it might be a hardwood. You become an expert on woodworm in this salty air.' She made a little face at the cloud of dust sent up as she moved the papers.

'I could bag all this up and have a look at it,' Amber said, getting more excited. She wondered if any of it would refer to the mysterious child, Jago. 'I might go through it, where it's readable – it might relate to history of the cottage.'

Ellie was examining the stove. 'This is so cute. But it's low, you'd have to be sitting down to cook on it.'

'I'll just use it for heating,' Amber said. 'I want an induction hob over by the window.' She grinned at Ellie. 'Now let's have a look in the other side.'

'Where?'

Amber tapped the plasterboard beside the chimney breast. 'There must be another alcove there, there's at least a foot of space.'

She attacked it with the hammer, making Ellie jump then laugh.

'What's in there?'

They peered into the gap, empty right down to the floor, where an unpleasant smell wafted up from some things that looked like mushrooms.

'Do you think that's dry rot?' Amber said, almost in a whisper.

'No. I think dry rot would have been visible all around the room. But it's pretty damp.'

'I could put logs here, ready for the stove,' Amber said, visualising a modernised kitchen next to the antique range. 'Maybe I could put a tiny table in, like Betty has next door.'

Ellie looked at her, eyebrows raised. 'You sound like you're planning to live here.'

Maybe I am. Amber smiled a little. 'I don't know what my dad has planned. But I should make it as nice as possible for whoever does live here.'

. . .

By the time Lewis arrived early on Monday, she was able to make explicit her plans for the chimney wall, and she had bagged up all the debris from the alcove. She'd managed to get the one wormy shelf out and break it in half, throwing it out to the yard.

He looked over her work and the neatly bagged-up plasterboard she'd knocked off. 'Nice job. I still don't think that old stove will be usable. It looks like the rust goes all the way through in places. I suppose you could weld new bars on the firebox...' He didn't sound hopeful.

'Well, I'd like to try,' she said firmly. 'What are you doing today?'

'Prepping walls, putting on beading and filling a few big holes,' Lewis said. 'Next week we'll start plastering and hopefully you'll have some walls and ceilings a week after that. So we will just be here for half a day today.'

'That's great.'

'Patrick was asking after you last night. I saw him down the pub with Ben.'

Ben. The name made her heart skip a little. 'How is Patrick?' she asked, almost afraid to hear the answer.

'He's not exactly happy, but he seems a bit more resigned. If you called him, I think it would put his mind at rest that you haven't been doubting your decision.' He smiled, tilted his head. 'You haven't changed your mind, have you? Don't mind me, I'm just an old romantic.'

'No second thoughts, no,' she managed to say with a small voice. 'But we've been best friends for so long. I miss that.'

'Some people make brilliant marriages with their best friend,' he said, running his hand down the uneven edge where she had removed the plasterboard.

'Not me,' she said, tears itching her eyes.

He winced. 'Not me either,' he said. 'I had to wait until the right bloke came along.'

'I'm sure it was worth the wait.' She smiled at him, even as the tears spilled. 'The attic room?'

He rolled his eyes and half smiled. 'Do you mind? I was having a moment. Attic room, yes. Come and have a look.'

She gingerly climbed the ladder over the stairs into the room at the top of the house that was free of smoke damage and mostly boarded. 'What would it be like to sleep up here? I suppose it would look over the fields behind, very private.'

'Too cold in the winter, too hot in the summer,' Lewis said. 'It needs insulating and a modern window, which really means planning consent and building control, a proper conversion. It's quite solid, though. Good boards. Hopefully the joists are OK.' He stamped vigorously. 'No real bounce.'

'It would be a three-bedroomed cottage, then,' she said.

'You'd have to put space-saving stairs where the airing cupboard is,' he said, 'but then you won't have enough space for a bathroom upstairs.'

'Maybe just have a loo and sink between the bedrooms,' Amber mused out loud. 'And keep a bathroom downstairs like Betty's.'

'You're getting very invested in this tatty old house,' Lewis said, looking at her with amusement. 'I've been inside the gardener's cottage at the manor on West Island. It's a four-bed detached house, it's gorgeous and it's basically yours. Yet you've fallen in love with this tiny place. Down you go, lovey, careful.'

'The gardener's cottage is lovely, yes,' she conceded, concentrating on not falling down the ladder. Honestly, her attachment to the gardener's cottage had faded. It had been just a dream, along with sharing her life with Patrick. 'But it's not meant to be mine. I think Beehive Cottage is full of potential.'

Along with her whole life.

'I want to do a good job with this cottage, then Dad will be able to get his money back, at least.'

'Well, once we've plastered the kitchen properly, you can

sand that cupboard door and we'll see what can be salvaged of the shelves.'

'Great. I'll let you get on,' she said. 'I'm off for a walk. Oh, one more thing. Do you know anything about a ghost? People say this place is haunted.'

He shrugged. 'It has a bit of an atmosphere, doesn't it? Maybe there's something in all that stuff that will give you a clue,' he said, pointing at the bags of paperwork.

'That's mostly mouse nests and mould,' she said, but the idea was already making her curious. 'I'm going to take a look, sort through it.'

'Something else Patrick said,' Lewis added as she reached the door, bags in both hands. 'Ben mentioned you were asking about a book. Patrick's going to look out ones that have articles about Morwen. Maybe he'll drop some over, if that would be all right?'

Her heart lurched, it felt like it dropped into her stomach. 'Oh. Great. Yes, that would be fine.'

26

NOVEMBER 1943

Georgie had underestimated the attitudes of the islanders. Clemmie seemed shocked that she would even consider having a single man staying in the house.

'*I* wouldn't do it,' she said, leaning back against the school fence. 'Not even for the rent.'

'He's not paying rent,' Georgie said. 'He's very ill – it's charity. He needs looking after. Martha Ellis is coming to help nurse him.'

That seemed to mollify Clemmie a bit. 'Well, she's a respectable woman. Did you know she took in a rescued Dutch sailor at the beginning of the war?' she asked. 'Of course, she's married. But I still think you should have a lock on your bedroom door, or stick a chair under the doorknob.'

'I'm married, too. Honestly, if he had the energy to try anything, he'd have to get by the two children first,' Georgie reassured her, aware that other women were listening. 'Even if I had a spare chair. He's very gentlemanly. He was educated at Cambridge.'

She wasn't sure the islanders had much reference for the word, not for a 'furriner'. Come to think about it, there had been an article about people from Cambridge being arrested for spying in the newspaper she had edited.

'People have been saying he's been interviewed at the garrison,' Clemmie said with relish. 'Twice.'

'And they let him go, so he's been safely vetted,' Georgie said, waving to Dolly as she came out of the school. 'I'm more concerned that he'll give us all his horrible cough.'

She walked home, trying to work out how she was going to make rations for three stretch to four, but when she got back she could see that he wasn't going to eat much. By sunset, a bang on the door brought Mrs Martha Ellis, a fisherman's wife in her forties who came with bones and a few carrots to make broth, and some fillets of pollack, straight from the trawler, for their tea. Tommy came in late with several good bits of driftwood and a graze on his knee from playing football, and he didn't seem to mind the man sleeping in his room too much.

'If he doesn't have anywhere else to go,' he said, stacking the driftwood outside the back door and being chivvied back in. There was a cold, wintery wind drifting into the kitchen. 'Poor chap. It will be good to help someone else after all the help we've had,' he said, looking up at her. 'The Christian thing to do, the vicar would say.'

'Yes, exactly,' she said, and hugged him. He wriggled away after a few seconds. Georgie wanted to hold on to him forever. He had brought her so much comfort these past months, with wisdom beyond his years. She had enjoyed his company, too, and was dreading the day he would have to leave to board at whichever school he would end up at.

'I hear you've been helping down at the quay,' Martha said to Tommy. 'My husband says you're strong for your age. Maybe you'll be a fisherman one day.'

'I'd be too scared,' he said, glancing sideways up at Georgie for a second. 'It's so dangerous to go out in the storms.'

'Yes, we did lose a trawler at the beginning of the war, the

Island Queen,' she said. 'And there have been a few wrecks since, and a couple of lives lost. We're all fighting in our own way. I'll go up and see your invalid, shall I?'

'Would you mind?' said Georgie, chopping vegetables to go in the broth with the bones. 'I'm not sure whether he needs to see a doctor.'

Georgie fried the transparent fillets of fish and served them up with some potatoes left over from the day before with a few scraps of kale. The children cleared their plates.

'Where am I going to sleep?' Tommy asked. 'We can't all share – your bed isn't really big enough even for you and Dolly. I suppose I'll have to camp on the floor down here.'

'No, I'll do that,' Georgie said, racked with guilt. 'You've got school in the morning.'

'I'll be fine,' he said in a gruff voice. 'It will be like camping with the scouts. Or I could make a bed up in the attic.'

Georgie shook her head. 'It's a good idea but it will be so cold up there,' she said, as Martha came back in. 'And we need to fix the leak first.'

'Your lad is welcome to stay with us,' Martha said, smiling at him. 'I'd offer to have your Frenchman but my William has a weak chest.'

'That's a lovely idea. How is Mr Seznec?' Georgie said, clasping her hands together in an irrational wave of anxiety.

'It's a nasty cough, and he needs looking after, you were right there.' She looked at Georgie, very directly with sky blue eyes. 'It's going to cause some talk on the islands. I'll do what I can, but he's a young man living under your roof, no matter how ill he is. The best thing you can do is get the doctor over and get him back on his feet, back to the big island.'

'He's lame as well,' Georgie said. 'The Germans shot his legs from under him when he was escaping France.'

Martha nodded. 'I saw. Well, I'll come over tomorrow and

check on him – it's your newspaper day, isn't it? I'll help him with the broth and the pot.'

Georgie smiled involuntarily. The islanders really did know everything. 'Well, thank you. That would really help. I'm at home the rest of the week, doing paperwork for Mr Seznec.'

Martha looked over at Tommy. 'Would you like to come and stay, then? We'll have some cocoa before bed, and Mr Ellis plays the fiddle.'

'Can I?' he said to Georgie. 'It would be nice to sleep in a bed and I can go straight from there to school.'

'All right. We'll make a bedroom here for you in the attic over the weekend,' Georgie said.

'I can probably lend you some blankets and a mattress,' Mrs Ellis said. She lowered her voice. 'It might be better to get him home as soon as the Frenchman feels better. For decency.'

Georgie gave up arguing about her reputation, kissed Tommy goodbye despite his rolling eyes and huffing, and thanked Mrs Ellis. 'I think you persuaded him with the idea of a warm bed.'

'It was the cocoa,' he said, and grinned.

After she had tucked Dolly into bed – who was full of worries about the stranger in the next room and was afraid of his muffled coughing – Georgie stepped in to check on Hugo.

'How are you feeling?' she murmured, seeing he was awake.

'Do you have an outhouse?' he said, his voice rough and his eyes red.

'We do, but it's outside and you are in no state to get all the way down the stairs. There's a pot under the bed, I don't mind emptying it.'

'*I* mind you emptying it,' he said, wheezing another cough, shaking with cold.

'Don't be silly,' she said briskly. 'Imagine I'm a nurse.' She laid a hand on his forehead. 'You're still terribly hot. I'll get you some aspirin, and you should really take a blanket off. I'll call the doctor in the morning from the post office.'

'It's just a cold,' he said, but she shook her head.

'It's influenza. I had it back in London, it's serious. I felt like I'd been run over by a milk cart, everything ached.'

'Oh,' he said. 'Influenza.'

'I can't have you dying up here, think what the islanders would say? In the meantime, don't be such a baby. You could do with some fresh water to drink and a few fresh handkerchiefs for that cold.' She tried to keep her voice as matronly as possible, but couldn't keep it up. She smiled at him. With his rumpled hair he looked younger, except for the beginnings of a beard. 'Let someone look after you for a day or two and you will be back on your feet in no time,' she soothed.

It was only when she lay in her bed next to a sleeping Dolly that Georgie went back to worrying about that single pencilled line in his papers.

He was French, wasn't he? Breton, he would insist. He *had* been telling the truth about his background, hadn't he?

Maybe he would use the German spelling for Munich. Maybe it was harmless.

Maybe.

27

PRESENT DAY, 31 OCTOBER

Amber had put some sheets over the kitchen table and floor in Shambles Cottage, before unpacking the papers from the cupboard at Beehive. The documents were welded together into stacks by years of damp. She'd looked online for advice on easing them apart, and had laid out as many as she could to dry overnight.

As she opened the window to let the cool evening air carry away the smell, she caught sight of the postcard she'd received from her parents, who seemed to be very much enjoying her honeymoon. With a resigned sigh, she sat down to sort through the papers. They looked like legal documents; she found a few pages of wills from the 1920s and 1930s. The island names jumped out at her. One Flora Ellis, born 1842, had intended to leave her estate of one quarter share of a house to be divided equally between all her grandchildren. They must have each got a few pounds when she died in 1944. *Shillings*, she corrected herself, reading through the details that would include great-grandchildren too. The house was valued at three hundred pounds, and Flora owned just a quarter of that. Times had been so hard then. Amber wondered how Georgina and her children had managed.

In the middle of the bundle was a packet wrapped in oiled card or something waterproof. It was glued shut with bindings made of cloth and smelled so *old*. She cleaned it off and turned it over. It was probably just full of dusty legal papers, but it was a link to the past. Still, she stood up to get a knife to slit the glued tape when a tap at the door made her jump.

'Coming!' she said, looking down at her dusty top. She must stink like mouldy mouse droppings, she thought, as she brushed another couple onto the sheet of drying papers. She opened the front door.

It was Patrick, his dark curly hair cropped shorter than when she had seen him last, his round cheeks a little thinner, paler. Her mouth fell open, and she was sure she had gone red right to her hairline. Even her ears burned.

'Oh,' she stammered. 'I wasn't expecting you.'

He smiled at that, a sad, crooked version of the sunny smile she knew. 'Ben said you were looking for books on the history of Morwen,' he said in his soft voice. 'And your father texted me about how the cottage was coming on. I hope you don't mind? These are from the manor library.'

'Oh. Thank you, come in. I'm sorry about this,' she said. 'The place is in a bit of a mess.'

'I don't mind,' he said, wiping his feet on the mat before walking into the living room. 'This is cute.'

'It's just a holiday let,' she explained. 'They're plastering Beehive Cottage. Sit down,' she said, waving to the tiny sofa. 'I'll put the kettle on.' She looked at her fingers. 'After boiling my hands in bleach. I'm sorry about the smell.' She disappeared into the kitchen, stepping between the drying piles of papers spread over the floor, and washed her hands thoroughly.

When she returned to the living room, he was looking

through a paper at the top of a stack. She looked down at the crown of his head. *I don't know how to talk to you.*

He looked up. 'How have you been?'

'Oh, you know,' she said, then saw the tears in his eyes, the hard lines around his mouth as he pressed his lips together. 'Terrible.' Tears sprang into her eyes at the memory of waking up crying in the middle of the night, the physical yearning to see him, hug him.

'Good,' he said. 'No, I don't mean that.'

'Yes, you do,' she said, sitting on the arm of a chair. 'And you should, I deserve it. I won't say I'm sorry, because it doesn't start to cover it.'

'I just keep thinking that you never loved me,' he said, his words clipped.

'I did love you,' she said. 'I can't explain what went wrong.'

He nodded, then handed a couple of paperbacks over. Her fingertips brushed his hand; they were icy cold and the shock almost made her drop the books. 'I thought we could go back to being friends,' he said, with difficulty. 'But I'm not sure I can do that.'

She nodded. 'Will you stay on the islands?'

He shook his head before spreading out his hands. 'I don't know. I want to. I love the manor, but that was when I thought...'

One day, the manor would be hers, and therefore *his*. She hadn't thought he would be thinking so far ahead.

Of course he was. He was thinking of middle-aged them, with children and a couple of Labradors, just like her parents. Patrick had often talked in terms of *always* and *forever*.

'I think they knew you were the perfect custodian of the gardens,' she said, realising it herself. 'Marrying me would just be the icing on the cake. I do hope you stay. You are a great asset to the place, and maintaining the manor has always been a team effort.' Her father's cousin was the hotel manager, and they had a lettings manager who ran all the property along with a team of support staff. She remembered the solicitor with a jolt. *I must check how Betty's case is progressing.*

'And you think you can run the manor with me as garden designer and manager, one day, when your parents retire?'

She walked back into the kitchen to make the tea while she thought of an answer.

'You and your partner. Or family,' she said, putting the cup down with care. 'Because that will happen too.'

'Just not with you.' He glared at her. 'You're so cold about all this.'

'I was never going to settle down and run the hotel,' she said, tears springing easily to her eyes. 'And I'm not cold at all, it was the hardest decision I've ever taken. I've agonised over this, cried myself to sleep, walked all over the island to try to understand all my doubts.'

He looked a little less angry. 'I've been doing that, too.' He looked down at the cup. 'Are you seeing anyone else?'

'Of course not!' she said, flexing her left hand. It was aching, which was strange after such a good recovery in recent weeks. Her neck was tense, and she could feel it impeding the movement in her arm. She rubbed the hand, trying to relax her shoulders. 'That's the last thing I want right now.'

'I know Ben was helping you. He's a nice guy.'

'Yes, he is,' she said. 'But I'm not looking for a romance right now.' She did miss Ben, though – his good nature, his joking and light teasing. 'We were working together on the house.'

'Ben said he found out a few things about Beehive Cottage,' he said. 'The family that owned it before yours were rich, the Prestons. They owned property in Bath and Cheltenham, they made their fortune from spa hotels in the Victorian times.'

She jumped up. 'I've seen papers with Preston on, I'll have to follow that up.'

'Since before the war, they used the place as a holiday

cottage for the family's children. They would install a nanny and the kids there while they stayed up at the hotel.'

'That big one at the corner of the island?' Chancel Hall Hotel sat right at the tip of Morwen, below the ruins of a lighthouse. She hadn't been able to afford to eat there but remembered going to a wedding there as a teenager.

'Yes, but something happened. One of the kids that stayed in the cottage might have drowned another boy. Accidentally. You'll see the case is outlined in a couple of the books.'

'I did read something online. How do you *accidentally* drown someone?'

'By being so terrified you hang onto them, I suppose. That's how the legend goes.'

Amber couldn't imagine how frightening it would be, to go to someone to help them but then they push you under. She had always been a strong swimmer, but she knew how treacherous the cold Atlantic waters could be. 'So the boy who survived was staying at Beehive Cottage before the war?'

'Exactly. The local family felt the authorities hushed it up at the inquest, that the family somehow paid off the islanders and got away with the scandal because it was a poor kid who died.'

Amber sat down again with a jolt. 'You must come over and see the cottage for yourself when it's done.'

His expression dropped. 'I don't need to see the cottage. I just wanted an excuse to see you,' he said, his voice growly and soft. 'I can't stand it, I miss you so much. Sometimes I just want to run away, get away from everything that reminds me of you.'

She didn't know what to say to that for a moment. 'Maybe you should take a holiday,' she said. 'Maybe a break would help.'

'I might go home, see my parents. I thought it would help to see you but it's almost like you're just standing there, telling me over and over that you don't love me.' He was looking at her like she had kicked him.

Apologising was not going to make it any better. 'Thank you for coming over,' she said. 'I know it was hard. But I think you should go back now.'

He stood up abruptly, almost knocking the tiny table over. 'You're really not going to tell me you regret what you said, that you've changed your mind?'

Amber shook her head. 'I feel awful that I hurt you. But I won't change my mind. I know it wouldn't work.'

'If they hadn't spent so much time fixing your neck and arm, you would have gone through with the wedding,' he said bitterly.

'If I hadn't hurt myself, I wouldn't have got engaged in the first place,' she said softly. 'I was lost, terrified.'

'You want something that doesn't exist,' he said, his voice flat. 'You'll never find it. Some fairy tale version of love.'

'I hope you're wrong,' she said, taking a deep breath and standing as tall as she could. 'But if you are right, I'll still have music, even if I can't play at the top level any more.'

He nodded once. 'That won't keep you warm at night.'

She waited until he had walked away and shut the door to the court before she sat down and covered her face with her hands, lost in tears.

28

NOVEMBER 1943

Hugo was shaking with fever and rambling a little in the small hours of the morning, so Georgie wrapped herself in a blanket and watched over him. The fluid words he muttered were incomprehensibly not French, although they didn't sound like her limited memory of German either.

She got to know every plane of his high cheekbones and strong chin in the single candle flame. He had always seemed slight to her, but his shoulders were wide, he was just thin. His legs were twisted and bent where they had healed badly, the skin covered with livid scars. She wondered why he hadn't been properly treated – perhaps he hadn't reached a hospital in time. The thought of him so ill was unbearable. She couldn't save Jim, but she was afraid to leave Hugo in case he died.

By early morning he was deeply asleep and she woke from a doze curled up on the chair she had placed in the corner. She slipped over, laid a hand on his forehead and realised it was cooler and the fever had broken, but he didn't wake. She slid out of the room to lie down next to Dolly for an hour or two before she had to get up.

She didn't get much rest before Martha Ellis arrived with

Tommy and went upstairs to check on Hugo. Georgie scrambled into clean clothes and went downstairs to cut some bread for Dolly's breakfast.

'Was it nice staying at the Ellises?' she asked Tommy.

'It was warm,' he said but didn't elaborate. 'Patience is back at her school now, but she's coming home early in December – she promised to help me work through the mathematics problems my teacher can't help with.'

'You could ask Mr Seznec, when he gets better.'

He made a face. 'He's not going to die, is he? I heard Mrs Ellis say he wasn't but...'

She smiled at him. 'I'm sure he isn't,' she said, hoping she was right. 'Have your breakfast.'

'Mrs Ellis brought some potted crab for you,' he said, reaching up to one of the shelves for a plate. 'She makes her own. Can I have some too?'

'You can,' she said, looking at the stove. It wasn't worth lighting just for hot water for tea, but Hugo would need some, too. She started snapping sticks to place in the tiny fireplace over a screwed-up sheet of paper. 'I'd better offer Martha some tea as well.' Georgie peered at the remaining few leaves in the bottom of the tea caddy. She would have to ask Hugo for his ration if he was staying.

Martha came down, nodding to Georgie. 'He's down to skin and bone; I don't think he's been looking after himself properly since he was shot. He needs the doctor in case it goes to his lungs.'

Tommy looked over at her. 'When he was shot by the Germans?'

'He was trying to stop the Germans invading his homeland,' Georgie said. 'They were shooting from the air at people who were running away to get to the sea.' It was all he had ever said about it but it must have been agony – and terrifying – being so badly injured.

She could see Tommy revising his opinion of Hugo already.

'We can look up in the loft soon,' he said. 'We can make it into a room, if we use that ladder.'

'It's not very safe,' she demurred.

'You always say I climb like a monkey,' he said, grinning, and bit into his crab paste sandwich. 'This is lovely, Mrs Ellis.'

'Well, you can help me and the boys come crabbing, if you want. We're sick of sardines and the like,' she said, rolling her eyes. 'What I'd give for a few rashers of bacon.'

The rations allowed a little bacon but the ship hadn't brought any for several weeks.

'I'd better get ready for work,' Georgie said, glancing at her watch. 'If it's safe to leave Mr Seznec.'

'Yes, you go ahead. I'll take Dolly back with me, she can walk up with my boys,' Mrs Ellis said. 'You get off to work, Mrs Preston, I'll be back to keep an eye on him. Perhaps you'll call at the doctor's house to get her to visit.'

'I will. Please call me Georgie,' she begged. She'd asked her several times before but she hadn't responded. Despite her kind actions, she seemed reserved around Georgie.

'Well, all right, Georgie,' Mrs Ellis replied. 'You'd better call me Martha. I thought you wouldn't stay long, to be honest. I thought one of the Prestons would take you in.'

'We're staying,' Georgie said. *The Prestons don't want us.*

Bob Alden made her welcome at the newspaper though, although the tide had made it impossible to get there before eleven.

'We've got some ministry stuff to include today,' he said, poring over a letter. 'I was hoping we could rephrase, it's very wordy. Would that be allowed, d'you think?'

'I don't suppose anyone is going to check,' she answered, taking the sheet he offered. 'Goodness, what a lot of nonsense this week. I'm sure if we did an editorial, we could make it much more understandable.'

'I don't mind you having a try.' He looked over his glasses at her. 'I hear you've been harbouring a dangerous alien.'

She laughed. 'Honestly, he's lived here for months, haven't any of you bothered to get to know him?'

'Well, he's French, isn't he? Did you have to take him home with you? It's caused a bit of a stir.'

'He might have developed pneumonia if I hadn't,' she said. 'He has a horrible case of influenza. I'm doing some filing and sorting for him. I couldn't leave him to sleep in an unheated shop.'

'Probably not,' he said, but he didn't look convinced.

'Anyway, I found something I thought you might be able to explain,' she said, rummaging in her bag for the single sheet. 'There was some sort of tragedy related to Beehive Cottage, a while ago. I don't know why solicitors would be involved in a tragic accident.'

He squinted at the paper, adjusted his glasses on his nose. 'I remember this. My father wrote a piece on it every week for months.'

'It involved a child, Jago Carney.'

'I knew his brother,' Bob said. 'Jago was hailed as a hero by the islanders.'

'So why was there so much controversy?'

'As I recall,' he said, tapping his front tooth with his pen, which he did when he was concentrating, 'there were three children staying at the cottage with an old woman, their nurse, I suppose. The two boys went for a swim one afternoon at Seal Cove but it was blowing a bit, big waves straight off the Atlantic.'

'And a boy got swept out. I heard that.'

'Young Jago Carney dived straight in. He got to the older boy easy enough – by his own brother's account he managed to calm him down, got him swimming along the beach so they could get out of the current.'

'But something else happened?' It made Georgie cold to think of it.

'We don't know exactly what. Jago's brother said a wave broke over their heads, and the visitor panicked. He held on to Jago. He fought back, but he kept getting pushed under.'

'That's dreadful. But why was it such a mystery? They were both children, no one could be held to blame.'

'After the visitors made their statements to the police, something happened. The coroner's inquest was held over here, even though the drowning happened on Morwen.'

'How did that happen?' she said, realising the truth as soon as she said it. 'The islanders think the Prestons paid people off.'

'They got the inquest moved from Morwen to St Brannock's, got some London lawyers over. Somehow, everyone's story changed by the time of the inquest, except Carney's family. But when the coastguard found the body, they saw the marks on his face and neck. My father wrote the story up in the paper and didn't care about the consequences. That boy was pulled down, scratched and bruised.'

'How did the Prestons take the newspaper story?'

'There were threats against my dad, as I recall. A couple of letters saying they would sue for libel. Even the doctor changed his first report, said the scratches were from rolling on the beach.'

Georgie was horrified. 'That's so awful. Did they name the boy who did it? I mean, it wasn't really his fault exactly, but if it wasn't for him, Jago would have survived.'

Bob hesitated for a moment. 'Dad only dared print the name the first time. After that he was gagged by the court. James Edward Preston.'

She had a sick feeling in her stomach. 'Jim.'

Jim had never told her about the terrible event when he was

eulogising about the cottage and the joyful times he'd spent on the island as a child. She had wondered why he stopped going each summer, but his answer had been that he went away to school.

She shut her eyes as the thought of his drowning in the Pacific shot into her head like a flashbulb.

'My husband.'

29

PRESENT DAY, 1 NOVEMBER

There wasn't much Amber could do at Beehive Cottage at the moment, except for fetching coffee and clearing up after Grant and Lewis, and she was frustrated.

After a stint sorting through the papers, she headed over to the cottage to see how the work was coming on. Her heart leapt at a familiar voice.

Ben. She'd been trying not to think about him, about the way he used to duck under the door frames and look back to smile at her, about how her skin tingled when he stood close to her... She schooled herself not to grin when she saw him.

'Morning,' she said breezily, leaning around the front door. 'What are you doing here – I thought you were at the manor?' *Protecting Patrick's feelings.*

'Ben's going to resurrect the frames and the windowsill,' Lewis said.

'You can help if you like,' Ben said, breaking into a smile. 'Chip your nail varnish some more.'

'She's been pretty good, actually,' Lewis said, surprising her. 'No trouble. And she's filled up a hundred bags and dropped them down the quay.'

'A thousand,' she said, hefting her good arm. 'My muscles are lopsided now.'

As Lewis walked back upstairs with Grant, her smile faded. 'What about Patrick? I thought you were sparing his feelings by avoiding me?'

'He's left for a couple of days,' he said, looking serious. 'Off to do a quote for a design job. But he apologised for thinking there was something going on between us. I explained.'

Right. Not that she planned on indulging her little attraction but still, it would have been nice to know that that someone had liked her.

'Did he tell you he came over?'

'He did.' He winced. 'He's not taking it very well but I can't blame him. My housemate says he'll need a lot of time to get over it. Some formula, that it takes half the length of a relationship to really recover.' He shrugged. 'Lizzie reads a lot of women's magazines.'

'Maybe he does,' Amber said, feeling worse that she was starting to feel ready to move on herself. 'So, what can I help with?'

'Measuring and cutting,' he said. 'Have you ever used a circular saw?'

She shook her head. 'And I'm not going to. The vibration alone...'

'I wasn't that hopeful,' he said. 'No, you'll be fetching and carrying, sanding and scraping, same as before. And, of course, you'll be doing all the coffee runs.'

A tap on the door made her turn. It was Betty, looking a bit subdued. 'Could you pop next door and help me with something, Amber? Nothing to bother the boys with.'

'Definitely. Get your own coffees,' she said to Ben, smartly. 'Come on, Bets, what can I help you with?'

Betty waited until she got inside and shut the door behind

Amber. 'You won't believe it, lovey,' she said, shaking her head. 'Look at this letter.'

Amber took the paper from Betty's trembling hand. 'Sit down, Betty,' she said automatically.

'No! Read it.'

It was from the solicitor who had been chasing Betty's savings. The police, once they found out it was an active scam and the thieves hadn't yet covered their tracks, had managed to identify a whole nest of them.

'Read the bit at the bottom,' she said. 'The bank is going to refund my money because those terrible people stole thousands from their customers.'

Amber's smile grew. 'Look at that. There's a reward, Betty, from a big American bank that has been losing money to those crooks, too. Ten thousand dollars.'

'I don't care about that. My savings will be back in my bank and the bills are all going to be paid,' Betty said.

'Listen. *Ten thousand dollars!*'

'Where on earth would I spend dollars?' Betty said. 'An American at the airbase once gave my mother two dollars for some pies she cooked for his platoon, and she never could spend it. I've probably still got them somewhere.'

Amber laughed, dispelling some of the awkwardness that she'd felt around Ben. 'The bank will turn it into pounds for you. You could treat yourself, go on holiday somewhere.'

'I wanted to visit my daughter in Penzance a few years ago,' Betty said. 'But I'm not sure my old bones would do well on the boat.'

'You can fly! Take a helicopter, it lands in Penzance – you could just get a taxi at the other end.'

Sadness crossed Betty's face. 'My husband went to the mainland when he had his stroke, they took him by air ambulance. By the time I got there on the boat, he was dead.' The bleakness in her voice made Amber reach out and hug her. Her bones were bird sharp, projecting through her cardigan.

'This is quite different,' she said. 'It will be lovely. I'll put you on the helicopter, and your family can meet you. It's just a few minutes.'

Betty stopped shaking as much and pulled away, wiping her eyes with a snowy handkerchief from her sleeve. 'Well, I haven't got the money yet. I'll think about it.'

'You can stop worrying about your bills,' Amber said. 'And maybe have the heating on a bit more when it gets cold.'

'Oh, I don't want to dip into my savings,' she said, her voice firm. 'That's for my old age.'

Amber couldn't help smiling as Betty collected her shopping bag and stick from by the front door and set off down the hill. She walked back into Beehive Cottage, where Ben was measuring up the front door.

She gave an exaggerated sigh. 'Coffees, then? I suppose that's all I'm good for.'

'Do you want to save the front door?' he said, tapping a paper with his pencil. 'It's not original and it got pretty scorched.'

'I suppose we have to?' She looked at the document. 'Oh, it's not listed.'

'It's a rubbish one, probably from the sixties,' he said. 'Look at it, the panels have shrunk and cracked in the heat. It won't provide much insulation.'

'Do you think we could get one from a reclamation yard? And could we put a proper wood burner in here?' she asked, looking at the small opening. 'Now we've cleaned the flue out.' The acrid smell of the tarry soot still lingered, taking her back to the day she helped with the chimney.

'Definitely, if your dad comes up with the money. It will need a flue right up to the roof. So will the kitchen one, if you want that to work.'

'Can't we just connect it up as it is?'

He gave a hollow laugh. 'If you want another fire,' he said. 'It took Lewis and Jake two days to get that chimney ready for the sweep, it was worse than this one. No, you need a proper flue and a safety certificate.' He glanced back at the kitchen. 'I don't hold out much hope for it passing, to be honest. I think we should just take it out and scrap it.'

'But...' She trailed off, feeling the tug to the house. 'It's just, I like this house. I feel comfortable in it.' The tune she'd been working on was trickling into her head intermittently, even with the banging and conversation coming from upstairs. 'It suits me.'

He half smiled at that. 'I thought you were used to jetting all over the world, staying in the most glamorous places?'

'I am,' she answered. 'Well, staying in the cheapest hotels and sharing a room with another musician, usually. Worrying about my violin on every plane ride. We played a fundraiser in Ukraine and slept in a youth hostel, in January.' She shook her head. 'You've mixed me up with Patrick...' as the sadness hit her. 'He always gets gorgeous suites in fantastic hotels.'

'Do you miss it, that world?'

'Honestly,' she said, thinking it over, 'I'm not sure. I miss the music more than the concerts.'

'But you are playing again.'

'Sort of. Exercises, a few practice pieces. I have to go up to the hospital next week and they'll stress-test my neck and arm and increase my exercise regime.'

He smiled down at her. 'I think we can add some sanding and painting to your exercise regime.'

On the way down to the café to pick up some coffees, Amber bumped into Ellie and Zillah, who were walking up the hill singing. Amber waved. 'Looks like you're having fun, are you off for another walk?'

'Yes. And no,' Ellie said sheepishly. 'I've come to ask a favour.'

'Oh, of course,' Amber said, matching her steps to Zillah's and taking her little hand, sure she'd want to swing. 'Where are we going, Zillah?'

'School,' the toddler said, 'and sheep.'

'There are a few sheep in the school field at the moment,' Ellie said. 'But the main thing is, my friend Charlotte was hoping to talk to you. You'll see when you meet her, she's the teacher.'

'Sure. The boys can wait for their coffee.'

It was a delight to walk up the cobbles at Zillah's pace, to stop to stroke a ginger cat along the way, pick up a few fallen leaves that had already filled up the ruts of the lane.

The school was a small, modern building that sat next to an old cottage with arched windows like a chapel. Charlotte was in her thirties, tall, dark-haired and immediately welcoming.

'Nice to meet you, Amber. I just wondered if I could ask your opinion,' she said, smiling back into the single classroom. 'Billy, can I borrow you for a minute?'

Seven children looked curiously up at Amber, including the red-haired child she recognised from the posters and her first trip over on the ferry. He was sat in a reclining wheel-chair, covered with a blanket, his expression interested but sleepy.

A slim boy with dark eyes stepped forward, looking appre-hensive. Amber smiled to put him at ease.

'Tell Miss Marrak,' Charlotte urged, 'what we were talking about the other day.'

'I want to learn the violin,' Billy said, all in a rush. 'Or the cello. I play a bit of piano in the church. We all like music.'

'How old are you?' Amber asked.

'I'm eight,' he confided. 'Merryn is seven, Kai is six. Is that too young?'

'Not at all. I started even earlier. What sort of music do you like?'

He rattled off a lot of contemporary music: hip-hop and rap, rock music with a strong beat. She suggested a few solo performers who had videos online, and a few classical pieces. 'It's best to see them being played,' she said. 'Then you'll know if you'd like to play them yourself. But to start with we'll play really easy stuff.'

She'd enrolled in a Suzuki class at four, playing real tunes from the start, igniting her passion for music. The monotony of scales came later, at music academies, and almost killed the love for a while until she discovered performance.

'But I don't have a violin or a cello,' he said, looking up at her with amazing, deep brown eyes ringed with long lashes.

'We don't know what instruments to get,' Charlotte said, putting a hand on his shoulder. 'We're complete beginners, neither of us play.' When Amber frowned, she explained. 'Billy and Beau, his big brother, are my sons. They live with me and my husband Ash in the village. Of course, if Billy takes up an instrument, it would be good to get lessons for the whole class, but the islands don't have a music teacher at the moment.' She smiled down at a little girl who led Zillah over to a small table. 'And Kai loves music – anything to get him moving is good.'

Amber had always had private lessons – it was one of the reasons they had lived in London so much of the time. 'So, you want some advice about what to buy, how to get started?'

'All of it, tuning, maintenance, and basic playing.' She looked hopefully at Amber. 'I know it's a lot to ask.'

'No, it's not, of course I can help! I have a couple of kids' sizes back on West Island. I have a three-quarter size cello, too, if the kids would like to try one, and a keyboard and a few hand drums. We could do a few lessons to get you started, while I'm still here... We can do some singing and clapping today, if you like, just for fun.' Her imagination was fired, she could see music as the action of playing, as she had learned. Kai was talking with Merryn, smiling, but one hand looked weak as he leaned sideways in his chair. She started to think about how he could experience the violin, too...

Her own words rang in her head, even as she questioned them.

While I'm still here?

Was she really going to leave soon, and if so, what would she do with her life?

30

NOVEMBER 1943

Tommy and Georgie clambered up the old ladder to the loft room which ran the whole width of the house. The slates were nailed on, but a few were askew. Georgie could see where water had crept in and stained the floorboards under the leaks.

'We will have to get someone to fix the roof,' she said, running her hand along one sliver of daylight. 'We need to look after your estate, now you're a householder,' she teased.

'With Daddy,' he reminded. 'Just a share.'

'Yes, but we have to look after it for us, and him,' she replied after an awkward pause.

He knelt down in the corner and pulled out an old nest at the end of a joist. 'Birds must be getting in under here.'

'You're right,' she answered. 'We'd better block that hole before the spring.'

'We could make this into a proper room,' he said, getting excited. 'Maybe I could have it as my own place.'

'Maybe you could,' she said, running a finger around the edge of the small window. 'But we don't even know if you're going away to school yet. You might not be here in term time.'

'I think I should stay here,' he said, jutting his chin out just like his father had. It made her chest ache; he was growing more like Jim every day although he had inherited her dark colouring. 'Especially if you're going to take in lodgers.'

She laughed at that. 'You don't mind Mr Seznec, surely! If we'd left him back at the office, he'd have frozen to death by now.'

Tommy shuffled his feet a bit, sweeping dust across the floor. He lowered his voice. 'I don't like the way he watches you.'

'Since he's been asleep most of the week he's been here, I can't imagine why you would say that,' she said smartly, but a small blush rose to her cheeks at the thought. Since she'd found that little line in German, she had bigger worries. But she had noticed Hugo watching her, as if he was trying to puzzle her out. As if he was trying to gather information.

Tommy looked down at the floor to the bedroom below, where Hugo was probably lying asleep. 'When we talk about school stuff, he asks questions. Sometimes.'

'I'm sure he just wants to get to know you better, to understand what you need to learn,' she answered. 'I think the ladder is too steep over the stairs, and much too dangerous if someone does fall. How about we put it in the linen cupboard? It's not as if we have many spare sheets or blankets. A new ladder, maybe even some new stairs could go in there.'

'They would have to make a new hole in the floor,' he said, frowning. 'I don't know how to do that.'

'When we get someone to mend the slates, they can tell us. Then we wouldn't have any unexpected animals on the top floor,' she said, looking around. A bundle of spiders' webs poorly concealed a dried rat. 'Poor little thing,' she said, gingerly lifting him by his tail. 'He probably starved up here.'

Georgie brushed away some of the dust on the window,

revealing the emerald of the field behind, the brambles and shrubby trees in the hedge now losing their leaves.

Tommy put his arms around her and she held him as he buried his head against her. He was trying so hard to be the man of the house, but he was still only a child.

She kissed the top of his head. 'If Daddy comes home, you would need to move up here anyway so Dolly can have your room. We'll need to make room for him.'

She could feel him relax into her arms. 'And if he *doesn't* come back?' he whispered.

'Well, then, we will manage. Let me see if I can find someone who can do the work. Is that all right? After all, it is your house.'

He smiled, but there were tears in his eyes.

Dolly hardly recalled Jim – she almost never talked about him now – but Tommy was carrying all his fears around with him.

'I still don't think I should go away,' he said, detaching himself as if pretending the moment never happened.

'Well, I think Daddy would expect you to do your very best to get an education,' she said firmly. 'Because he valued that highly. He wanted what was best for you so you would have lots of choices for jobs when you're older. Do you have any ideas about what you would like to be when you grow up?'

He started down the ladder like a monkey, and when it was Georgie's turn, she had to climb down one rung at a time, trying not to look at the potential fall down the stairs.

'What did Dad want to do, when he was my age?' he asked at the bottom, by the linen cupboard.

She opened it, peering in. It was deeper than it was wide, and if they took some shelves out, it would allow some steps to sit at an incline. They lifted the ladder in to store it, and shut the door.

'He trained as an engineer,' she said, brushing dust off her hands and skirt. 'But he's an inventor at heart.'

'Me too,' he said, firmly. 'I'd like to invent things. Or maybe I could be a vicar,' he said, turning to run down the stairs, whistling through a gap in his teeth, taking Georgie's breath away.

31

'You could put a space-saving staircase right there,' Ben said, as Amber tried to move the shelves out of the deep cupboard. 'You can see that's where the ladder was, originally.'

'I think the loft room could be really lovely once it's insulated,' she said, puffing a bit as she wrenched the old shelf out. 'There, just the last one to do.' She hit it from underneath to get it loose. It was only afterwards that she realised that her neck, shoulder and hand didn't hurt at all.

'Even if it's not a proper bedroom, it could be a hobby room or something,' he said, squinting up at the ceiling of the cupboard. 'Is that the hatch?'

'It's just a square in the boards, but better than the other one over the stairs. Can we get the stepladder?'

By experimenting with the ladder, and forcing the old hatch open, she could see where a narrow staircase might go. It wouldn't be much more than a fixed ladder, but there was room to fit a loo and washbasin behind it, between the bedrooms. Lewis had created a modern bathroom off the kitchen, but going downstairs at night was hardly perfect, whoever ended up living here. She climbed up to the top and stepped into the attic.

'Here, take the coffees,' Ben said, passing up two pumpkin spice lattes and following her up.

'This could be a music room,' she said, seeing it in her mind's eye. The ceiling was a good height; she would have plenty of room to play and she could store equipment and instruments around the edges. She sipped her drink, the steam rich with cinnamon.

'It might get too hot in the sun,' he said, looking around. 'It's big, though, the whole footprint of the house.'

'Look,' she said, 'this all needs proper lining and the window needs modernising. I'll need ventilation up here, and insulation will keep it warm in the winter, too. And a thermostatically controlled heater will do the rest.'

He didn't reply, and when she looked at him he had a strange expression on his face. 'It's as if you're thinking you'll be living on the island long term.'

'Well, I might be,' she joked, 'as I'm probably going to be the island's new music teacher.'

She explained how she was going to give the children a few lessons to give them a chance to explore making music, once she had collected enough instruments.

'This is about Kai? Is Beau involved?'

'All of them, including Kai,' she said, frowning. 'Who is Beau?'

'Billy's older brother. Beau just started at the high school, so he's a weekly boarder. He's been learning guitar from Elk.'

'It's Billy who wants to learn the most, but they are all interested. I'm going to get them started like I did, trying actually playing something rather than reading music or doing scales. There are some good online resources for kids.' She grinned at him. 'Who knows, I might start my own youth orchestra on the islands. And maybe drag Elk into teaching guitar, too.'

'If you stay.' There was a note in his voice, a little stern.

She was taken aback by his tone. 'If I stay,' she said, uncertainly.

'When I was little,' he said, leaning against the chimney wall, 'I desperately wanted to play cricket but none of the sport teachers knew the game. It was one of those things on the islands – if there wasn't someone to teach you, you couldn't do it. We only took French or German because our language teacher knew those, but I already had a smattering of Spanish and really wanted to learn.'

It was a sobering thought. 'My dad has long bemoaned the lack of science education on the islands. No physics, not much chemistry. He was a biochemist, before he inherited the manor,' she explained.

'I think visitors always see the positives – the sea, the beaches, the quaint cottages and villages – but don't realise how restrictive it can be here. If you can't afford to get off the islands, I mean.'

She took the hint. 'I was lucky, I went away to school. But it's one of the downsides of such a small population.'

He sighed, stood up straight and took her empty cup. 'I'd better get back downstairs. I have door linings to fit and kitchen units to put together.'

She looked out across the back field through the window, the last seedheads thrashing around in the wind. 'Can I help?'

'If you think it's OK. I thought it was better if we didn't work together?' he said, but moved closer.

'I will try and resist your charms,' she said lightly, but his eyes grew intense. They looked darker in the shadows of the loft. 'Don't,' she whispered, involuntarily.

'Don't what?' he asked, then shook himself. 'See what I mean? I can't concentrate, you're a distraction. Why don't you check the tide and see when you can get those musical instruments for Billy.'

She nodded, and started down the ladder. Her heart was

beating faster at the thought that there might be something building between them.

It was all nonsense. Anyway, she couldn't forget that his housemate Lizzie liked him, and they spent a lot of time together. They looked perfect for each other.

And Amber still hoped to be off on a world tour at some point, so could there be any future in a new relationship, teaching at the school or even keeping the cottage?

32

NOVEMBER 1943

After Georgie took the children to school, she stopped by the shop as she had seen the goods ship coming in. They were still unloading sacks of coal and logs, and she reserved one of each and picked up her post – just a simple envelope. Her heart lurched in her chest as she recognised it as an official letter.

She sat on a bollard on the quay to open it.

It was from the War Office.

We regretfully inform you that extensive searches by the US navy have conclusive evidence that your husband Captain James Preston was lost at sea and is therefore believed to be deceased...

She slumped forward, unable to read any further.

Jim. Jim, holding baby Tommy to his face to kiss his tummy. Jim, in uniform, so proud at going to fight for his country in whatever capacity he could be useful. Jim, his strong arms locked around her as they said goodbye, afraid it might be the last time.

Now she knew it had been.

She couldn't help it; tears were streaming down her face. She looked to the Sound, at the brightly coloured buoys, most of the smaller boats having been trailered up the slipway and parked in front of the church. The same sea, the same lurching and dropping tide that would be pure blue in the Pacific but was no less deadly. She knew now how terrified Jim had once been, when he almost drowned at Seal Cove.

'Mrs Preston?' Margery Pascoe, from the school, was leaning towards her. 'Georgie? Are you all right? Can I get someone for you?'

Georgie closed her eyes, took a deep breath and scrabbled in her pocket for a handkerchief. 'I'm sorry, I've just received terrible news.'

'I'm sorry.' She was a thin, tired-looking woman with thick dark curls that almost looked as if they were draining her of vitality. 'Do you want to pop in for a cup of tea? You look so pale, and our house is just up there.' She pointed.

As Georgie stood, her head swam, and she bent down to grab the bollard for support. 'Perhaps – just for a moment, if you don't mind. That's very kind of you.'

She took the offered arm to support her past a few houses and into a cottage no larger than her own, but warmer and cosier. 'Come and sit down,' Margery said. 'I have the kettle on.'

Georgie hugged her coat around her, suddenly freezing, even though she was next to the stove. 'This is very kind of you,' she repeated as she looked around the room. She knew Margery had several children, one still at the school on Morwen and two were at the secondary school.

'The shop mentioned you'd had an official letter,' Margery said, putting a steaming teapot on the table with two cups. Everything was so humble and chipped, yet the effect was so welcoming Georgie felt tears prickling again.

She tried to word the impossible, vile news as gently, as politely as she could. There wasn't a way, she discovered. 'It's the notification that my husband has died,' she said baldly. 'He's been missing for months now. He was on an American ship in the Pacific. It was sunk.'

'That's terrible,' Margery said, her own eyes filling up with tears as she poured the tea. 'That's awful news.'

'Before, he was just missing...' Georgie's tears were flowing freely now. 'The worst thing is, I have to tell the children,' she said, and hiccoughed a sob. 'Take away their last hope. How do I tell them?'

Margery pushed the dark brew with just a little milk in towards her. 'Children understand far more than we think,' she said.

Georgie sipped the tea; it was warming and comforting. 'They'll give me a death certificate now.' That sounded so final.

'The vicar's wife said you were waiting for a war widow's pension.'

That was a grey thought, no comfort at all. The word *widow* conjured up a version of death for her, too. 'I hoped so much to hear he was alive.' She surprised herself that she said it out loud. 'But they stopped his wages just before I came here, so they already thought he was gone.'

'Of course.' Margery Pascoe had a world of compassion and understanding in her eyes that made Georgie start to cry again. 'I'll just hang my laundry out, you sit here and get warm. I think you're in shock, my dear.'

Shock. It seemed ridiculous – with all the messages she'd received about how Jim was missing and presumed dead, the number of times she'd told everyone from Aunt Alice to herself that he had almost certainly died – that now she was so distressed she was shaking with cold. She wrapped herself in her arms and gave in to the knowledge that he was gone.

Margery came back and looked Georgie over with a mother's eye. 'I think I'd better walk you home,' she said. 'My husband will bring your wood and coal later, when he comes home from work. You look like you need to lie down.'

'I need to buy some food, for Mr Seznec and the children's tea.' Hugo would be waiting for her to bring home something for breakfast, too.

'I heard you were still looking after that solicitor.' She stood back and looked Georgie over. 'He has the flu, doesn't he? You don't look well either.'

'Yes, but...' The possibility that she had it too dawned on her. 'I'm sure it was just the letter. The shock.' She shivered.

'I know what it's like,' Margery said, sliding her own coat on. 'You spend hours looking after your family when they're sick, then you're in no state to cope with it yourself.'

'Well, I can't be ill right now,' Georgie said, standing, the room wavering and dipping. 'I've got so much work to do.'

'Maybe so,' Margery said, 'but the sooner you look after yourself, the sooner you'll be better. We know about how dangerous the flu can be, after the last war. Make me a list, I'll run down to the shop for you. I can get your lodger a bit of breakfast, and you can lie down. Clemmie will pick up the little one and your boy can help make a bit of tea.'

Georgie couldn't argue, she felt dreadful, and just hoped against hope that it wasn't influenza. The children were too young to cope on their own, and what if they got it?

She shut her eyes at the thought of Tommy and Dolly getting ill, remembering children dying of the Spanish flu when she was a little girl. And they couldn't afford to lose their mother. Not now.

She sobbed into her handkerchief, overwhelmed, as Margery wrapped her up in her coat.

33

PRESENT DAY, 2 NOVEMBER

Sitting at the bank with Betty, hearing all the good news, had been a great way for Amber to start a new day. They returned to Betty's cottage and Amber put the kettle on.

Betty was still very suspicious about rewards in dollars, reserving celebrations until she actually saw them as pounds.

'So, that's a few hundred pounds, is it?' she said, her eyes narrowed.

Amber got her phone out and tapped in the query. 'Today that would be eight thousand and twenty pounds,' she read. 'And eighty pence.'

'My goodness,' Betty said, looking at her draining board. 'I can definitely afford a new mug, then,' she said, inconsequentially. 'That one's got so many chips, it cuts my lip sometimes.'

'You could choose a new one if you visit your daughter,' Amber suggested. 'When you catch a helicopter to Penzance.'

Betty tutted and shook her head. 'What nonsense, spending money on all that.'

'Three hundred pounds, there and back. For a proper holiday with your daughter. You could stay over for a few days,'

'Oh my,' Betty said, still wrestling with the thought. 'And you would take me to the helicopter airport?'

'I will deliver you to the heliport,' Amber said, laughing. 'It will make the pilot's day to know you're a new passenger. You'll be a seasoned traveller by the time you get home.'

Betty topped up Amber's tea and her own, in her 'posh' cups with saucers. 'I think I will give the money to that poor little boy, young Kai,' she said. 'He's my second cousin's grandchild, it's terrible for them. Have you seen all the appeals?'

Amber remembered Kai's eyes lighting up as she played for the children, helped them tap out a rhythm and talk about learning instruments. 'I have. I don't think you should give away all your savings, though. There are others who can help him,' she said.

'Well, if we all thought that, the poor little lad would die, wouldn't he?' Betty reasoned. 'He just needs a special treatment they don't do on the National Health. I could help a lot, even if I just give him *five* thousand.'

Betty's generosity was humbling but made Amber feel awkward. In her heyday, five thousand would have been easy to find, but now she was struggling to make the rent. Perhaps the islanders did expect her family to spread their largesse a bit more widely, though.

'Maybe I could ask my dad for some more,' she said aloud, and sipped the tea.

Betty didn't quite scoff but there was a little noise. 'Don't you think they asked? I suppose if they – your family, I mean – can't keep giving. I know they already support the air ambulance and the lifeboat.'

Amber let the idea sink in. 'How much do Kai's family need? And how close are they to getting it?'

'I don't know, dear,' Betty said. 'I do know they were trying for twenty-five thousand pounds at first but it's gone up. I don't know how on earth they could raise that in time. They need it before Christmas.'

'Let me look into it,' Amber said.

That tune was playing in her mind's ear again, soaring like a lark, diving into waves in melancholy harmonies. She shut her eyes and the image from her dream replayed itself, the perfect, slightly smiling child being washed in by the sea. 'Do you know what Kai's surname is? The appeal will probably be online.'

'He's an Allen, there are a few of them on the island. His mum works in the shop, his dad is a fisherman. He's only six.'

Just a baby. She couldn't get a signal on her phone. 'I'll have to go down to the quay,' she said, still staring at it.

Inside, something familiar was building, something like the stress and anxiety she experienced before a big performance or a competition.

Excitement at a challenge.

There was a poster in the shop window, so Amber went in to talk to one of the women working there and came away with much more information. Kai Allen had an inoperable brain tumour. At least, he had had surgery but it had grown back. He needed special radiotherapy that was unavailable in the UK unless the parents could pay for it privately. The alternative was to join a waiting list to be treated abroad.

The germ of an idea, sparked in Betty's kitchen, was growing, crowding out other thoughts. She could organise a concert. She knew enough young musicians who wanted exposure. She could get it videoed, stream it online. She could be the musical director – she had the perfect venue at the manor, if she could just get a few world-class players to visit the islands. It would create massive exposure for little Kai. The target seemed modest compared to some of the appeals she had played for.

She wanted to get back to jot down her ideas. She had been

at a fundraiser organised by an Italian singer friend; she knew she could call on her for advice. One of her good friends from music college was now a celebrated virtuoso cellist. He always loved an excuse to come to the islands. But time was tight, and most musicians filled their schedules years in advance, not weeks.

Yes, but we all scale it back after November so we can spend time with our families.

Amber walked along the quay, dialling the manor without thinking. She remembered too late that her parents still had several days of their holiday – her honeymoon – left.

Patrick answered the phone, not Nickie, the manager. 'The Manor.'

She took a deep breath, shut her eyes for a moment as her heart flip-flopped in her chest. 'Hello, Patrick. It's Amber.'

'OK,' he said, cautiously. 'Is everything all right?'

'It's fine,' she said, and winced. 'I mean, it's as well as... Look, could you check if the hotel is booked up in the first two weeks of December? I need two, three days of the restaurant, ballroom and the bedrooms.'

'I see.' His voice sounded strained. 'Are you planning another wedding?'

Ouch. She took a deep breath, tried to keep her voice as calm and businesslike as possible. 'No, I'm hoping to organise a fundraiser with a few musicians.'

'What's the money for?'

She explained about Kai Allen, and proton beam therapy and how much money he needed, breathless as her words tumbled out. 'It's got a good success rate for cases like his,' she said, breathless at the end. 'I just need to get it filmed and put it out as an appeal. He'll die without it.'

'You could get the local news broadcasters involved,' he said. 'Maybe I can ask my friends from the Chelsea Flower Show to recommend videographers. And social media experts.'

'If you could.'

'I think it would be very worthwhile. If you don't mind me – us – working together?'

'*I* don't mind.' She had to bite her lip and turn out of the wind. 'Would it be too weird for you?'

'Maybe uncomfortable at first, but we have to get along if I'm staying at the manor,' he said. 'You can't stay away from your family home forever.'

'OK,' was all she could say at first. 'Thank you.'

'Come over tomorrow once you've got a few dates and people in mind. And talk to the child's parents – you'll need to get them on board.'

In her enthusiasm, she had forgotten them. 'I will.'

She rang off. As she looked over at the white-topped waves splashing up the quay wall at high tide, she felt a surge of something. Relief. It had been lovely to hear Patrick's voice without bursting into tears.

The following day, she called Ash, Charlotte's husband, to help her carry five instruments up to the school for their first impromptu lesson. He was charming, a slim man in his thirties who worked as a diving instructor.

'Rather you than me,' he said as he saw her falter at the door. 'They're great kids but the islands breed them opinionated.'

'As I was,' she said, smiling back.

There were seven children including Kai, and Billy's brother, Beau, who had been kept home from the high school especially. She hoped, after all her years of learning the violin, that she could teach it, too.

It proved much easier than she thought. As she took her own violin out of its case and put the bow to the strings, the children fell completely quiet, and remained so until she had finished playing three short, easy pieces.

Ash, Charlotte and Kate, the classroom assistant, all helped the children explore the small violins and the three-quarter size cello, which was a bit big even for eleven-year-old Beau, but he managed to get some creditable notes out of it.

Kai Allen had a weakness in his left side, but managed to play a few notes on the cello when she held it for him. He was small for his age and pale, a legacy of recent surgery, but laughed at every sound he made on the instruments. Amber enjoyed helping Billy find a comfortable position to hold down the strings with his left hand and bow with his right, and she noticed he had a natural ability to adjust his hold to hit the notes.

'You're going to be good at this,' she said as he screeched out a few wails from the violin, before she noticed his parents' expressions. 'It gets better,' she said, laughing. 'Honestly. He's confident enough to give it some welly, really hit some notes.'

After a few hesitant attempts, Beau scraped out some reasonable sounds from the cello, and one of the girls, little Merryn, was happy to dance around with the smallest violin and get a few odd noises out of it.

Finally, she got all the children together to beat out some rhythms by drumming their knees and stamping their feet, and then she got them singing. Kai's voice was sweet, and strong enough to float above the percussion, moving the adults to tears.

Amber had recorded a little video on her phone for Charlotte to send to their parents.

'When can you come back?' Ash asked.

Amber looked over at Charlotte. 'Would the same time next week be OK?' she asked, hesitantly.

'If you don't mind,' Charlotte said, helping Billy put his violin back in its case. 'Why don't we try it for three weeks, if you've got the time?'

'I'll make the time,' Amber said. 'It's been lovely showing them the basics. It's lovely to be able to play an instrument. Have you ever thought about asking Elk to teach a bit of guitar?'

Charlotte caught her lip between her teeth, looking at Ash. 'Guitar isn't on the curriculum,' she said slowly. 'But he'd be good, except—'

'He's a bit of bear?' Amber laughed. 'You should see him at the pub, he's so patient with beginners. It's worth a try.'

'Could you ask him? I really don't know him, but he's good with Beau,' Charlotte said.

Amber smiled as Merryn hugged her around the waist. 'I'll talk to him,' she said. 'And we'll keep singing.'

34

NOVEMBER 1943

Of course, it *was* the flu. Georgie could barely stand when she got home, and was unable to argue about crawling up the stairs and onto the bed. Hugo met her at the bedroom door, looking anxious.

'What happened?'

'She's caught the flu,' Margery Pascoe said briskly. 'And *you* still look very poorly to me. Get back to bed, maid, and I'll bring you up something to drink.'

Georgie lay down on her bed fully clothed, her throat raw. She wanted to cry, scream, anything to let out the rage and grief that had built up inside her since she saw the letter. But somehow she was frozen. She heard Hugo walk towards her.

'I'm so sorry I made you ill, too,' he said, his voice cracked. He started to cough again.

Georgie turned over to reach into her pocket. She pulled out the letter and held it out blindly. 'It's not just the flu.'

She shut her eyes as he took it, not wanting to see his reaction.

'I'm so sorry,' he said, before the storm broke inside Georgie, washing up inside her, making her sob like a child. She turned away from him. She heard Mrs Pascoe shoo Hugo away, then come and sit on the edge of the bed, rubbing her back.

'Poor maid,' she crooned, over and over. It was comforting but nothing could stop the tidal wave of feelings Georgie had kept banked down since she first found out Jim was missing. At some point she fell asleep, then woke up just as the light was going. She could hear Dolly laughing downstairs, and Tommy's voice as well. She tried to sit up, but the room whirled about her as if she was on a merry-go-round. She felt so sick she lay back down.

The sound of feet on the stairs reassured her.

Dolly pushed the door open. 'She's awake!' she cried, and Tommy held her back.

'Gently, Dolly,' he said, balancing a tray with one hand. 'Mrs Pascoe made some barley water,' he said, putting a glass beside the bed. 'And Mr Seznec made some soup, he says it's from Brittany.'

'Hugo is downstairs?' she managed.

'And Mrs Pascoe is going to help out as well, and so is Clemmie,' he said. 'There's some aspirin in the bottle and I thought you might like a cup of tea later as well. You have to drink plenty, you told Mr Seznec that.' He frowned. 'Is it all right to call him Hugo? He says it is but I wasn't sure.'

'Hugo is fine.' The horrible news had taken up residence in her stomach, making her feel even more sick. 'Tommy – I'm sorry – could you get me the ash bucket and take Dolly downstairs? I'm afraid...' She retched, and put her hand over her mouth, lying back down and closing her eyes.

'Right away.'

When he returned a few minutes later, she leaned over the bucket for a few moments, but she wasn't sick. 'You need to go downstairs,' she said. 'I don't want you to catch it.'

Tommy's eyes were red and swollen, his face tear-stained. 'Hugo told me,' he said, his voice wooden. 'About Daddy.'

She nodded, retched again, but the urge was fading. 'It was such a shock,' she said, choosing her words carefully. 'I so hoped...'

'I know,' he said. He looked out over the garden but she could see his shoulders shaking. 'I prayed every night.'

She sat up on the pillows, pressing a handkerchief to her lips as the room spun. 'It will get better. There are some things I have to do, and the blasted pension people to contact. Hugo can help me with that, and the bank.'

'I could help,' he said, looking older and more strained than she had ever seen him, a little echo of the young man he would become. 'I should help.'

She choked back her need to protect him. 'Yes, that would be very kind, thank you. But not right now. If I can just get over this stupid flu, we can sort everything out.'

'I just don't know what to do,' he said, looking down to his hands.

'I *do* know what to do,' she said slowly, seeing his wet face. 'You are still young, darling. We will share the burden, but Daddy would expect you to concentrate on your school work.' She took a deep breath. 'There is a will. I'll go through it with you, Hugo will help—'

'I don't want Hugo,' he said, his face twisted.

'Why ever not, darling? When he's better. He is a lawyer.'

'We don't need him,' he said, turning, his face creasing with the effort not to cry. 'We need Daddy.'

'Yes, we do,' she murmured. She opened her arms and he snuggled against her, folded up on the edge of the bed. He had grown so much, his back and ribs were sticking out now, all his puppy fat gone. 'But all we have is Hugo, who is our friend,' she soothed. 'Just a friend who is very kind and helpful. Especially as he cooked the soup.'

'Dolly likes him,' he mumbled into her. 'I couldn't tell her about Daddy.'

'That is my job,' she said, smoothing the hair back from his broad forehead. He was almost the age Jim had been when Jago had died, and she hadn't processed how she was going to tell Tommy about that either. She wouldn't want him to find out from someone else on the island.

She drank the soup and the lukewarm tea and finally managed some of the barley water with some aspirin. Eventually, she struggled downstairs on her way to the outhouse, to see Hugo reading in the most comfortable of the chairs in the kitchen with a sleeping Dolly on his lap. Her round cheeks were bright red; Georgie hoped she hadn't caught the influenza as well.

'She looks very hot,' she said, clinging to the back of another chair. 'Is she feverish?'

'That's because I'm still too hot,' he said. 'She's been fine. I think if they were going to catch it, they'd be ill by now. I'll take her up to your bed. Tommy says he'll be all right in the loft – he's borrowed some blankets from the scouts and a mattress from Mrs Ellis. I'm surprised you didn't hear them bumping it up the ladder.'

'Thank you. I must have dozed off.'

Hugo still looked very pale. By the time she came back from the outhouse, he had returned from putting Dolly upstairs, and was putting a little more wood on the fire. 'I took her shoes and socks off but she's still in her clothes.' He filled the kettle and put it on its stand to heat. 'Tea made *me* feel better,' he said, managing a smile.

'Will I ever feel better?' she croaked, past her sore throat, feeling the hollowness that had settled inside her when she got the letter.

He waved at the chair. 'You should sit down,' he said. 'You

look like you're about to fall down, and I could barely carry your *daughter* up the stairs with my bad legs.'

She smiled at that, then sat, hugging her cardigan around her. She resisted the urge to rock, to fall into crying again. 'I still can't believe it,' she whispered. 'But I know it's true.'

'Bad news is hard to accept. When I left home, in Brittany,' he said, in a calm, flat voice, 'I was with my fiancée Anna and my sister. We were heading for the coast at first, and I joined the volunteer defence league. We were helping a group of women and children with push carts and perambulators. Most wanted to stay with families in the north, hoping the Germans wouldn't invade.' Georgie could feel her heart beating faster at the strange tone in his voice. 'We set up defences across the roads, demolished some small bridges, tried to slow the Germans down.' He swallowed audibly. 'We never exchanged a shot with them, they stormed instead straight through our column of villagers, babies, old people. I saw Anna fall...' His voice ran dry, and he looked down into the clenched fists in his laps. 'I couldn't get to her. My sister was injured, but was hidden with some of our neighbours and friends. They surrendered a day later. I was already fleeing for the coast, to stop them there. We imagined the British would hold the line, drive them back, anything. But all they could do was evacuate themselves and us.'

'At Dunkirk?'

'There were evacuations all along the coast. I was shot on the beach at St Malo, by a machine gunner in a plane. I was scooped up and rescued along with other defenders.' He looked up. 'They didn't expect me to make it.'

'Oh, Hugo.' She reached out a hand, and for a moment, she could feel his warm strength sustaining her. 'I am *so* sorry.'

He let go first. 'We have all been injured in this dreadful war,' he said sternly. 'And we all continue to endure, and contribute where we can. I honour your husband's sacrifice, *your* sacrifice, and I will do what I can to help his children.'

Something had shifted between them, as if they had somehow found they were related.

'Thank you, Hugo,' she said, shivering.

He filled the teapot up. 'You keep telling me to drink, now I do the same for you,' he said, his accent stronger now he was emotional, tears in his eyes.

35

PRESENT DAY, 4 NOVEMBER

Amber's plans for the fundraising concert were filling her thoughts. She had researched Kai Allen's condition and had arranged to meet his mother, Zoe.

Amber sat in Zoe's kitchen, watching as the careworn young woman absent-mindedly folded baby clothes and T-shirts. The sweetness of washing that had been aired outside scented the room.

'Kai used to love bouncing,' Zoe said as she stared out the window at the trampoline in the family's small garden. 'The surgery left him lopsided; he hasn't dared jump yet. He can barely walk.' She looked exhausted. She was pale, her blonde hair wispy and floating around her face. Kai must get his ginger colouring from his father, Amber thought.

'You have another child?' Amber asked.

'Lara's at nursery two days a week, she's one. It gives me time to spend with Kai, and take him to appointments. His dad's got him today. They've walked down to see my mother.' She looked up, and for the first time, there were tears in her eyes. 'We're spending a bit of time apart, but he's still a wonderful dad. We just never seem to be on the same page. I'm fighting for this new treatment, but he...'

'The proton beam treatment,' Amber said, watching Zoe closely as she took the basket of washing out of the room. She returned with a leaflet, which she handed to Amber.

'They have already assessed him for the treatment – it was more than five thousand pounds just for the scans. We've raised about seven grand towards the therapy already, but the islands have such a small population and it's an expensive place to live. If we owned our house, we would have some equity to release, but we rent. Now I can't work any more, with Kai and the baby at home.' She shut her eyes for a moment, tears spilling down each cheek. 'I want to spend as much time with him as possible, in case all we can do is make a few more memories.'

'What does your husband want?' Amber asked.

'Liam wants someone to wave a magic wand so he can have his lovely boy back.' She sat down and cradled her mug. 'Kai's regressed since the first surgery. He's back in nappies, and he needs the special buggy if we go out anywhere. He barely sleeps, he just wants me to tell him stories, or stroke his back all night. I'm so tired. I think Liam already feels we've lost Kai, the Kai we had.'

Amber sipped her coffee, hardly knowing what to say. To offer something that might not work seemed so unfair, and she wondered how much of this fundraiser idea was her own ego desperate for the limelight. She was pretty sure that was what Patrick was thinking. But inside, she had such a need to help, and use the connections she had to do something good.

'What's the timescale for the treatment?' she asked, putting the cup down, watching Zoe's reaction.

'Soon. We've already asked your father, Sir Michael. He put five thousand in already.' Her voice was clipped, harsh.

'I'm afraid he's spent a lot on improvements and extensions to the garden,' she said. 'And then he spent a lot more on my wedding. Which I cancelled, in case you're the only person on the islands who didn't know. He and my mother are away on my honeymoon.'

'So, how can you help? I thought you were a famous violinist, but you seem to have given that up.'

'I had an injury, it needed surgery. A lot of surgery,' Amber said, thinking back to how lucky she had been that her treatment *was* available for free. She also knew that if she had needed private treatment, her dad would have sold something, mortgaged something, to raise the money. Kai's problem was that his family were poor. It wasn't fair. 'I would like to organise a concert to help raise funds for Kai.'

Zoe shrugged. 'That's very kind, but the window for treatment is very small. They say that by January it might already be too late. Christmas would be the last available week. But the slots fill up fast and we can't book one until we have at least half the money.'

'Which would be...?'

Zoe opened a drawer full of papers and pulled out a battered letter. 'That's the total.'

The final figure was over thirty-eight thousand pounds. 'Wow.' Even while she was staggered by the total, she worked back in her mind through the list of friends and colleagues she could call upon. 'Well, I can definitely hold a gala at the manor on either the sixth or the ninth of December. If we can get some early tickets sold as well, we might be able to get to halfway point sooner and you can book the treatment. My friend Billie does music videos for Lukas Bright and the Scat Cats, and she thinks we might be able to sell the rights to the concert to a platform for a fee. They'll make more money from selling it to networks, and they have to pay upfront. All of which normally takes months, but she's happy to get out there and make a noise, especially as she will be telling Kai's story.'

Zoe managed a small smile. 'I love the Scat Cats, I saw them at the music festival.'

'Let me contact the festival manager, Eleanor Markham. She might be able to put us in touch with other sponsors,' Amber said.

Tears were running down Zoe's face now, and she wrapped her arms around herself. 'I don't know what to do. It all sounds so wonderful, but if the fundraiser doesn't work, I think I'd feel worse.'

'We have to make it work,' Amber said taking Zoe's thin hands. 'I will make it work. I wish I could just come up with a quicker idea.'

'But why would you help?' Zoe said, snatching her hands back suddenly. 'You don't know us, you don't know Kai.'

The dream of the boy, his tranquil face at the water's edge, leapt to mind. 'Please let me. I mean it, I need to do this. And I've met Kai.' She struggled to find the words about how she felt when she spoke to him, helped him hold an instrument, saw the joy when he managed a note or two. 'He's such a lovely boy. He needs to have this chance,' she managed.

'Oh.' Zoe looked dubious but there was a lighter look about her, her shoulders were less hunched around her ears. 'What would we have to do?'

'Press, interviews, videos. Billie's happy to come over and help you with that, we'll start a campaign and you can do little videos each day for social media. Funny, light videos, nothing dark. Make people see what you would be losing.'

'We tried all this at the beginning,' Zoe said. 'But people got bored.'

'Billie has over one million followers on her social media platforms,' Amber said. 'Imagine if we could get someone like the Scat Cats to share it, maybe do a little appeal themselves?'

Zoe's eyes widened. 'Wow.'

'The biggest problem is the time factor. We've got, say,

twenty-eight days to book that treatment slot.' She looked down at the letter. 'He needs five treatments – you'll be in hospital all over Christmas.'

'There will be other Christmases,' Zoe said, her eyes shining with tears again. 'But you need to know something. There's a sixty per cent chance this treatment will work, significantly lengthen his life, even the possibility of a cure.'

As Amber let that settle into her mind, her stomach lurched. 'But a forty per cent chance he won't benefit from it.'

'That makes it hard to raise money, as we found out when we went on a local radio show. People feel as helpless as we do, so they don't want to get involved. But,' she said, looking more determined, 'I'd want to do it if it was one per cent. He deserves this chance.'

'I agree. Leave it with me,' Amber said, jumping up. 'I'll talk more with Billie and get her to talk to you. She's got some ideas.'

Zoe looked up, frowning. 'I can't do it by myself. It's too much.'

'No, *we* will do it, and we will call on people to help. The concert will just be the icing, it's the *cake* we need.' Amber opened her arms and they hugged. 'It's a plan.'

Zoe let go, and her smile faded. 'It is for you. But I'm not sure how I'll manage with all of this. I've still got a very sick little boy who needs a lot of looking after.'

'Of course, we don't want to add to your stress. Let me meet your husband. I'll go and shout at Billie and the music festival lady and everyone else I can think of, and we'll take it from there.' She made a face. 'My dad's going to be surprised that he's donating the hotel for an evening, but he'll be cool with it. Once I explain.'

36

DECEMBER 1943

Georgie recovered from the flu much faster than Hugo. He was unable to return to his lodgings for several weeks, and when he contacted his landlady, she told him she had already let his room to someone else. He could pick up his box of belongings and clothes from her, but she had already abstracted the rent from his small stash of savings.

'I could take her to court,' he said gloomily, sitting at the kitchen table. 'She basically stole from me. She asked me to leave in the first place – she can't pay herself rent, let alone go through my things.'

'Well, you could mention that to the police,' Georgie said, snipping off a thread from her darning. 'But isn't her son one of the policemen?'

'And the local magistrate will throw me out as soon as look at me,' he said, looking down at his hands. 'Do I seem so different?'

She stared at his sharp features, deep-set green eyes, longer than average hair. 'I would say you look exotic,' she said. 'Where do your parents come from?'

'My father, from a town outside Brest, Plouzané. My

mother came from the island of Ushant and her mother was English.' He fell silent. 'My father is Jewish. I don't know if they are dead or alive.'

The silence built between them for a minute.

'I hope they are all managing under the occupation,' she said gently.

'I hope so, too.' He looked up at her, his eyes glistening. 'I just wish I knew they were all safe.' He put his head on one side. 'And you? Where are your parents?'

'Both dead now,' she said, trying to keep her voice light. 'Mother died when I was fifteen, she had consumption. Dad died a few years later from a weak heart. I think he would have liked Jim, I met him the following year.'

'That's sad,' he said, coughing a little until his shoulders shook. She waited for him to catch his breath again.

'It's just me and the children now,' she said softly, lost in the memory of the last time she saw Jim, the way his lips had clung to hers. Now she would never be kissed again.

'I should move out,' he said, his voice raspy. 'You have your reputation to guard now.'

'Why does it make any difference now Jim is dead?' she asked, managing a small smile.

'It will do. Your widow's pension application tells you to live an exemplary, moral life. Having a strange man in the spare room might be seen as inappropriate.' He sounded out the word carefully with his Breton accent.

'What nonsense,' she scoffed. 'Anyway, where else would you go?'

'Ah,' he replied, also smiling, leaning back in the chair. 'That's a question. Maybe back to the mainland. But I do have work here.'

She put another stick on the tiny fire and watched as it caught. 'How on earth did you end up on St Brannock's, anyway?'

He opened his eyes a little at that, looked over at her for a long time. 'I'm not sure I'm allowed to tell anyone,' he said awkwardly. 'I was supposed to take up a ministry job, here on the islands. But my leg injuries refused to heal sufficiently to take up my duties, so I stayed and did what legal work needed doing. I've been doing some paperwork for them while I recover.'

'Ministry work?' She lifted her darning up to the glimmer of the single candle. She thought of that German word, scribbled on one of his papers. 'What department?'

He sat up a little. 'Your husband worked in intelligence, didn't he?'

'He did. But I never knew what he did. He was very knowledgeable about electronics, radios, that sort of thing.'

'Well, the work I do is in intelligence as well. Translation.'

She looked up at him, the thought making her shiver. 'Is it dangerous – I mean, does it make you a target?'

'It might do. It has to be top secret and under the guise of the legal work I'm already doing. But there could be a spy on the islands, watching the garrison and the naval base.'

'The secret base we're not supposed to know about?' she said slowly. 'If you can do war work, I think you should. I want to help you in any way I can. But I need to ask you something first.'

He looked at her for a long moment.

'You want to know if I'm a German spy.'

She stared back at him, as the candle wavered and hissed. 'I saw something, a few words in pencil on one of your documents.'

'Do you remember where you saw it?'

She lifted it out of her own papers where she had kept it. 'I didn't want to believe you are working for the Germans. I *don't* believe you are.'

'I'm not. I'm working for British intelligence. Which I'm not really allowed to talk about, but since you've already found a piece of evidence...'

'Who wrote it, then?'

He gazed at her, the low light making his eyes deep, deep green, like the water in the Sound. 'The solicitor whose office I have taken over.'

'But isn't he dead?'

'No, he's in prison, awaiting trial for treason.' He reached across her darning and touched her fingers for a second, making her jump. She stared down at her tingling hand, wondering at the reaction she had to the contact. 'I'm going through the papers, looking for any proof of treason. The more evidence we have, the more pressure they can put on him to talk about spy networks and contacts.'

'Then you're sure there are other spies *here?*' The idea was terrifying. 'Surely not one of the islanders.'

'My predecessor was born and brought up here. They think he became a Nazi sympathiser at university. There could be others. The base has links to agents all over Europe – it's imperative that information is controlled.'

'I want to help.'

For the country, for the war effort, for Jim, to help carry out his lost mission.

Suddenly, she felt like she had a purpose.

To Georgie's astonishment, a gentleman in a scruffy brown suit and hat turned up the next afternoon, after Hugo had forayed out to the post office in the morning to phone his superiors and come back exhausted. Dolly, who had been playing with her toys on the living room rug, stared up in astonishment at the tall, blond man.

'May I speak with you, Mrs Preston?' he asked with a smile.

'Of course,' she said, letting him in. 'I'm sorry it's a bit... sparse in here, come through to the kitchen.'

'I understand you have Mr Seznec staying?'

'He went upstairs for a sleep,' she said, staring at the young man as he shook her hand. He had bright blue eyes, sandy eyebrows and eyelashes and looked about her own age. 'He's been ill. He's my employer.'

He sat down on one of her small kitchen chairs. 'My name is Captain Miles Macintosh. Broadly speaking, I'm in the same line of work as your husband was, in military intelligence. I am very sorry for your loss.'

He looked like he was genuinely grieved. 'Do you know any more about what happened to Jim?' she asked.

'I'm afraid not. The Americans have told us everything they could, but it was a savage attack. Many men were lost to the sea, and after a month or so, it was assumed that no more would be found alive.'

She nodded, hot tears streaking down her cheeks. She found that she wasn't embarrassed to be crying in front of this young man; he projected only kindness and understanding. She reached in her sleeve for her handkerchief and regained her composure.

'How can I help?'

'Mr Seznec is gathering information to help our covert operations, but he needs a base away from St Brannock's. People there seem to suspect that someone has German sympathies. They already suspect him of being an agent.'

She sat opposite him, dabbing at her cheeks and putting an arm around the curious Dolly, who leaned against her knee. 'What can I do to help?'

'If you were to continue letting him stay, you could help him sort through all the documents the solicitor tried to destroy, while keeping important records for the islanders. You're educated and, I understand, a good typist.'

She stared at him. 'I could. But his remaining would cause a lot of gossip.'

It was one thing to not care what the neighbours thought about her kindness to a sick and incapacitated Hugo, it would be another to have them suspect she was living with another man as her lover. She had never thought much about her reputation, seeing herself as more free spirited, but now she was bringing the children into it, too. And she wanted to be accepted by the islanders she had grown to respect and care for.

'Our intelligence suggests that you have a loft room you could convert. That might limit the gossip, but I'm afraid there will be some.'

'If the ministry of pensions suspects I'm sharing my home with another man, I won't have any money to live on,' she said, in a quiet voice.

'I'm afraid the war ministry might make the pension difficult. *We* will be able to pay you, but it would be through unusual routes. They would appear to be insurance payouts or support from your husband's bank, or rent from Hugo. You will accrue proper wages but we will only send them when it is safe to do so.' He spread his palm out. 'You do understand: if you start spending more than you could earn from your existing employment, people will suspect you are being paid by *someone*, perhaps the enemy.'

'Is that how it works with Hugo, too...? He seems desperately short of money.' As if he'd heard his name, she heard him moving around upstairs.

'People suspect him less while he's working for the islands, on very low wages. He has special knowledge that will help us get certain people – families in danger – out of Brittany.'

'Special knowledge?' she questioned, as she heard his feet on the stairs.

Hugo put his head around the door and half smiled, rubbing his eyes. His hair was sticking up at one side. 'I'm a native

Breton speaker, and I'm half Jewish – I speak Hebrew, too,' he said.

She looked at him, wondering if that was what the islanders on St Brannock's found alien, or if it was just his Gallic good looks and precise English accent.

'Many of our target refugees and intelligence gatherers are Jewish,' Captain Macintosh said. 'And our coded messages are also delivered in Breton, Cornish and Welsh. Hello, Hugo. I hope you're feeling better.'

'Hello, Mac. Better, yes, but I'm still lame. Which still rules me out for active service. For now, anyway.'

Georgie felt the words like a blow to her stomach. 'Surely not just "for now",' she snapped. 'You can barely walk.' The thought of another man in her life struggling in the black water at the dead of night made her feel sick.

'No, we have important things for him to do here.' Mac looked at them both. 'If you agree to this, you might be ostracised by the local people.'

'For what?' Hugo asked, looking from one to the other.

'He wants you to board here, to work from here even after you're feeling better,' she said, feeling tearful. 'He wants it to look as if I moved my new man in before I was even sure my husband had died.'

'Look,' Macintosh said, 'if you can convince the island that you are a landlady to an injured refugee, maybe you won't get the gossip we all anticipate. You're a strong woman, your neighbours speak highly of you. And it would enable Hugo to work for us while getting on top of the intelligence.'

'She's already found something useful,' Hugo said.

'I understand that the lawyer's records are important,' she said, looking from one to the other. 'But how does it help the war effort?'

'We're making a case against him,' Mac said gently. 'We

need to know if he's told the enemy about the missions of the base on West Island. And who else is involved.'

'The work is important for the local people, too,' Hugo said, stretching out his legs with a wince. 'Some of the documents are the only known copies of wills dating back fifty years. If they were disputed, people could lose their inheritances.'

'More importantly,' Captain Macintosh said, leaning forward, his elbows propped on his knees, 'we need to identify what messages were passed to the Germans and who they were sent to. Will you help?'

'Of course! But what would I actually need to do?'

'Read the documents with a sceptical eye. Note anything suspicious. We'll get you a typewriter, you can make notes. As well as continuing with the local work Hugo pays you for.' He looked over at him. 'We will give you enough funds to continue to pay Mrs Preston, but we dare not pay her directly.'

'While her reputation is shattered, she will be denied her rightful pension as a war widow,' he answered. 'She's barely scraping a living now.'

'I'll do it,' Georgie said, smiling faintly, the best she could muster. 'I'll have to manage without the pension. Hugo will live in the attic. I will be a harsh and demanding landlady and complain about him to all my neighbours. But I do have one request.'

'Anything,' Mac said, staring at her intently.

'You must wait until I've spoken to my son, before all this is confirmed,' she said. 'He may only be ten years old, but this is his house. It's his mother who will be the subject of criticism and gossip, with Hugo staying here. I will only do it if he agrees.'

37

PRESENT DAY, 11 NOVEMBER

Amber painstakingly organised the Post-its outlining the whole concert on the table in the living room. She barely registered the tap on the door, but got up to check after a second knock.

It was Ben, dressed in jumper and jeans instead of the tattered and paint-stained work clothes he usually wore.

'Hi,' she said, looking past him at Beehive Cottage. 'Are you working today? By my calculations it's Saturday.'

'No, it's not a work day. Although we're really pleased with how it's going. Do you want to see? You haven't been around all week.'

'I'm busy with this other thing,' she said. 'Come on in, I'll show you the poster. Eleanor Markham's designed it, it's great.'

She had printed off some of the graphics to present to her dad, due back from his holiday later that evening.

'Someone told me you were doing a fundraiser for Kai,' he said, moving the pictures around. 'Are you really going to raise the rest of the money we need?'

'*We* need?' she asked, raising her eyebrows.

'I grew up with Zoe's brother; he was my best friend at school as well as a cousin.' He shrugged. 'Kai started falling over around his fourth birthday party. We thought it was comical at first, but Zoe knew there was something wrong. We just felt helpless at first, then we hoped the surgery would save him but...' He shrugged. 'Then we heard about this proton beam treatment. But how can we raise the money in time?'

'What we need,' she said, 'is lots of rich people. The plan is to invite patrons to an exclusive concert with brilliant players, and keep them in luxury at the hotel. We'll donate all the profits from the tickets, and I'm hoping my parents will throw in the accommodation for free.'

He looked sceptical. 'Would that really make enough?'

'Well, the idea is to film the whole thing and sell it to a streaming service. They pay an initial fee, and then a royalty on each play. We will make the target, I'm sure of it.' She bit her lip, the enthusiasm fading as she thought of Kai. 'It has to work.'

'But won't the artists need paying? I mean, they don't know him.'

She sat at the table and rearranged some of the notes. 'I've got these people already interested. They will waive their fees and their share of the royalties, and they'll cover their own costs.'

He read some of the names. 'You are joking? Even *I* have heard of these people.'

'Young musicians have to compete for a small number of top slots, to enhance their profiles. It's coming up to the quiet break,' she said. 'A small, intimate concert with world-famous musicians and a few celebrities at a magical island retreat – the perfect pre-Christmas treat. These are my friends. Or friends of friends. And we can get promotion in the local press, even nationwide, to ask for donations towards a little boy's last chance. Publicity is gold.'

'At Christmas,' he said slowly. 'You're right. You might be able to do this. I'm in, of course.'

'What?' She wasn't immediately sure what he could do.

'I'm serious. I've known Kai since he was born. He screamed the pub down when they brought him in to show him off.' He smiled. 'He looked like a gremlin with bright ginger hair. What can I do?'

She thought fast, getting excited. 'We'll need to extend the stage. And we'll need help to set up microphones and cameras – we have a light and sound company doing the electronics, but...'

'Everything will have to be secured or concealed. Your dad won't want people drilling into sixteenth-century panelling. How much will this company charge?'

'We're offering a percentage of the takings, but I'm hoping the exposure is worth them donating their fee. They're a new company, very tech-savvy – they'll do drone shots of the whole island as well as the manor itself. It will raise the manor's profile. I know my dad will be happy with that.'

'Who does all the publicity...?'

She smiled. 'We have an expert called Billie Chang, something of a wunderkind in the social media arena. This is a perfect project for her – she never wants to do the same sort of thing twice and this is new to her. She's ready to launch as soon as I have my parents' say-so.'

He stared at the whole plan, set out over the table. 'Of course I'll do it,' he said. 'But what about Patrick?'

'Patrick and I have spoken about it,' she said, carefully choosing her words. 'He's supportive, but I still have to persuade my dad. I'm hoping Patrick will help me with that.'

'Will he want to work with you?'

'It's not about me or him. It's about Kai.' She looked at him. He was shifting in the chair, tense. 'Is everything all right?'

'Sort of,' he said, glancing up at her. 'I'm having a hard time sleeping recently.'

'I'm sleeping much better,' she said, laughing. 'Seriously, not trying to stay warm in the draughts and with that music...' She stalled, not sure if she wanted to talk about the melody that had been haunting her. 'What's the problem?'

'Lizzie, mostly,' he said. 'You know, we have been friends for a long time, but I haven't really seen her as girlfriend material. Best friend, really.'

'She really likes you,' she said, with a little pang.

'She told me. But I don't see her that way and now it's really awkward. Living in the same house right now is uncomfortable.'

'Oh.' She looked down at her hands, surprised to see the fingers tightened into bunches.

'We have a mutual friend who's losing her summer accommodation, and Lizzie suggested she has the box room. But it's tiny, really miserable, and it doesn't have a radiator. I suggested that it might be better if I store my stuff in the small room, and she takes my room.'

'But where are you going to stay?'

He twitched his mouth into what could have been a smile. 'I thought I would bunk at the job, Beehive Cottage. It certainly makes it easier to commute in, and I can work in the evenings on the small stuff. Maybe your dad will give me a bonus if we get it done quicker.'

She thought about it for a moment.

'I was hoping to move back in myself,' she said slowly.

'There are two bedrooms, it's just a houseshare. I'm not proposing—' He cut himself off, flushing red.

She managed a wry smile. 'Well, exactly. And I have this cottage for another few days. How long until we have actual heating?'

'The plaster's nearly dry, so we can put the panel heaters on soon. They will help air the place out, too. More importantly, the bathroom is warm, tiled and functional, and Grant has promised electricity to the new shower by Tuesday.'

She walked over to the window, looked out at the tiny court with its cobbles. 'If you can help with the fundraiser, you staying at Beehive Cottage would be helpful, too, so we have more time to work on it together. I'll clear it with my dad when he's properly landed, but I'm sure you can stay for free. They're flying back today.' It all made perfect sense, but... She sighed. 'But what about Patrick? And what will people say if we're essentially living there together?'

'I'll talk to Patrick again. I've already reassured him there's nothing happening between us. And it's not like we're moving in together – it's just temporary, till the cottage is finished.'

'OK,' Amber said. 'And I suppose a few more sly digs won't make much of a difference.'

'Right, then. Can I bring a few bits over now?'

She turned to look at him. 'Better than that. I'll give you a hand, if that would be all right. I could do with getting out of the house.' She was still anxious about how her father would react to her grand plans.

'That would be great.' His smile faded. 'Lizzie might not like it – she thinks I fancy you. Well, I do, a bit.'

'She's got to get over that,' Amber said. 'I think I'm going to die single and celibate. And you don't fancy me, not really.'

He laughed. 'Not now I've found out you're not a millionaire,' he joked.

She managed a wry smile. 'Nope. I am literally reduced to fundraising for charity.'

But the truth was, this didn't feel like a step back. She might not have millions of pounds to give, and she might not be able to rebuild her high-flying career. But with this fundraiser, she could use her skills, her passion, to help little Kai.

38

DECEMBER 1943

Tommy had reluctantly supported the idea to keep Hugo as a lodger, at least for the short term. Of course, Georgie wasn't able to explain what *other* work they were both doing, as she scoured the papers for more evidence of spying.

Now she knew she was definitely a widow, it was necessary to act like one. It was almost impossible to buy black fabric on the islands, but Georgie managed to send off for some dye to transform two of her dresses for going outside. She found it comforting to reflect her own grief outwardly, and made armbands for the children.

She had managed a carefully worded conversation with Clemmie, who was both sympathetic and a gossip, and could explain her 'strictly business' relationship with Hugo. Georgie had explained that even with a promised death certificate, her war widow's pension was months away at best, so she was offering Mr Seznec a room at a reasonable rate, breakfast and evening meal included. She managed to also imply that his rations would help stretch the children's diet and that he was virtually an invalid. Since he coughed all night and hadn't been seen outside much, she hoped it would be convincing enough.

It was easy to take on the persona of deeply grieving widow and become a bit reclusive, which gave her more time to help Hugo with the papers. Personally, she longed to get out in the fresh air, even in the biting wind over the coast. A trip to the solicitor's office had yielded several more boxes of tattered papers, carried back by Tommy, who was determined to help. She had a new focus, looking for pencilled notes, receipts for journeys that the suspect would have to explain, receipts for film and chemicals to develop pictures they couldn't find. They were building a case for the spy to answer.

She *was* grieving, but she hadn't expected it to be so tumultuous. She wanted to run down to the shore and scream at the sea, she wanted a grave to visit and sob over, she just *longed* for Jim to come back.

She didn't want to be stuck indoors doing paperwork, the stormy winter weather perfectly suited her mood, and when she could, she worked on digging over more vegetable beds on the school's new allotment. One of the land girls had shown the mothers at the school what to do, and a few scraggly plants were already growing, netted off from the pigeons. The chickens were growing healthier on more ground, and were turning over the dug soil in their new run, finding worms and slugs galore. A cockerel was arriving from St Piran's which might perk up the hens in the spring.

Hugo was a comfort in a strange way just by being there, just by being a man around the house. And he still needed looking after; he was weak and breathless, and the doctor had diagnosed him with bronchitis. She had taken his cigarettes off him and recommended rest and fresh air. As he couldn't walk without two sticks and wheezed like a pair of bellows when he tried, Georgie hoped the island wouldn't think of him as a threat to her reputation. Martha Ellis had also introduced him to a few local people who seemed to accept him, although the vicar's wife and her small circle were still distrustful.

Tommy seemed ambivalent about Hugo, and Georgie wondered what the children at school were saying. She couldn't tell him what Hugo's work was really about, so instead told him how the documents left at the office constituted the legal proofs of ownership and inheritance for all the islands, and many of them were the only copies available, going back hundreds of years. All had fallen prey to damage from mice and mould and damp.

Tommy asked if he could help, rather heroically as the paper stank of mouse urine and worse. She was happy to send him back to his homework instead, or out to play with his friends.

Tommy was then able to innocently spread the story that the Breton was as weak as an infant and definitely not a German, as the tale still occasionally ran.

For a small fee (and the opportunity to look around), old Mr Ellis collected Hugo's limited belongings from his ex-landlady, and he and his daughter-in-law Martha delivered them in person. Georgie was able to give them a cup of tea, explain how ill Hugo still was, and leave them at least certain that there was no illicit affair going on.

'That poor man,' Martha had said to Mr Ellis, 'he's so sick. I worried that he had congestion of the lungs at one point, and that probably would have been the end of him.'

'He's missing his family dreadfully,' Georgie had said, taking on a maternal tone. 'And his fiancée. He doesn't know if they are dead or alive.'

'It's not just us suffering in this dreadful war,' Mrs Ellis had said. 'All sides have their troubles.'

In addition to continuing to work on the paper one day a week, sorting out the legal papers whenever she could and digging over the new allotments at the school, Georgie was too tired to worry too much about any gossip people were spreading.

One afternoon, Mrs Anstruther approached her as she was working at the allotments, in her gardening clothes.

'I just thought I would have a look at the vegetable garden you are starting,' she said, very out of breath at the top of the lane. Georgie wondered, not for the first time, how she stayed so plump in the era of rationing. 'And you have managed to save the chickens, very resourceful.'

'I couldn't bear the thought of them just ending up in soup. They are this year's chicks – the land girl working on the farm at the back said they would lay for another couple of years.'

'I'm sure an extra egg now and then would help the children,' Mrs Anstruther puffed. 'I'm glad you're settling in, but I thought I should drop a word in your ear. Completely confidentially.'

'Is this about Mr Seznec, the Breton refugee?' She was saving them both five minutes of standing in the cold wind, going around the houses. 'Did you know he was crippled by the Germans, poor man?'

'I had heard something, yes, but my concern is, as a single woman—'

'I am not a single woman, Mrs Anstruther,' she snapped back. 'I am the widow of a war hero.'

'Hero?' she replied weakly.

'They are all heroes,' Georgie said, seeing the door to the classroom open. 'Oh, there's my Dolly, she looks like she's had a good day.'

'It's just, appearances *must* be kept up.'

'They are being kept up,' Georgie said, sweeping Dolly up into her arms. 'I am a widow with two children to support and perhaps months to wait for my pension. Which be a pittance and is heavily taxed anyway, so I am renting out a spare room we have created in the attic. Mr Seznec has been virtually driven off St Brannock's by a suspicious mob as if he were a Nazi.'

'It's just strange that he would come here, of all places,' Mrs Anstruther said. 'An Oxford-educated Frenchman?'

'Cambridge,' Georgie said smartly. 'He's a Breton, with relations in Ushant, which I'm sure you know has many connections to the islands. When he was treated at the base hospital, he was told that the islands urgently needed a lawyer, so he stayed to help.'

'Oh. I see.' Even as a mainlander, Mrs Anstruther must have come across the connections between the Atlantic islands and Brittany. 'It's just that someone saw a man visiting, Captain Macintosh, who is well known on the islands. He married one of our girls, Jenny Huon. Of course, her father did come from one of those islands off Britany.'

'Exactly. Captain Macintosh came to speak to me about my husband's passing. Captain Preston worked in the same department,' she said, making it up on the spot.

'Oh. I'm so sorry.' She seemed flustered now. 'I hope the visit was a comfort.'

'The truth is always comforting, in the end,' said Georgie, letting Dolly down and putting on her poshest voice. 'Thank you for your concern, but I know what I am doing. I am a lady in my thirties, not a flighty young girl.'

'Excellent. Yes. Well done on your vegetable garden, I look forward to visiting it in the spring.'

'If you have any old newspapers or peelings not needed for the vicarage gardens, we have a compost heap just there, by the gate,' said Georgie.

'I will let Cook know,' she said, smiling, the expression not reaching her eyes. 'Good day, Mrs Preston, and I am very sorry for your loss.'

39

PRESENT DAY, 11 NOVEMBER

Amber reached the manor just as her father came out. The castellated stone wall remained from the original priory, abandoned by the Benedictine monks in the sixteenth century after repeated raids by pirates. A handsome Tudor extension had been built on the site after the island was gifted to one of her ancestors. The huge, fortified door was ajar, her father waiting, tall, wide, clean-shaven after years of sporting a beard. He opened his arms for a hug, and she was almost lifted off her feet.

'Your honeymoon was spectacular,' he said, his eyes twinkling as he let her go and ushered her inside. 'It probably would have been wasted on you youngsters, though.'

Amber could feel her face warming up. 'I'm glad someone enjoyed it,' she said, glancing around. 'Is anyone else here?'

'Your mother's doing laundry.' He put his hands on her shoulders and looked into her eyes. 'How've you been?'

'Sad. Busy. OK,' she answered. 'I'm still sorry I didn't manage to call it off earlier.'

'Oh, well, it's done now. You didn't manage to bankrupt me – quite – and the holiday was just what we needed. Have you talked to Patrick at all?'

'I had to,' she said, walking into the living room and sitting down on the large corner sofa. 'I've taken on a project. Hasn't he told you?'

'We haven't been back long,' he said, sitting beside her. 'Something to do with music? How's the playing going?'

'I'm building it up,' she said, guiltily realising she hadn't done her exercises regularly since she started on the fundraiser, although she was playing for pleasure. 'I'm trying to organise a fundraiser for Kai Allen, the little boy with a brain tumour on Morwen.'

'They came to me,' he said. 'I was a bit wiped out by planning your wedding or I would have helped more. How short are they?'

She told him and he whistled. 'I can't help, love. That's too much. And why aren't the National Health Service paying, anyway?'

'I suppose they can't afford it for every child who needs it,' she said, and took a deep breath. 'Dad, you *can* help. Not by donating, I'm not asking for that. I would like to arrange a small – intimate – fundraiser, here. To hold at the manor, a concert.'

'How long would something like that take to organise?' he asked, incredulous. 'And how much would it cost?'

'The hotel has hardly any bookings for the week I'm thinking of. All I need is some bedrooms and the ballroom and restaurant. You could put on a great island dinner, and we'll invite some of our regular patrons back to a unique concert. With people like Pablo and Stefan, Mara Corsa, and possibly the Windward Trio.'

'You'll never get them at such short notice,' he said.

'Well, that's the great bit,' she said. 'I've already asked them. They're all coming back to the UK for Christmas. Most people will have engagements over the holidays, but the beginning of December is quiet.'

'Will *you* play?'

Amber shook her head. 'Dad, you know I can't. I can't rehearse enough to play something at that level.' She jumped up when she saw her mother walk in. 'Mum!'

They hugged. Her mother, Valerie, looked trim and very tanned, her dark hair cut in a flattering hairstyle. 'You look fantastic.'

'I feel fantastic,' her mother said. 'What's this I hear about playing?'

'She's organising a concert. I've told her she should play,' Michael said.

'Don't push her. Are you ready for that?' her mother asked, staring closely at her. 'You do look better. How is your neck? And are you still having problems with your arm?'

'No. I'm loads better,' Amber said slowly. 'But I don't know if I can get back to that level again.'

'If *you* play, I'll let you have the ballroom, the restaurant and the rooms,' her father said, staring at her unsmiling. 'But I want you to play something. Play along with your friends if you must. Play something simple and modern. I just need to know you'll perform. Do it for me.'

Amber's eyes filled up with tears. 'Dad, you don't understand...'

'Yes, I do. Do you think I don't know you? You're terrified to find out what you've been left with.'

There it was, in a nutshell. 'I'm not expecting much,' she said weakly.

'Maybe not. Which means you need to find out what you want to do with the rest of your life,' he growled. There was brightness in his eyes, too. 'Because you need something to do.'

'Maybe I'll become a builder,' she said, her laugh a little watery. 'I've been helping out a lot with the work at Beehive Cottage.'

'I heard,' he said. 'But you will play?'

'If you'll let me do the fundraiser.'

He sat back down and she sat between her parents. '*And* if you stop saying sorry about the wedding,' he said, looking over at Valerie. 'We've come to terms with it, your mother and I. If it's not right, it's not right.'

They seemed to share a secret thought and both smiled.

'Well, you look very happy,' she said, a little suspiciously.

'We are,' her mother said. 'Come and help me cook supper. Is it true you're teaching some music on Morwen?'

'There isn't a music teacher on the islands at the moment,' she said. 'So the kids don't get a chance to try it out. Who knows, a couple of them might become the next Luka Šulić or Nicola Benedetti.'

'Or Billie Eilish, or Ed Sheeran,' Valerie added. 'Singer-songwriter or composer.'

A few notes of what Amber had started thinking of as her ghost song ran through her head, and her fingers twitched, longing to play.

'Maybe,' she said. 'I'll try to play something for Dad, but I don't want to push it yet.'

He snorted, standing in the doorway. 'I know you played at the pub – the islands were all talking about it days later. How's the Goulding?'

'Better than ever. But that was just...' Wonderful, easy, painless. 'I played it on a borrowed fiddle,' she said, remembering. 'Now, can we get the piano in the ballroom if we extend the stage? I've bullied Ben into helping with that.'

'Ben?' Dad said, his voice flat.

'Yes, Ben. And don't start, we're just colleagues, there's nothing going on.'

His frown cleared. 'Well, that's all right, then,' he said as she walked out with her mother into the brightly lit family kitchen.

'Basically, you want the whole wedding package,' Valerie said. 'Ballroom, restaurant and good catering. Our chefs are all away until Christmas.'

'I can ask around the islands,' Amber said.

'Better still, I can,' Valerie said. 'The chefs at Chancel Hall will probably offer if I tell them what you're doing, and I know Erwan from Le Petit Bleu on St Brannock's would love to do a Breton course. It will be fish, he's a wizard with seafood.' She smiled ruefully. 'I'll be everyone's commis chef, I know that. I can get a couple of friends in to wash up, too. That little boy's story broke my heart.'

'Thanks, Mum,' Amber kissed her cheek. 'You're a star.'

'Not just me,' she said. 'You too. Someone's got to make all the bedrooms up and clean while I peel a mountain of vegetables and prawns.'

'I'll do the bedrooms,' Amber said. 'You remember what a good chambermaid I was as a teenager.'

'I remember you eating most of the chocolates we put out,' Valerie said, laughing.

'I can hopefully get a couple of volunteers to help,' Amber said, pulling out another book of Post-its and making notes. 'Because I'm going to be rallying and welcoming and organising, too.'

'So,' her mother said, putting the oven on. 'Tell me how you are? Really?'

'Really? I've been super sad about Patrick, and I feel awful that I let it get so far.'

'That was at least partly your dad's fault,' Valerie said. 'I remember you trying to talk to him – us – and everyone just thought it was wedding nerves.'

Amber scrambled to change the subject. 'You should see Beehive Cottage. It's really cute and the builders are doing a great job.'

'Well, Lewis is always reliable and Grant's a great electrician. Who else did your dad ask?'

'Lewis had a kid help at first, Jake something. And Ben's

been there from the start. He's local to Morwen so did a lot of the wrecking and prep.'

'That's nice,' Mum said, laying things out on the work surface. 'Which Ben is that?'

'Mum! You know perfectly well who Ben is! Ben Kevell.'

'Oh, the carpenter. Did he help in the sunken garden at some point? Nice boy, red hair?'

'That's the one.' She shook her head. 'Which reminds me. He's lost his room at the house he shares. He'd like to stay at Beehive Cottage and finish little jobs in his spare time.'

'Stay with you at Beehive?'

'No. I'm at Shambles, next door,' she said.

Her mother carried on dipping fillets of white fish in beaten egg. 'Hm?'

'After my tenancy runs out next door, I'll have to move back then.'

'You're both grown-ups. I'm not worried about your virtue at this late stage.' She made a funny face.

Amber stirred the seasoning into the flour and Valerie coated the fish.

'You and Dad had a good time, then?'

'Wonderful. Really lovely.' Her mother almost said something, then pursed her lips tightly.

'What?' Amber started laughing. 'Mum, what is it?'

'Let's just say, it was a very *romantic* holiday,' Valerie said, smiling back. 'When you've been married for thirty years, it all gets a bit dull. I started to think we were past all that.' Her eyes sparkled. 'It turns out we were not past all that at all. I can't remember the last time he even held my hand here on the islands, but he hardly let me go the whole time we were away.'

'So, my honeymoon—' Amber couldn't finish, she was so choked up.

'That holiday was so long and so luxurious, we absolutely spoiled ourselves. We treated each other, did things we never have time to do here. Swam in the sea at dusk, wandered around temples and museums, ate street food and went to bed in the afternoons.' She laughed to herself. 'Sometimes we even had a nap.'

'Mum!' Amber laughed. 'I'm so glad for you.'

'You were right,' Valerie said, her smile fading. 'If that's not what you felt for Patrick, no matter how much you liked him, then he isn't the one.'

'He was so nearly the one,' Amber said, tears starting quickly and tumbling down her face. 'Oh, Mum, I really did love him. But I knew it wasn't right.'

'Then you did the right thing,' Valerie said firmly. 'One day you'll find the right person, but there's no rush. You're so young. He will find someone, too, he's a lovely man.'

'I hope so,' Amber said, feeling for an edge of jealousy that was no longer there. 'Because he deserves someone gentler and more giving than me.'

'Says the woman who's organising a fundraiser to save a six-year-old's life.'

'There are no guarantees, Mum,' Amber said, her voice soft with tears. 'And all I'm doing is making calls and writing on stacks of Post-its. It's the least I can do. The surgeons gave me a second chance. I want the same for him.'

40

DECEMBER 1943

Georgie struggled to find a carpenter to help with adapting the loft room, but eventually the Ellises – George and Martha – came over to help. She couldn't understand the couple. They were at the centre of the village, related to half the islanders, yet were slightly more welcoming.

'People are a bit different here,' Georgie said, brushing more whitewash onto the repaired and lined roof. 'I mean, they are smiling and kind, but I know we're outsiders.'

'Us too,' Martha Ellis said. She craned her neck to look out of the window over the yard, to the field beyond. 'Carefully with Dolly, Nora!' she called. The window had had to be forced open by Hugo and Mr Ellis, but it was loosening up as layers of paint cracked off. 'We caused a bit of scandal a few years ago. We took in a half-drowned young sailor, just a boy really. A Dutch fisherman. But the locals thought he was a German.'

Georgie stopped painting, stared over at Martha. 'Goodness. Didn't you have the ministry down on you?'

Martha shrugged, scraped back a little paint from the window edge. 'They came, but they soon realised he wasn't a German. He'd lost his memory, poor lad, and very nearly his life. He was in the sea for hours, in November. He's crewing on a trawler now, he's a good fisherman. People like him, but he's more accepted over on the big island. He'll move to the mainland when he gets a ship.'

'And the local people...?'

'Well, you have to know that the same night, a Morwen ship was sunk by a German submarine. People were grieving, lashing out.'

'I didn't know. I'm so sorry.' She wedged her wet paintbrush into the corner of the ceiling, splashing herself a little. 'Oh, bother. It's not like I can easily have a bath!'

'It will come off easily enough, it's mostly lime. Glue is hard to find now, and even salt is short.'

Georgie looked at the thin paint running back into the bucket. 'I didn't even know what was in it before,' she observed. 'You see it on walls, but our decorator in London just bought it ready to paint.'

'Decorator, hm? Ooh, that's loosening up well,' Martha said, attacking the window frame with a scraper. More shards of paint in many colours flaked to the floorboards.

'Well, we had a big house,' Georgie said, suddenly self-conscious.

'Nice for you. How big?'

'Three storeys,' Georgie said shortly. 'Four bedrooms.'

'You must have had help with all those rooms.'

Georgie sniffed back a sudden sadness. 'We had a cook and a general maid. The maid, Susan, went off to a munitions factory in 1940. But Lena stayed with us, she'd been a maid in Jim's family for years and worked her way up. She was a marvellous cook. I miss her dumplings and her apple cakes.'

'What happened to her?'

'She was at the house when it collapsed. She was injured.' Georgie swallowed hard, her throat dry. She stared up at

Martha, her eyes watery. 'The bomb went off and blew the house down on the basement. They had to dig her out.'

'Lucky she wasn't in the upper rooms, then.'

'That's where I would have been, if I hadn't been with the children,' Georgie said, seeing the wreckage in her mind. 'After it happened, I left them in the shelter with a neighbour, while they were digging Lena out. It's the most brutal thing. It's the smell that stayed with me, while they were rescuing her. Rotten food, the smoke, chemicals from the explosive, gas, dead animals and probably bodies.' She dipped her face towards the cleanest part of her sleeve. 'I'm sorry, I shouldn't indulge myself with this maudlin remembering.'

'I understand,' Martha said softly. 'I was in a field hospital in France in the last war. The stench of mould and damp was horrible, but gangrene was the worst, and I sometimes wake up smelling it. Scents give intense memories, don't they?'

Georgie went back to painting. 'My grandmother loved lavender. I used to smell it on the landing in her house, long after she had gone.'

'My grandpa used this unusual tobacco,' Martha added. 'I can still recall it today. If I catch a whiff of it, I always think he's right there, behind me.'

They smiled at each other, both a bit teary-eyed.

'Well, time for a cup of tea and—' Georgie broke off triumphantly. 'Some biscuits!'

Martha put down her tools. 'My goodness, where did you get them?'

'There was a box of broken digestives delivered to the shop off the boat. Bob Alden at the newspaper got some, and picked me up some as well. His wife has lent me a tin for them.'

After they negotiated the ladder and the stairs, Georgie led the way to the kitchen. On the table sat the tin, decorated with transfers of the coronation of the old king, and half filled with an assortment of plain biscuits, which smelled delicious. She put the kettle over the tiny gorse fire, prodding it with a bigger stick, leaving it to catch. She had learned that a fire was a luxury to be lit just once a day, but late afternoon would mean she could reheat yesterday's casserole after she'd made a big pot of tea. There wasn't enough wood to heat water for bathing, though – she would have to make do with a cold wash.

Martha stripped off her heavy apron, revealing a floral one underneath. Dolly and Nora from next door had come in from the cold and were playing with dolls in the living room. Georgie had managed to sew a couple of them out of scraps of fabric, and they were very popular.

Martha put her head on one side as if she was listening. 'This is where that young boy stayed, when Jago Carney died.'

Georgie's stomach dropped. 'Yes. The young boy was James Preston. My husband.'

Martha didn't say anything, just sat on one of the chairs and held out her hands to the fire. 'People say they were best friends, that Jago spent all summer playing with him. He even went sailing with Jago and his brothers.'

Georgie turned to rinse out the teapot. 'I never knew anything. Jim never talked about it.'

'Some people blamed him.'

Georgie's hands stalled. 'So I heard.'

Martha rubbed her hands together. 'He was a nice enough boy,' she said. It seemed like she was choosing her words carefully. 'I mean, for a summer swallow.'

'Summer swallow?' *Oh, just a visitor.*

'The Prestons weren't well liked,' Martha went on. 'My sister-in-law, Louise, she worked for them every year, used to bring food in that she cooked at home. And they had a maid, who used to sleep up in the attic with the nanny.'

'Where was the nanny, when the boys were on the beach?'

'There was James, and his cousins Rosalie and Richard, as I remember. The boys were playing on the beach and the girl was with the nanny. They were told not to go in the water. The local boys warned them that the tide was on the turn, it was very high that day. A strong offshore wind from the east – that's unusual at that time of year.' She shook her head. 'There's no one as arrogant as a young boy growing into manhood. My eldest son joined the navy at fourteen as a boy, third class. He died a year later at the beginning of the war. He thought he was invincible.'

'I'm so sorry.' Georgie measured out the tea with a shaking hand, filled up the pot with boiling water. 'I can't believe Jim never told me,' she said. 'He should have.'

'Likely he was ashamed,' Martha said. 'He had to give evidence at the inquest on St Brannock's, too.' She pressed her lips together as if trying to hold back words she wanted to say, but couldn't.

'That must have been difficult if he was just eleven,' Georgie said, checking on the girls. Nora was plaiting Dolly's long hair and threading the last of the daisies in it.

Martha nodded her thanks as she was passed the best cup and saucer, and added a little milk.

'Well, it's all over now. We have bigger things to fret over.'

Georgie breathed in the fragrant steam. It was strange how a simple cup of tea could stop the world, allow thoughts to tumble out. 'Tell me, please,' she said, staring into the steam. 'I'd rather hear it from you than anyone else.'

'Well, this is just what people say,' Martha said, slowly. 'You'd have to talk to your Mr Seznec about the truth of the matter.'

'Which is?' She looked at Martha, who was looking away.

'They said James told the police the story, honest like, on the day poor Jago went missing. The gig lads saw a bit, the boys on the beach, even his cousin all gave the same story. A rip tide snatched the boy – your Jim – away, Jago went in to guide him along the beach to where the current was weaker. But the current was stronger than the boys had ever seen, pulling both of them out.' She shook her head. 'He drowned before the gig found them.'

Georgie found she had been holding her breath. 'That's a terrible story. But what is "the truth of the matter" that Mr Seznec knows about?'

'By the time they found the body, and arranged an inquest, the Prestons had changed their story. They claimed James Preston had seen the younger boy in trouble and went in to help him. The boy – your husband – testified that he was trying to help Jago.' She looked away for a moment. 'They didn't come back after that. They rented it out to a widow for a dozen years or so.'

'I've heard about the inquest. But *Jim* lied about it?'

Georgie could hardly believe it. Of course, the Prestons had the best legal advice, they would have wanted to cover up a tragic mistake. Maybe she would do that for Tommy, in the same circumstances?

No. Not only Georgie but Tommy would want the truth told, no matter how shameful.

41

PRESENT DAY, 18 NOVEMBER

Amber finally had Wi-Fi and was able to field queries from halfway around the world, as rain misted down the kitchen window at Shambles. Her closest friends were on tour in Australia, due to fly back just three days before the concert, so it would be a bit close with time. Not to mention killer jet lag, she thought – one thing she didn't miss about touring. Oh, and the food, because they always ate after the concert, basically whatever the hotel had left.

The hard physical labour of helping the builders had kept her moving and built her muscles back up. Her recent check-up had been good, she was making excellent progress and her posture while playing was much improved.

She had started a proper practice regime, and although she had to take extra time to warm up, the muscle memory was good. She could tackle some of Bach's trickier pieces now. She had also played 'Niel Gow's Lament' but couldn't quite capture the magic she had found in the pub. She finished each practice session with the piece that had built from snatches of melody in her head up to a spiralling song that built to a lovely finale. In her head, she could already hear a cello part, a viola, maybe a piano or harp... She put the instrument back in its case and wiped her eyes; the music always made her cry. The dream of the little boy in the surf was fading now, but she felt intuitively that the music was somehow connected to him.

Someone banged on the door and opened it without being asked, stepping out of the rain. 'Are you coming to work?' Ben called through. 'We're tiling the kitchen today.'

He had been polite but more distant now they were neighbours. She was feeling quite awkward about moving into Beehive next week now.

'How hard is tiling?' she asked. 'I can spare a couple of hours.'

'Piece of cake,' he shouted back. 'I'll stick the kettle on.'

She had never been self-conscious about her music before, but he must have heard her. She quickly changed into her work clothes.

As she pushed open the door to Beehive Cottage, she noticed something different. The heating was on, and it was *warm*. It really lifted the atmosphere in the place.

As Lewis had finished the plastering, it was just Ben and Amber in the house, their movements echoing and singing around each small room.

The kitchen was bright now, new spotlights in the ceiling blazing onto worktops she had chosen weeks ago. A simple white kitchen would bounce as much light around as possible, and she had chosen a flooring the colour of the local slates.

'I *love* it,' she said. They had kept her out of it for the last fitting. Her rescued old stove looked fabulous in contrast with the modern cupboards, and someone had painted the old alcove door a slate blue to match the floor. 'I really do.'

'And,' he said, whipping a piece of paper from one of the drawers, 'certificate of safety for the chimney. Actually, both chimneys. Your dad has a wood-burning stove for the front room being delivered on Thursday, along with a large bag of logs.

We'll have to stack them out the back though, so I'll clear up the yard for them.'

'Oh, thank you,' she said, smiling so hard the corners of her mouth pulled.

'You'll have to come over and play your violin here,' he said, with an awkward smile. 'Christen the place.'

'I'm still a bit self-conscious.'

He shook his head. 'You sound *amazing*.'

'The violin has had a fantastic overhaul. It makes me sound so much better than I am.'

'Oh, it just sits there and sings, does it?' he said, grinning.

'Almost,' she said, laughing back. 'It's like my oldest friend, it just always forgives the odd squeak and twang.' She looked around the new floors, the untidy edge where the new plaster met the wood. 'What about skirting?'

'I'm doing that today if you can get on with the tiles.'

The tiles, also carefully chosen from a catalogue, were much brighter and warmer in real life. She loved them straight away. Ben had already fixed a level batten onto the wall, and showed her how to start.

'It's easier than it looks,' he said, putting the first three tiles on. 'We know the first row will be straight, so we'll just build off them.'

It was easy, although she took twice as long as he had to carefully select each tile, smooth on some adhesive, and settle it in place. She carried on, building a rhythm, and humming the harmony for the cello part.

'That's really nice,' he said, peering around the doorway. 'What is it?'

'It's just a song I'm writing,' she answered, sticking her tongue out to concentrate on fixing the tile, level and square and in just the right place. 'It's a practice piece.' *Except that I'm writing parts, hearing the orchestration.*

'It sounds sad.'

'It really suits my violin.' She stopped and walked through to where Ben was working. 'It's about Jago Carney,' she said.

'Jago. There's a memorial on the beach at Seal Cove. I heard the story as a kid, a warning not to wade out too deep.'

She nodded, watching him mark a pencil line on the wood. 'I keep having a weird dream about this little boy, I think he drowned. I didn't remember anything about Jago before I got here, it might be him.'

He sawed off another piece of mitred skirting in a flurry of sawdust. 'You could have heard about him, when you were a child. You did spend *some* time on the islands.'

She shook her head. 'I can't remember being told. Anyway, the kid in the water is much younger, five or six maybe.'

He stopped measuring. 'Kai Allen's age.'

'But the dream started when I stayed here. To start with, it was just a sound. I just thought it was the wind blowing in. Before you mended the windows,' she said wryly, 'it was a little breezy.'

'I thought you would bail after that first night,' he admitted, laughing.

'You should have known better,' she said, returning to the kitchen to stare at the tiles, trying to lose the image of the boy, floating by the edge of the water. She just wanted to wade in and pick him up, breathe life back into him.

Ben had followed her into the kitchen. 'I'm sorry. You look really upset.'

'It's the boy, it's Kai. The music,' she said, closing her eyes to conjure the first haunting notes, 'is like an earworm, I can't get rid of it.'

'Just play it,' he said.

'I can't. It wants more instruments – oh, listen to me! I'm making it sound like it's got a life of its own.' She realised with a jolt that maybe if she played it, recorded it, shared it with some of her friends, she might be able to finish it. 'I have a friend, a cellist. Perhaps I'll send her a copy and ask her opinion.' Only she didn't want to. She wanted to write the score then get her to play it.

'Do what you need to do,' he said, looking over at the tiles. 'Because you're no tiler.'

'What?' She smiled at him as he pointed out the tiniest of flaws, where four tiles had almost, but not quite, lined up. 'Well, I think it's pretty brilliant for a first go. And anyway, it's my kitchen—' The thought took her breath away. 'Did I really just say that?' she breathed, more to herself than to him.

'Apparently so,' he said, looking back at her. 'I'm just joking. They are handmade tiles, they're always a bit irregular. You've done a great job. But I ought to mention that your dad has a couple of potential buyers coming to view the cottage after Christmas.'

'He does? Why didn't he tell me?'

'Maybe he knows you've got a bit attached,' he said.

She took a deep breath in and blew it out. 'It's fine, he's right. My priority is the concert.'

Ben was standing closer to her now; she could feel his warmth. 'What happens if the concert doesn't cover Kai's treatment?'

'It will. I'll keep going until it does.' She could feel the pressure in her chest, as vivid as the compulsion to play music. 'He might die,' she reminded him, as much as herself. 'But this is his best chance.'

'He might die even with the treatment,' he said.

He reached out a gentle hand, flecked with sawdust, to touch her cheek and wipe away a tear.

'I'm sorry,' she said, sniffing and trying to smile, but it fell flat. He was closer now; she could see where he'd missed a spot shaving, and a tiny mole by the side of his mouth.

She moved forward and kissed him, not thinking, just

reacting to something that seemed easy and uncomplicated. He kissed her back, slid an arm around her waist, kissed her again.

Then he pulled away. 'We shouldn't,' he said, his voice shaking. 'Patrick.'

She touched a finger sandy with tile adhesive to his lips. 'Not right now,' she said, her own voice husky. 'But maybe another day?'

He wrapped his arms around her harder then, and she let herself be swept away by the sweetness of it, the warmth of his kisses. He managed to break away first.

'Soon, then.' He smiled, and it was like the sun breaking through the clouds.

Tears still drying on her cheeks, she smiled, too.

42

DECEMBER, 1943

Hugo kept his continuous cough, and struggled to walk around the town. It lent some credibility to her letting him stay in her house as an invalid. Days passed as Georgie pored over the papers, finding odd receipts and pencilled notes for Hugo to analyse, for them to discuss. They continued the illusion that he was renting the attic once she and Tommy had done their best to make it warm and dry. Martha Ellis had lent them a narrow bed she had in her house, which had belonged to her deceased elder son, which was more comfortable for Tommy as Hugo still couldn't climb the ladder.

Georgie had grown close to Martha, although in a different, pre-war life they would never have met. Perhaps Martha would have sold her fresh fish on the quay while they stayed in comfort at a hotel. Now, they bonded over their grief, and their communication was easy. Sometimes, Georgie was able to mind Martha's younger boys while she did a shift at the cannery. At other times, Dolly stayed over with the Ellises while Georgie tackled the stacks of papers from the office as well as the newspaper work.

Tommy was working hard to prepare for his entrance exam

for Jim's old school, and towards the end of the autumn term was helped by Patience Ellis returning from the grammar school. They got on well, the older girl serious and focused and aiming to train as a teacher herself one day. Tommy seemed to have grown up, too. She had written to Jim's old school and they had sent a labyrinthine application paper for a full scholarship.

'But I still don't know if I want to go,' he said, puzzling over his own handwriting by the light of a smoking candle.

Georgie took her needlework scissors and trimmed the wick a little. 'Better?' she asked, trying to thread her needle by its brightness. 'Why wouldn't you want to go?'

'I still think I should stay here,' he answered, crossing something out with his pencil. 'Oh, bother. When was the Battle of Bosworth Field again?'

'Fourteen eighty-five,' she dredged up from her memory. 'Henry the Seventh won and Richard the Third was killed.'

'Hacked to bits,' he said with some relish.

'Well, Shakespeare made him out to be such a villain,' she said, setting another stitch. Keeping the children's clothes in order, especially as cloth was scarce and the children were growing, was a weekly task. 'What don't you like about the school? Daddy loved it there.'

'I think that would just make me sad,' he said, his voice flat. 'And if Hugo's going to be here, I think it would look better if I was here, too.'

'A chaperone,' she said, just a little laughter in her voice. 'Well, thank you. But I don't need looking after.'

'That's not how our neighbours will see it,' he said, looking up at her. 'I don't think that's how Great-Aunt Alice will see it either.'

'Well, if Great-Aunt Alice could send us a few pounds now and then to help from her vast fortune, we wouldn't need a lodger,' she said, giving up on the sewing. 'It's too late to light another candle now. Why don't we get ready for bed? We can tidy up tomorrow.'

'Mummy,' Tommy said, blotting his pen and putting his pencils away. 'I heard this story about Dad. At school.'

'What story?' She put her hand on his shoulder. 'You know you can tell me anything.'

When he looked up, his eyes were full of tears. 'They said Daddy killed a boy when he was my age.'

She took a shaky breath. 'Of course he didn't! He got into trouble in a rip tide, which is why I don't want you to go in the water at Seal Cove.' He stood up and hugged her, putting his head against her shoulder like he always had since he was little. 'The boy who died tried to help, but in the end, Daddy nearly drowned, and the other boy – his name was Jago Carney – *did* die. It wasn't anyone's fault. Daddy didn't get into trouble, it was an accident.'

He shrugged and turned his head away as a tear tracked down his face. He scrubbed it off on his sleeve. 'I just wish I'd known about it before.'

'I only recently found out myself,' she said gently. 'Please don't worry about it.' She changed the subject. 'Now, what on earth are we going to do about Christmas?' The question had been causing her to cry at night as her grief returned, memories of Jim with the children before the war... She swallowed hard. 'I haven't come up with any firm plans. I've saved up some sugar and butter rations, the shop will hold some back for me. I hope we'll have a bit of cake, anyway.'

'It would be nice to get Dolly a present,' he said. 'But there's nothing in the shops even if we had the money.' He looked sad then, like a little boy who knew he wasn't getting a present either.

'You leave that to me,' she said, already drafting a letter in her head to the now hated Great-Aunt Alice. 'Who knows, I might even get that pesky pension.' She could write to friends in

London to see if they at least had a little fabric to make Dolly a toy. Her sewing skills had developed, from her lacklustre efforts at school to semi-professional darning. She had had another thought: perhaps she could make a draughts set for Tommy, or better still, backgammon. She thought she remembered how the boards were laid out, and the same pieces would do both. She could make the board out of her gas mask box. 'And I have an appointment to see the bank about Daddy's money.'

She really didn't hold out much hope, but the ministry had paid Jim the last of his back pay, and she was at least entitled to that. Whether it could be transferred to the island bank before Christmas was another matter; everything was so slow during the war. It would be lovely to buy Tommy a book as well, or replace the penknife he had lost in London.

She heard Hugo's steps coming down the stairs and looked around. 'We're just clearing up,' she said, smiling at him. 'We've been talking about Christmas.'

'In Brittany we burn a special Yule log on the fire, on the day before Christmas. And after midnight mass, we share our meal with all the animals, dogs and cats.'

'You eat at midnight?' Tommy said, incredulous.

'Indeed, my family used to. And the children left their shoes by the fireplace, hoping *Tad Nedeleg* would fill them with little gifts and sweets.'

Georgie looked at Tommy. 'Like our Father Christmas, I suppose. Do you cook goose?'

Hugo shut his eyes. 'Ah, a goose, my mouth waters already, and cheese, and some fish. It varies from town to town. But always, the very best wine of the year. My mother was never converted, so we celebrated Christmas.'

'Now *my* mouth is watering,' Georgie said. 'What do you like to eat most at Christmas, Tommy?'

'Chocolate,' he said. 'And fruit cake.'

She smiled at him, reached over and squeezed his hand.

'Next year, or in the years after when this blasted war is over, we will have a mountain of good food and presents for all.'

Tommy hesitated, glanced over at Hugo. 'I suppose you will be back in France by then,' he said, uncertainly.

'Brittany, not France,' said Georgie automatically. 'Who knows? Perhaps we'll visit Hugo on holiday.' She turned to him. 'You might be settled in Brittany by then.' She remembered, too late, his mention of a fiancée when they fled the invasion. Would he even want to go back to a place that held the memories of so much loss? 'I'm sorry.'

The expression on his face was sad, tragic even. 'Who knows what the future will bring? We must pray for better years ahead. Perhaps, a new beginning, for us all.'

43

PRESENT DAY, 29 NOVEMBER

Amber worked on getting the rooms ready for the concert at the manor, and the process acutely reminded her of making plans for the wedding. It didn't help that she kept obliquely bumping into Patrick, although he didn't stop to talk. She couldn't stop thinking about those kisses with Ben either. There was a gleam in his eye now, from time to time. In hers too, probably.

Ben was working on extending the stage and Grant was running cables to microphones and lights. Billie, the social media wizard, was on the island and had already filmed brief snippets of Kai's life, contrasted with interviews with his parents. She had also recorded a lot of the preparations, which would become a time-lapse video, and interviewed several of the artists and guests in anticipation. Amber had a zing of excitement when she saw a video online of a celebrity talking about the music concert, and another when she saw how many views that snippet received.

A famous pop star had had a baby with a similar brain tumour; he was coming over and bringing his surviving children. Zoe was already excited about meeting him, even though it raised the spectre of this treatment either coming too late or not helping. Amber lay awake at night imagining how easily little Kai could slip away, also acutely aware that Patrick was sleeping in the gardener's cottage next door. The kiss with Ben sometimes intruded, confusing her.

Every day meant more enquiries, more problems to be solved. Vasily would bring his viola but would it be insured? (Yes). Kerry wanted to bring her spare instruments, would there be room? (Probably). Could Simon's Song do a whole one-hour set? (No, twenty minutes, four songs only, including both their number-one hits).

Broadcasters were becoming interested and sent reporters to talk to Zoe and now Amber. Soon, with just one week to go, the hard campaign for funds would start, but the fund had already jumped up to eighteen thousand, and Zoe and Liam had been able to pay the deposit and book Kai's proton beam therapy. The next available treatment slot was on the eighteenth of December.

Little Kai would have a chance to extend his life, or even be cured, in the month over Christmas. The most important month of his young life.

Hotels and holiday lets across the islands had offered accommodation for free for the many technicians and the small orchestra, and donations were coming in from the islanders. It was as if Kai's diagnosis had paralysed them before, but now there was a specific plan, they were fully behind the venture.

Amber looked back at her notes. Tickets to book, people to tell, things to organise. She longed to lift her violin, play for an hour, work on the song, but that all seemed a long way away.

She made her way to the dining room and was met by Patrick. She sighed; she just couldn't cope with anything else. She longed to be able to slot her private life onto Post-its and lists, too.

'I thought I'd come and help,' he said.

'Thank you,' she said, her voice coming out small. 'I'm ready for some food now. Has Mum got dinner on?'

'They're going out to eat,' he said, his eyes a little luminous in the dim light. 'I was going to heat up some pizza. If you'd like to join me.'

No. She took a deep breath, thought quickly. Maybe he was just trying to be friendly. Trying to just be *friends.*

'I have to work,' she said. 'But a couple of slices would be lovely.'

'They left some wine as well, and your mother bought ice cream. She didn't entirely leave us to starve.'

They walked through the manor to the private quarters.

'I'll just go change,' she said. 'I'll be down in a few minutes.'

She could feel his gaze on her as she walked up the stairs. Being around Patrick was so uncomfortable now, especially when she was thinking more and more about Ben.

She took some time to shower and change into a relaxing but homely jumper, and slippers. No point dressing up for him, especially as she could almost feel an agenda in the air.

Down in the kitchen, she bombarded him with information about the appeal before he could say whatever was bothering him.

It wasn't until she had a mouthful of food that he spoke.

'No regrets, then, now you're back here?'

She shook her head.

He continued. 'Cancelling the wedding didn't have to split us up.'

She swallowed with a suddenly dry mouth, and took a fortifying sip of wine. 'It did. I understand it better now,' she said, looking across the breakfast bar at him.

'One day you just decided you didn't love me?' He frowned shook his head. 'I'm sorry, I'm still trying to understand, not get angry.'

'I'll always love you.' The words fell out before she could

stop them. 'I mean, you'll always be someone I care about, deeply. But I'm not *in* love with you.'

He propped his elbows on the surface and put his chin in his hands. 'You could have told me,' he said. 'I thought we could tell each other anything.'

'So did I.' She smiled sadly at him.

'I just wanted to make sure there wasn't an ember left before I told you. I'm leaving the island in the spring.'

'Oh.' It came as a blow, strangely. 'I'm sorry. You don't have to... Mum and Dad will be so sorry.'

He shrugged. 'I'm an asset for the manor at the moment, and I'll still oversee the planning for the garden going forward. But I need a more central base, not stuck on the island being reminded of our dream. I've got commissions coming in, I need a fresh start.'

Almost out of habit, she was about to ask eager questions about what he would be doing next, but managed to pull it back. 'I'm glad.'

'I'll be around for the fundraiser. In fact, I've got tickets for a couple of my wealthiest clients. They've promised to support the appeal. Do you know how much money has been pledged or tickets sold, so far?'

'Enough for Kai's treatment to be booked,' she said. 'Now we're going for a bigger appeal to complete his treatment. Anything raised over the target will help more children on the waiting list.'

He fiddled with a crust on his plate; he hadn't eaten much. 'It's funny. During our three years together, I never would have pegged you for a philanthropist.'

She smiled. 'Neither would I. Enough people have called me selfish over the years. Self-absorbed has been mentioned, too.'

'That's the artistic life, isn't it?' he said, staring at her. 'Total focus.'

'It's the only way to get right to the top,' she said, managing a shaky laugh. 'And now all that's over.'

He raised an eyebrow at that. 'You could work your way back.'

'Maybe. But I don't know if I want it any more.' There it was, the disturbing thought that interrupted her when she was playing, and when she was speculating about Ben when she wasn't insanely busy. 'I mean, music is still central, but I'm not sure if *performing* is.'

'After all those years travelling and playing and building your portfolio?'

'After all those years living out of a suitcase trying to make my way to the top?' she said, placing her hands in her lap, pressing her fingers together. 'I never stopped to find out if I still wanted it.'

'So, what would you do instead? Teach?'

'Maybe.' She laughed. 'I have already given a few lessons at the school. But no, I don't think so. I want to explore other kinds of music, maybe do some composing and create new styles.'

'I never wanted us to break up,' he said slowly, then sipped some wine. 'But I also didn't want to make you unhappy.'

'*You* never would have,' she said, leaning forward. '*I* was making myself unhappy. I just wasn't in the right place.'

'And you never would have been. Not with me.'

Tears filled her eyes. 'No. I'm sorry.'

'Do you think – no, that's none of my business.'

Thank goodness he hadn't asked if she'd met anyone else because she really didn't think she could lie to him. 'I'd better go. I have a fundraiser to run, and a concert to organise.'

He glanced up at her, his eyes shining with unshed tears. 'Don't you miss being up on stage, getting all the applause?'

'Funny enough,' she said, surprising herself, 'I don't. I do miss playing, though, I miss falling into the emotion that comes with the music. I'm practising again.' She smiled. 'Kerry is playing one of my favourite pieces. I'm looking forward to the concert, but that niggles a bit.' She flexed her arm. 'She'll probably do a better job than me anyway.'

'You played in the pub on Morwen.'

She jumped. 'Oh, you're kidding! Is there anyone on the island who doesn't know?'

'Elk was up here with your dad, talking about the sound setup. He was raving about your performance.'

'Raving, no,' she scoffed.

'Don't run yourself down. He said something like you *became* the music.'

That's what was happening recently, with what she was calling 'The Lament of Jago Carney'.

'It's still in me, somewhere,' she said. 'To be honest, I started to lose some of that, working in the orchestra. It's no longer about *your* interpretation of the music, more about being perfectly matched to the others. The vision is the conductor's.'

'I feel a bit the same,' he admitted. 'Working in just one garden has been a joy, really getting my hands dirty again, I've loved it. But there's a limit to what I can do. Most of the garden design here was already defined by two hundred years of previous head gardeners. Your father won't appreciate me changing the layout, going with cutting-edge planting or new vistas.'

'You mean, cut the monkey puzzle trees down?' She grinned. 'You've always said they obscure the best view in the garden.'

He laughed with her. 'I'd be out there with a chainsaw tomorrow if I could,' he admitted.

'Well, I love them,' she said. 'They are part of my childhood and part of the island now.'

His smile faded. 'So, we're OK? You and me, just friends?'

'We're good,' she said, but looking at him, his eyes picking up the low light, his dark hair flopping forward, she momentarily wished they could walk upstairs together and see what happened.

Then Ben's lopsided grin popped into her head, making her catch her breath.

'You said Mum left ice cream for us?' she asked, sliding off the bar stool.

'She got the roasted pecan and honeycomb you like.'

'That will help me go back to my calculations,' she said, sorting through the freezer. 'She has berry and clotted cream, too, if you fancy it.'

'No, thanks.' He was standing a bit close. 'Do you need any help with your paperwork?'

She shook her head.

'Then I'll say goodnight,' he said, hesitating. Finally, he leaned forward and kissed her cheek. 'Just friends.'

She managed a twisted smile. 'Goodnight, Patrick.'

44

DECEMBER 1943

A week before the children broke up for the holiday, Tommy came home with a letter from his teacher.

'But the eleven-plus exams are normally in the spring,' she said, looking again at the enthusiastic phrases his teacher had used.

'Miss Cartwright thinks I should try it now,' he said. 'Didn't she explain in the note?'

'She thinks if you pass with good scores, it would be easier to get into Daddy's school, or you could board at the grammar in Truro.'

'I don't want to go to Daddy's old school,' he said, his mouth set mulishly like Jim had always done when he thought he might not get his own way. 'It's too far. I need to be close by, for you and Dolly.'

'No, you don't,' she said, gripping his shoulders. 'You need to go to the best school I can afford, my darling.'

He shrugged her off. 'But I probably won't pass anyway.'

She stared into his eyes, veiled by his dark lashes, before he looked away. 'I need you to do your absolute best. Not just for

Wycliffe but for grammar school, too. Your father wanted you to have a profession.'

'Like he did?'

She sat down, pulled him closer so she could hold him around the waist. 'Darling, I need to tell you something, if you're old enough to keep it a complete secret. No telling even your best friends.' He turned to look at her, then sat in the chair next to her. She dropped her voice so Dolly wouldn't hear in the room above. 'Daddy worked in intelligence.'

'I thought you said he worked for the government,' Tommy said, frowning.

'He worked for the Special Operations Executive,' she murmured. 'He helped operatives get to where they needed to be, even organised rescues when people were in trouble.'

Tommy's mouth and eyes were open with astonishment. 'He was a *spy*?'

'He worked with spies,' she said. 'He had a fantastic education and he used it to help his country.' She brushed away a tear from under his eye. 'Right up to the end. What would he have wanted?'

Tommy looked at his feet. 'That I do my best,' he mumbled. 'For you and Dolly.'

'And for you, my darling. So that you can have a prosperous and happy life.'

He hung his head for a moment, then nodded. Tears dropped into his lap and he began to sob. She wrapped him in her arms. It was a comfort to hug him.

He slowly grew quiet, but stayed in her arms.

'I went to talk to Reverend Anstruther,' he mumbled, as he pulled away and rubbed his face with his sleeve.

'Why?' she asked, getting up to push all the remaining embers into the stove and add a bit of plank. There had been a wreck off West Island; wood was washing up all over the islands. Thankfully, no one had been killed.

'I just wanted to talk about Daddy to someone new,' he said, his voice high. 'I know everyone says he's dead, but I thought I would know if he was. It just feels like he's still there somewhere.'

'I feel like that sometimes,' she said, staring into the flames she had liberated. 'Other times I'm so sure he's dead it feels as if he was a dream, that he was never really here.' She smiled at him, the light weaving around them as the candle burned down. 'You'd better light another candle so we can manage the stairs.'

'He told me that Jesus is everyone's loving father,' Tommy said. 'That he will be my father now.'

Georgie, whose faith hadn't survived the war, recognised something ardent and passionate about the expression on his face. Her own father had been a lay preacher. 'Grandpa Preston would be very proud of you,' she said.

'Grandpa used to talk to me about God, even when he was very old and ill,' he said. 'He was never afraid of dying, was he?'

'No. He was very sad to be leaving all of us, though,' she said.

'Do you think Daddy felt like that? When he was...?'

Jim suddenly seemed more vibrant to Georgie than he had before. 'Daddy's last thought was probably: "I can swim to that island we saw three days ago," she said, smiling at Tommy's face, which glowed red in the last of the fire.

'I think Hugo likes you,' he sighed. 'I know it's selfish to be upset when he would look after you. If I went away.'

'He would be a *friend*.' She took his shoulders and gave him a little shake. 'I will look after myself,' she said. 'And Dolly, and you and even Hugo if I have to. I brought us here, rebuilt a home out of an empty shell. I've brought enough money in to keep us warm and fed. I'm doing useful work at the paper, too – the islanders need those bulletins.'

'So, you *don't* like Hugo?'

She let go, feeling a cold hollow in her belly. She shook her head even as the thought of Hugo reminded her how much of a pull she felt towards him.

'He's my... shipmate. My comrade in arms through this terrible war. I suppose we always feel close to someone in the trenches with us.' She blew out the old candle before it released liquid wax out of the bottom of the holder. 'Look, I don't know what's going to happen in the future, but I do know we have to behave as if there is going to be one. I will plant my vegetables up at the school, raise a few hens, help with the newspaper and file all of Hugo's mouldy papers.' And lie awake longing for Jim's warmth, his laughter, his voice. 'But for now, we should just let ourselves get used to missing Daddy.'

'So I should do my examinations, and try my best.'

He led the way up the stairs. The door to Hugo's room was shut, and she was glad he wouldn't have heard their conversation.

'I think you would always try your best.'

'Miss Cartwright said she would lend me a few old test papers to look through,' he said, at the ladder to his own room.

'Then we have a plan. I'll help you where I can, but I think your best help would come from Hugo. While he is still staying here, anyway.'

She kissed Tommy before he went up into his attic room, and he rolled his eyes. 'Mum!'

'I love you,' she whispered, as she started to close the door.

'I love you too,' he answered and the door clicked shut on the latch.

45

PRESENT DAY, 4 DECEMBER

Amber waved at the first of her friends to arrive. Kerry, tall with a head of electric red curls and colourful coat, had come with several cellos. She explained she wouldn't be sure which one she wanted to play until she knew the room's acoustics, and what amplification and recording equipment would be available.

'How on earth do you get on and off an island?' she said, puffing as she stepped off the boat onto the stone jetty with the help of Patrick, who had come down to help, and Tink, the boatman.

'I play a violin,' Amber said, grinning.

She ran into the hug offered by her friend. 'Oh, sweetheart, I was so sorry your wedding didn't turn out. Did he snore all night, hog the covers, sleep with other people?'

'You can ask him, he's carrying your bags for you,' Amber said, laughing at Patrick over her shoulder. 'But for me, none of the above.'

'Oh, sorry,' Kerry said, releasing Amber and shaking Patrick's hand. 'Nice to meet you. I'm Kerry.'

'I guessed,' he said, grinning.

'My reputation preceded me, then. Excellent.' As Patrick started up the steps towards the manor, she turned to Amber. 'You let *him* get away?'

'The prevailing opinion is that I've gone mad,' Amber said, hefting a heavy laptop bag. 'Is that it, Tink?'

'For this load,' he said. 'There are two more people waiting. We'll get them all over before we lose the tide.'

Kerry carried the last cello, protectively guarding it when Amber tried to help. 'No one else carries my best baby,' she said, following her up the hill towards the oldest part of the manor. 'Seriously, I thought you were joined at the hip to Patrick at one point.'

'While I was ill, I suppose we were,' Amber said. 'But it just wasn't right.'

Kerry's eyes flashed in the security light outside the manor. 'I love that you live in a castle.' She nodded towards Patrick. 'Do you mind if I chat to him? He seems rather nice, and we know he likes musicians.'

'No, of course not. But he's not like that...'

Kerry was no longer listening as she pushed her way into the original hall of the manor, with flagstone floor and oak panelling reaching into the carved rafters.

But it seemed he *was* like that. Maybe he felt released by their last heart-to-heart chat, but she wasn't sure how she felt about him openly flirting with her friends, who, as they turned up, seemed to gravitate towards him.

By eight o'clock, the manor held five of the world's most promising young classical musicians. And Amber.

Vasily dinged his glass with a spoon in the middle of dessert, peering over gold-rimmed glasses. 'Right. Now you have to tell us the important stuff.' Involuntarily, Amber glanced at Patrick. 'How is the *playing*?'

'Coming back,' she said. 'Better than I expected. I might even get close to where I was.'

'Waiting in the wings,' said Vasily, brushing dark hair off his forehead, 'for one of the old guard to drop dead and leave room for us.'

She was surprised at the frustration in his voice. 'Not you. You're headlining all over the world.'

'Playing the same old stuff,' Kerry intervened. 'If we want to do a pastiche of light classics, we could all get on tour.'

'Not me,' Théo said. He was a violinist from South Korea she was relying on to take her place as first violin. 'I'm recording more and more. Film music, computer games. I love it, I'm even doing a bit of orchestration.'

'I've been thinking about composition,' Amber said slowly. 'I've always done a bit, just to liven practice up. But now I'm thinking I could do more. Write some stuff for people like you to play.'

'What genre?' Vasily asked.

'New classical. Mood pieces. I have a four-part piece I'm working on.'

'Right. We'll have a look at that,' Kerry said, picking a piece of fruit out of the platter in the middle of the table. 'It's time for you to get back into the life. We miss you. And none of us are very good at sympathy or visiting hospitals.'

'OK, I'll print off the music for you all tomorrow,' Amber said, excitement building. 'Well, for a first violin part, so that's you, Théo, and a viola part for Vasily. And of course, a cello part for Kerry. I'll busk along with you.'

'A proper string quartet,' Kerry said as they walked through to the lounge, where her friends were gathered around the fire, chatting to her mother. 'Old school.'

'I've been thinking about adding vocals, too.' Amber let the idea unfold.

'You've been on the islands too long,' Vasily said. 'You'll be writing pop ballads next.'

'Actually, I might write it as a wordless piece, a *vocalise*.

The voice as an instrument. I was thinking of writing it for a woman's voice singing the melody. I've been sort of humming it a lot.'

'Go on, sing it,' Vasily said, staring intently, leaning forward.

'I couldn't!' She laughed out loud, then noticed how close Patrick and Kerry were sitting, him staring into her eyes. It made her cross, but she couldn't blame him. Then she realised she was a bit annoyed, but not hurt, not jealous – just annoyed that he would move on publicly in front of her friends. 'I'll play it to you tomorrow, get some feedback. Be kind.'

'You'll play it at the concert?'

'No! I mean, I'll play it after breakfast, before you all rehearse. I don't have my violin here.'

Vasily's eyes were almost as intense as when he played. 'That doesn't seem entirely fair. I mean, we've travelled all this way, to play for you, and you won't play for us?'

'You're playing for a little boy who needs special treatment,' she managed to say.

'I don't know him, I came for *you*. I want to get you back to music, even if you end up a country singer.'

She laughed, tears thickening her voice. 'I rather like country music.'

'Me too, but you are a *fantastic* musician. I don't just mean your playing. You personify the music, you always have, even when we were at college. Play it now.'

She nodded, unable to speak, realising the whole room was staring at her. In the past Patrick would have jumped up, protected her, softened the opinions of others, but now even he was looking questioningly at her.

Théo nodded. 'I'll get my instrument. And I don't lend it out to anyone normally.'

'I'll get the music,' she managed, finally. It would be easier to play than argue.

· · ·

Amber played her composition while her friends and colleagues were lounging in front of roaring log fire, drinks in hand. The room was mostly lit by fairy lights on the enormous tree her father had had delivered by boat the day before, the scent of pine filling the room. She didn't have time to warm up, so the first few squeaks and groans from the instrument made her wince, but somehow the magic of the piece grew in her fingers, in her frame, in the bow and the taut strings. She let the images come, of the wind ruffling the seagrass at the edge of the shore, of the stone hut on the beach, half washed away, of the waves stroking the sand. The drama built; she let the image of the boy come in painful flashes, floating just out of reach in the shallows. The music grew and surged, she was lost in it now, the strings biting her fingers, the buzzing of the bow. By the time she came to the end, tears were spilling down her face.

There was a long silence in the room, then applause. She had never been prouder of something she had created.

'Obviously, you could all do it better,' she said, handing the violin back to Théo.

'No, you just need to practise with musicians,' Kerry said, from the sofa next to Patrick.

'I've written parts,' she said, waving the hastily printed sheets.

'Well, that's handy,' Vasily said, removing the papers from her hand. 'Let's have a play with it tomorrow, straight after breakfast. It will help us all warm up for the programme rehearsal, before all your celebrity guests arrive.'

46

DECEMBER 1943

It took another week for Georgie to work through all the legible documents. The small amount of extra rent she accepted from Hugo and his rations had helped her to at least put a few things away for Christmas. She left Tommy at home with Hugo, working on carving a model out of driftwood.

She walked down to the quay, in knitted tights because the wind was biting. Dolly's hand was warm in hers as she skipped along beside her. Georgie waved at George Ellis, working on his boat, and he waved back. She smiled at Mrs Brundle, Clemmie's mother-in-law, who was working at the shop. This was her community now, even if they were a bit dubious about Hugo boarding at the cottage.

A young woman, who looked like she was in mid-pregnancy, was pushing a baby in a perambulator along the quay. Georgie now knew all two hundred residents of the island, and was puzzled by the newcomer.

She smiled. *I'm thinking like one of them.*

'Are you Mrs Preston?' the young woman asked, approaching her. 'I'm Jenofeve Macintosh, Mac's wife. I have some notes for you to transcribe. I work at the base, too.' She looked around the quiet quay. She smiled at Dolly. 'I wondered if we could talk?'

'Of course. Would you like to come back to the house?

'Could we go for a walk first? Anything to get my daughter to sleep.'

Georgie fell into step with the slim young woman, pale hair braided and wound around her head as Dolly ran ahead, pigtails flying.

Georgie glanced into the pram, seeing a baby staring back with cornflower-blue eyes and two teeth in a wide smile. 'She's lovely. What's her name?'

'Isabelle. She's nearly one. We think she's lovely but she screams like an air-raid siren if she's cross. She should be asleep. We left the house early to get here.'

'To see me?'

'My parents are the Huons – they live in one of the coast-guard cottages. I brought the baby over from Westy to see them. Mac said you should be on the island today, and asked me to give you the papers.'

'Thank you,' Georgie replied, looking ahead down the path as Dolly bent to pick up leaves.

'Is Hugo well?' Jenny asked.

'He's better, just that annoying cough.'

Jenny rummaged in her bag at the end of the pram. 'I forgot, the boatman told me to give this to you, too, to save the postman delivering it later.'

The postmark was from London. 'The last letter I got told me my husband was... The notification,' Georgie said, trying to keep her voice level. 'I'm a bit nervous to open this one.'

'Would you prefer to be alone?' They stopped at the gate to the churchyard and Dolly ran back.

'Come on, Mummy! There are sheep!'

'Yes, there are,' she said, looking down at the letter. 'No, stay, please. I should just do it, it's probably not important.'

It *was*, however, completely unexpected. Great-Aunt Alice had been admitted to hospital in Cheltenham and wanted to see Thomas as soon as possible.

Not a word about Dolly, she noticed, and nothing personal about herself. 'It's my husband's great-aunt,' she said slowly. 'She's unwell, it doesn't say how seriously. This was written two days ago by her solicitor. He wants me to contact him. But I can't just get off the island and take the children to Cheltenham.'

'Poor thing,' said Jenny. 'Is she very old?'

'She is. Jim used to say she was at least eighty, and that was years ago.' She folded the terse note into the envelope again. 'I'll call the solicitor. She never wrote back when I told her that Jim was…' She still couldn't easily say the word. 'Dead,' she finished. It jolted in her skull like a hammer blow.

'Perhaps she wants to leave the children something,' Jenny said, her face concerned. The baby started fussing, so they walked on slowly, Jenny bouncing the pram on its springs.

'Maybe,' Georgie said. She didn't hold out much hope. Dolly ran back and presented Georgie with a perfectly flat piece of slate off the shillet path along the beach. 'Thank you, darling.'

'Put it in your pocket,' Dolly demanded, and when the treasure was stowed, she ran off to find more.

'If I ever fall in the sea, I'll drown! My pockets are packed with Dolly's shells and stones…' The thought of Jim and Jago drowning stalled her voice again.

'I wanted to meet you after Mac spoke to Hugo.'

'Oh?'

'Hugo says you're terribly sad and lonely.' She smiled a little as she added, 'I think he knows a lot about loneliness. He has been for a long time. The islanders don't really trust him, you know.'

'I know he left his family and his fiancée back in Brittany.'

'We have some bad news for him,' Jenny said, wincing a little. 'He asked us to use our contacts to investigate what happened to his family. We've only just confirmed that his fiancée, Anna Le Brizec, died from her injuries. His sister survived, though. No one knows what happened to his parents – they have either been taken by the Nazis or they are deep under cover.'

Georgie let the news about Anna sink in. For a moment, a dark flicker of relief made her feel ashamed, disloyal. 'I am sorry.'

'Mac and I both think the news might be better coming from you,' Jenny said.

Georgie couldn't think straight, filled with emotion. Sadness for Jim, for Hugo, for herself and the young woman who Hugo had loved.

But something else too, curving darkly, uncomfortably, in the back of her mind. *He's free.*

47

PRESENT DAY, 6 DECEMBER

Amber walked back into Beehive Cottage early in the morning on the day of the concert, to pick up her violin. Ben was padding around in shorts and T-shirt, making coffee in the shiny new kitchen. The cottage felt warm and smelled of toast, but there was a hint of frost on the outside of the window.

'Oh, it's you,' he said, with an enormous yawn. 'I thought you'd stay at the manor today. I supposed I ought to get dressed.'

'You look very fetching in your negligee,' she said, smiling at him as she picked up her violin case from the corner of the living room. 'I just came back for this so I can join in rehearsals. I wasn't sure I'd be playing at first, but I caved to pressure. Just second violin, though. I've got Théo Ducasse playing first, he's amazing.'

'I'm glad you're playing,' he said. 'Because I really want to hear your lament played properly, with an audience. But I hoped you'd be out the front.'

'I'm not ready for that,' she said, accepting a cup of coffee from him. She had done nothing *but* play that melody; she wondered if she could have at least tried it. But it seemed daft to have one of the world's leading virtuosos right there and not ask him to play. The song deserved the very best. 'I'm in the quartet.'

Ben took his coffee upstairs. She opened the violin case and checked the instrument, realised it could do with a bit of attention and took it to the attic to clean the built-up rosin from the strings.

The new space-saving stairs going up to the loft were narrow and cramped, but the room opened out into a light space with views over the field behind and the spine of the island, and the vast expanse of sky. Grey clouds were dotting the pale blue sky, but the winds were light – perfect for the itinerary organised for the guests. Helicopter rides around the islands, and the hotel pool was freshly heated. A buffet would be laid out for them in the dining room. The musicians were free to mingle – it would hopefully be a treat for them, too. The rehearsal was in one of the barns, normally used as a yoga studio, so the other guests wouldn't hear or see anything before the concert. She got a cloth under the violin's strings to polish it, her mind drifting to the music she would soon be playing.

The bang, when it came, made her jump. Her heart thudded. 'Ben? Are you OK?' For a horrible moment she imagined him lying unconscious somewhere, maybe at the bottom of the stairs. 'Ben!'

Carefully placing the instrument back in its case on the shelf, she raced down the attic stairs to the landing.

'Amber!' He appeared on the ground floor, staring up at her. 'Was that you? It sounded like something collapsed.'

'I'm fine. What was that noise, then, was it next door?' He disappeared and she ran down the stairs in her socks, suddenly anxious about Betty.

She could hear him shouting outside Betty's door. 'She's not answering,' he said, a little pale. He banged again, shaking the frame.

She pushed in front of him. 'She never locks it,' she said, turning the handle to open the door. 'Betty!'

There was an acrid smell, like hot metal, inside the hallway.

'That's electrical smoke,' he said, as he charged up Betty's stairs two at a time. 'Bets!'

Amber checked the kitchen and looked around the back yard. Despite the early hour, Betty had already hung some laundry on an airer. Her handbag was missing from its usual spot by the door. 'I think she's gone out,' she said when he returned.

'Maybe down to the shop,' he said, hair flopping into his eyes. 'What was the bang, then? Nothing's out of place.'

'What is that smell?' she said, wrinkling her nose. The odour had grown stronger, even though the front door was standing open. The smoke alarm began shrieking overhead, deafening her. The stink of hot metal was everywhere.

'I'm going to check her electrical appliances upstairs, you do downstairs,' he shouted. 'Don't touch anything, in case it's live. Just switch everything off at the plug.'

She searched the ground floor, sniffing and switching off everything. Betty had very few appliances, just a TV with an old DVD player, a radio in the kitchen and kettle and toaster. The fridge-freezer looked and smelled OK, so Amber left that on. 'I can't find anything amiss,' she called back, looking through floral net curtains at the yard outside. 'The heaters all look fine, the cooker's off.'

But the curtains in Beehive Cottage did appear to be swaying.

He bounced downstairs. 'Well, something happened, her clock radio is blinking.' He pressed a button on the smoke alarm, which muted it, but another alarm was sounding, almost as loud. 'Maybe it was a random lightning strike.'

Her heart rate jumped into her throat as he met her eyes. 'Lightning? Like last time—' she said, racing to the door.

Smoke was pouring out of Beehive Cottage in great strands, billowing around her as she stared into a wall of darkness in the doorway of the cottage.

'Call 999,' Ben shouted, as he pulled his T-shirt over his face. 'Now!'

Amber had frozen, but she broke out of it to grab him as he hesitated in the doorway. 'No! Ben, you can't go in there. The fire brigade will be here soon.' The heat made her duck, the smell caught in her throat and she started coughing.

'I *am* the fire brigade,' he said, his face distorted as he tugged her further back.

'It's too dangerous. It's just a house,' she argued as something hit her in the pit of her stomach. Her Goulding.

It was as if Ben had read her mind. 'I've got to get your violin. Where is it?'

'In the attic,' and she had to grab him harder as he almost pulled her off her feet. 'Ben, no!' She wrestled her arms around his waist, pulled him back half a step. 'Please,' she said, in a softer voice. 'It's just a bit of wood. It's just stuff.'

'It's been your life. It sounds like...' He swallowed. 'It sounds like your soul, singing. You need it for the concert, too.'

Tears snapped into her eyes. 'That's the nicest thing anyone has ever said to me,' she said.

He stopped pulling against her and turn to face her. His kiss caught her by surprise, even as tears crowded her throat.

At one time, the prospect of losing the instrument would have felt like a gouge being carved into her heart. But now, in this moment, she was intoxicated by Ben. It felt right, he felt like the Goulding did to her. Part of her. It didn't require thinking or negotiation, she was just home.

'What on earth is going on?' They pulled apart. Betty had dropped her shopping bag and was staring in horror at the doorway to Beehive Cottage. 'Oh, not again.'

Now Ben was calling the fire brigade, and Amber hugged

Betty. 'Your house is fine, we checked. And with three feet of solid stone between our houses, it should be all right.'

'Like last time,' Betty said, her voice flat. 'It's that ghost, isn't it?' Then she looked up at Amber, eyes sharp, icy blue. 'Why were you kissing Ben?'

'Because I love him,' Amber said, her brain finding the words as she spoke. 'I'm *in* love with him.' Because it was true, because every cell in her body was drawn to him.

'You aren't going to leave him at the altar, too, are you?' Betty said, staring at the smoke, and moving back a little, pulling Amber with her. 'Come away, lovey, you don't need to see this. I know you love the house.'

Amber allowed Betty to pull her back into the gateway to the courtyard. She could see Ben bouncing on his toes, as if he still wanted to go in. She could feel the pull herself, imagined the flames licking at the two-hundred-year-old wood of her beloved violin, coiling around her beautiful new kitchen, racing up the old steps. Soon they heard boots stamping up the hill as two men appeared – boatman Tink, wearing overalls and holding a fire extinguisher, and another man she didn't know in uniform and carrying equipment.

'Tink, Ed, there's a violin in the attic, I need to get it!' Ben shouted.

'Out the way, Ben!' Tink shouted. 'Get into your gear.'

Ed grabbed the extinguisher and disappeared into the smoke, making Amber scream involuntarily. Then the world stood still as Ben donned the protective gear and followed Ed inside.

And as the smoke swirled about him, she saw the red flicker of flames at the base of the stairs.

48

APRIL 1944

Georgie opened the door to the sunny courtyard, to a woman in a tweed suit and matching hat, with scuffed but polished shoes and a sour expression. She looked about forty, but her lips were thin, pressed together as if judging the tiny house and its shabby door.

'Mrs Preston?' Georgie hardly had time to frown before the woman stepped forward. 'May I come in? Miss Bilsgate, Ministry of Pensions.'

'I would have preferred a prearranged appointment,' Georgie said, but the officious woman seemed to be coming in. Short of physically pushing her away, Georgie couldn't do anything, so she took a step back.

'This is a spot inspection,' the woman said, gazing around the room, looking at the low ceiling, the bleached fish box with Dolly's toys, a salvaged table serving as a desk and covered in papers. On it was the milk jug, jammed with daffodils that the children had picked for her from the school field. 'May I sit down?'

'Come through into the kitchen,' Georgie said, 'it's the only place with chairs.'

At least the place was clean, every utensil and pan washed up and put away – not difficult as they had so little. She waved Miss Bilsgate to one of the seats. She brushed a few grains of salt from the table into her hand and put them in the sink, then took the other seat. 'What is this about?'

'We have received intelligence that you have breached the conditions of the war widow's pension,' the woman said, looking uncomfortable in the stained chair.

'The pension I haven't yet received,' Georgie reminded her. 'Although the ship my husband was on went down in the Pacific over a year ago. Hundreds of miles from land.'

'We have received reports that you are behaving in a way that contravenes the regulations of the pension.'

'Reports? Who from?' Georgie couldn't believe any of her neighbours or anyone from the school would have made a complaint.

'I cannot discuss them personally. But someone whose opinion is highly regarded.'

'I see. Mrs Anstruther, the vicar's wife. A bitter, sad old tabby who has nothing else to do but judge her husband's congregation.'

'But you aren't *part* of her husband's congregation,' Miss Bilsgate said primly.

'I was unaware that the pension requires regular church attendance,' Georgie said smartly. 'In what way do you suspect I am contravening your requirements?'

'To put it delicately, Mrs Preston, you appear to have a gentleman friend.'

'What? No, Miss Bilsgate, I do not.'

She was drawn to Hugo, and would watch him when he was absorbed in their work; she thought he was beautiful. But she had never spoken to him in any way that could be considered inappropriate, and he treated her with great respect for her mourning. But she was starting to dream about just taking his hand, just feeling his warm skin, and seeing what happened.

'I have reports that your *friend*, the one you deny, is not only visiting but actually living here. Also, that you are about to inherit some money from an elderly relative, which may invalidate your claim.'

'Firstly, my son will inherit a sum, in trust for his education, not accessible to me or, in fact, to benefit my daughter.' Georgie folded her arms. She couldn't win this argument so she might as well enjoy it. 'In the year since my husband died, and in the six months since I stopped receiving any of his wages, I have been forced to take up paid employment and also rent out a spare room to a member of the local naval base. This has enabled me to feed my children, while the government left us to starve.'

Miss Bilsgate tittered angrily, a spot of red on each cheekbone. 'Some women have relied on charity instead of renting out their... homes. What kind of a message are you sending your children?'

'I hope I am teaching them to be resourceful and charitable, Miss Bilsgate,' Georgie said calmly. 'Mr Seznec was dangerously ill when we took him in, and he continues to suffer from ill health. In fact, he is recovering from an operation at the moment.'

The procedure, at the US base hospital on St Brannock's, had been to rebreak one of his shattered legs and wire the bones into a much better position. After two weeks of pain and with his leg in traction, Hugo now was encased in plaster from his hip to his toes. She could already see that his foot was in a better position, and his leg looked longer.

'Did I hear my name?' Hugo stood in the doorway, on crutches, having just come in from one of his short stumbles around the village.

'This is Miss Bilsgate,' Georgie explained. 'From the war

widow's pension department. Apparently, Mrs Anstruther believes I am living with a lover.'

She looked up at Hugo, arrested by the green-blue eyes, the intense gaze as he stared back at her. She held her breath, and she wouldn't have been surprised if time had stopped. All she could feel was her heart pounding in her throat.

'I see,' he said, finally.

'We don't need the stupid pension,' she managed to choke out, suddenly. 'I refuse to live like a penniless nun just to get a few shillings a week.'

Hugo raised his eyebrows. His mouth was turning up into a smile, different from any smile she had seen him give before. Uncomplicated, without his usual stress or pain.

'Hugo, I would like you to be my – gentleman friend.'

'I fell in love with you,' he murmured, 'the first time I met you—'

'Well!'

They ignored Miss Bilsgate's explosion.

Hugo's words resonated in her like a bell chiming in the same key. *Can I love two men at the same time?*

Yes, she could. Jim had always said love was unlimited, like a muscle. The more you loved, the easier it was to love more people.

And she was certain Jim would have wanted her to be happy.

'I love you, too, Hugo,' she said, smiling through her tears. 'I just need some time...'

'Take as much as you need,' he said. 'Let the children take their time to grieve their father, too. Should I move out?'

On some level, Georgie registered that Miss Bilsgate had stood, was saying something, was walking out of the kitchen and clunking the door shut behind her. Hugo got up to go after her.

'No! Stay with me...' She met him halfway, steadying him on his crutches, laughing through the tears and kissing him. She had wanted to do that for months now, but without truly allowing herself to imagine it.

He managed to get one arm around her. 'I don't think I can hide this now, if I stay here,' he said, his eyes as dark as a stormy sea. He was a lot taller than her, and she had to look up to stare at him openly, see the tiny scar by the corner of his mouth, the flecks of emerald in his eyes. 'What will Tommy say?'

Her heart lurched out of her euphoria at Tommy's name.

'Oh.' They pulled apart reluctantly, his hand staying on her shoulder. 'I don't know.'

'He needs a friend,' Hugo said. 'He already has a father.'

She shook her head. 'Jim went away after Dolly was born. We saw so little of him after that, and now he's been dead for a year. Tommy relies on you. It took him some time to adjust, but now he models himself on you.'

Hugo winced. 'An invalid.'

'A war hero, like his father,' she said softly. 'A kind and decent role model. We mustn't try to hide anything from him.'

'No.' He let go of Georgie and reached for the crutch leaning against the table. His face fell. 'Staying would be at the cost of your reputation.'

'This is a war,' she said, brushing her lips over his. 'And this is 1944 not 1920. Times are changing.'

49

PRESENT DAY, 6 DECEMBER

Amber walked onto the stage, giddy with energy and adrenaline, as the two-hour concert came to a close. She held her violin in her hand to the applause of the audience, ready to play her Lament. She walked over to her music stand, but Théo was in the way.

'What are you doing?' she hissed, trying to smile so the audience wouldn't see her confusion. She had brushed her long hair straight; it still smelled of smoke when she moved.

'This is your piece. Don't tell me you don't know it. You breathe it every time you talk about it.'

She stared at him as he smiled at her. 'I can't... I didn't rehearse it...'

'No. The rehearsal was terrible because you and I were playing the wrong parts.'

She turned, the idea spinning her brain. She hadn't rehearsed the lead, she couldn't remember the opening notes... But the music was there, waiting on the stand.

Amber turned towards the audience, to a sea of fairy lights and spotlights, dazzling for a moment. She fumbled in her pocket with her free hand for her introduction notes, and stepped up to the microphone.

'Thank you all so much for coming to support this brilliant cause. We want to finish with a piece of music I wrote here, on the islands, about a tragic thing that happened to a little boy, long ago. A boy called Jago Carney. He drowned on our neighbouring island, Morwen, a hundred years ago. No one was able to help him, but hopefully we can save another child here tonight by getting him the treatment he needs.'

She looked around the flushed faces, holding wine glasses, or phones to record her, seeing Zoe Allen smiling through tears beside a cameraman recording the concert, streaming live around the world.

'These islands are special places,' she said slowly. 'They create special people, and attract special people. This piece is called "The Lament of Jago Carney", and is dedicated to Kai Allen, the little boy we are fighting for. He's not well enough to join us, but many of you have met him.'

She returned to her place, caught the other performers' eyes and nodded twice, coming in on three with the first, plaintive notes. There was still a whiff of smokiness coming off her violin, after its rescue that morning from the scorched cottage.

Amber's belongings in the yard had made a pathetic pile; most of them had survived, as had the oiled paper-wrapped bundle from the old kitchen cupboard as it had been stored away from the flames. Most importantly, Ben had finally rescued the violin. Thankfully, there hadn't been any furniture to catch fire yet, but the consumer unit in the kitchen had burst into flames. It could have been a lot worse, but the damage was mostly cosmetic.

Grant had been loud in his condemnation of the set-up of

the shared electricity supply. 'I told you to get your supplier to sort that out!' he had shouted down the phone. 'Is there any more damage?'

'Smoke everywhere, and a bit of damage to the stairs. But it's OK. Anyway, I have to get to rehearsals. The concert's tonight.'

'I know, and I'll be there. But I ought to come over first and make sure everything is safe and look at Betty's electrics, too. I'll get Ben to help me, if you can spare him.'

She had grabbed what she needed and piled it into a bag. Tink, his face soot-stained, had smiled at her. 'I've got a boat if you need to get back.'

She breathed out a huff of relief. 'Oh, could you? I know the tide's falling fast.'

'It's almost a full moon tonight,' he said. 'The tides are higher. But your concert should have a fantastic backdrop of the moon over the water, if the weather stays fair.'

She had followed him down the hill, just waving quickly to Ben, wanting to go back and kiss him goodbye, thank you, lots of other thoughts and feelings.

He nodded back as she had headed down the hill, and she knew what he meant.

Not now. This is all about Kai.

Now, the memory of the fire faded as the music took her away again, soaring over Théo's second violin as he joined in, inviting the viola to echo...

A small part of her marvelled at how the piece all came together as it had in her head. She wrote this. She could write music. And, as she felt her fingers glide over the strings, measuring the pressure and movement of the bow, she knew she really could still play.

The cello and viola gave a powerful depth under the violins, a surprise blending together of the other instruments. Her fingers danced over the notes as she thought of them. They played in harmony, her mind singing through her violin. She felt dizzy, and had to remind herself to breathe through. The song reminded her of Kai as well as Jago. And of Ben.

Ben's kisses and the way he looked at her was the final piece of her puzzle. She had been looking for that all her life, the love that flowed through the music.

The lament was about Jago, but it was also about the people who had loved him, and the terror of the child who had inadvertently killed him. She was swaying, even dancing as the music washed over her, as the crescendo approached.

The quartet were perfectly together, filling the room with so much sound it felt pressurised. They finished together, too, in a huge wave of music, letting it break over the audience and leaving them stunned for a few seconds before the applause thundered back.

People were standing up, stamping, cheering, and Amber was laughing with relief and joy. She fell into a group hug with her friends.

She kissed Théo on the cheek. 'Thank you, thank you!'

'That's the first and last time I give away the limelight,' he said, kissing her back. 'Let's go.'

They walked to the front of the stage and took a bow. It was a strange mixed audience: celebrities, friends, musicians who had already performed, technicians and film crew. Her father was still clapping, tears streaming down his face; Elk and Charlotte and her boys from Morwen; Betty in a smart dress and coat; the firemen who had turned up at the last minute and been given tickets. At that moment, she loved them all.

After staying long enough for the film crew to catch more of the reaction, she put her instrument back in its case and slipped off into the curtains acting as wings to the impromptu stage.

The one that Ben had built for this moment. She knew he would always support her, whatever she wanted to do.

She slipped through the kitchen into the garden, freezing cold but beautiful, the stone balustrade glittering with the beginnings of a frost.

'Patrick.' He was hunched over in the middle of the terrace, but turned slowly.

'You were wonderful,' he said, his eyes glittering in the low light coming from the house. 'That's what's inside you. That's what I saw, fell in love with.'

'But—'

He didn't let her finish. 'But somehow all you did was struggle against the whole world.'

'I was ill. I was unhappy.' Other people's music, no matter how intoxicating, eluded her. In an ensemble or an orchestra, she was always constrained to do what other people chose, how they connected with the music. It had been a poor fit for her, she realised now, because nothing had ever given her the feeling that the lament had. She took a deep breath. 'I'm not going to say I'm sorry. I couldn't do anything else.'

'I know.' He looked out across the gardens he had worked on for months. 'I shouldn't have asked you to marry me. Deep down, I knew I wasn't making you happy.'

She put a hand on his arm for a moment and he turned to her. 'It's not just that, it's not that I wasn't happy with you. I know now that a relationship should be more than that, it goes so much deeper. I think you want more than that, too.'

'So this really is goodbye,' he said.

She stared at the gleam in his eyes, the sad curve of his mouth. 'Now you will be free to find the person you want,' she said. 'And so will I.'

'Let's not pretend,' he said, his voice sharp, 'that you haven't already found him.'

And she had. But it was different. Ben was occupying a

different place in her heart, one she hadn't even known was there, where the music bled into people and emotions.

'I hope so,' she said, turning away, breathing in the sharp air as she started to shiver. Now she needed to find Ben, to celebrate this moment with him. 'But the important thing is what we did for Kai, all of us.'

EPILOGUE

Amber arranged the tattered pages into some sort of order inside their oiled card shell on the table in the kitchen in Beehive Cottage. The sun was spilling in from the living room, now replastered and smelling of fresh paint, and a bee buzzed in and out of the open window. 'Fifteen, sixteen, where's seventeen... Oh, it's missing.'

'What are you doing?' Ben padded in, fresh from the shower, in jeans and T-shirt.

'Trying to make sense of the papers that were locked in the kitchen cupboard. I had to cut the binding open in the end. It's a draft of a book by the woman who used to live here, Georgina.'

Ben sat on the sofa, stretched out, made a face. 'It smells bad.'

'It's just rancid oil and smoke. Once I've got them in some sort of order, I'll photocopy them so they won't smell so much. I think the original belongs in a museum.' She picked up the slim volume from her father's library. 'Betty told me about it, her mum had been friends with Georgina back then, and then I found a copy back at the manor. It's a light-hearted history of living on Morwen during the war. *And,*' she said triumphantly, 'she lived *here.* This very cottage.'

'And that's what you've found, a draft of the book?'

'No. More than that, what I've found is the *whole* story. She just published a few anecdotes, but this is the real deal, her actual memoir. She worked for the intelligence services with a Frenchman, Hugo Seznec. If that's how you pronounce it.' She pulled page six over to her. 'Listen to this: *When my husband James went missing, I was lost, terrified for myself and the children. We had nowhere to go and no money to live on. Jim's wages stopped before we reached the island. We were penniless.*' She sat back, letting Georgina's vivid voice speak again. '*But we found ourselves, our real selves, how resourceful we all were, once we had to be. We created a home, I found work. Thomas worked hard for, and achieved entry into a prestigious school, and Dolly was comfortable growing up on the island.*'

'This is *the* James Preston? The boy who drowned Jago Carney?'

'It must be. Listen.' She turned over more pages until she reached a page with Hugo's name all over it.

'*I didn't realise I could love two men, side by side. My sadness at Jim's death, as well as our joyful memories of him, became a topic of conversation most days. Hugo, on that first Christmas, laid an extra place at the table for Jim, and wouldn't allow any argument. I found it comforting, I know Tommy did, too.*'

'I'm just looking up this Hugo Seznec,' Ben said, scrolling through his phone. 'He married Mrs Georgina Preston after the war. He became a barrister and they moved to London in the fifties. Did she keep her name?'

'Maybe. She seemed like a formidable person. Is there anything about her children?' Amber looked through the pages for more mentions of Hugo.

'Oh. There's an obituary. *Mrs Georgina Preston-Seznec,*

known to everyone as Georgie, died 3 January 2001, widow of Hugo Seznec QC of Brittany... Wow, it's a long obituary, I'll send you a copy. *Survived by her son, the Right Reverend Thomas James Preston, Bishop of Lichfield* – wow – *Dorothy Preston, now Blackburn, and Marigold Preston-Seznec, now Lippett.*'

'Wow. A bishop? She writes about her son when he was still a kid.' Tommy came across as just a little scamp in the prose, falling in the sea and going out for rabbits with an air rifle. She pushed the papers away for a moment and rubbed her eyes. 'The writing is so small, they must have been saving paper.' She smiled at him. 'How's the song going?'

Ben made a face and put his hands over his eyes. 'It's embarrassing,' he said. 'I'm going over to Elk's this evening to play around again, put down a few tracks.'

'It's going to be released,' Amber said. 'It isn't my fault the record company loved the demo we recorded so much they want you to sing on it. And you did write half the words.'

'You wrote *all* the music. You should have to sing it.' He sighed. 'They'll get a proper singer to release it as a single, anyway.'

'I'll be too busy playing the violin. The single will make money for the charity even if you do it. The video we put out went viral.' They had recorded it in the attic on her phone, just the two of them. It had managed a million views and raised thousands more for the fund, enough for several more patients to benefit.

'How's Kai doing?'

She smiled. 'He's just started bouncing on the trampoline again, but Zoe makes him wear a bike helmet. Just in case. Elk's started him on the ukulele, Zoe and Liam haven't thanked me for that.'

'He could barely stand before. And they think it's gone?'

'If not, they've bought him a lot of time.' She went back to her notes, frowning at an odd line on the page she was reading. 'Where's that little book?'

He picked it up and read the title. '*Stories of an Island in Wartime* by Georgina Preston.'

'It's full of sweet stories about growing vegetables and the chickens getting out and invading the church, that sort of thing,' she said. 'But *this* old manuscript we found in the kitchen is serious stuff. Listen to this. *Tonight, Hugo has to join a mission to retrieve operatives and refugees from Plouguerneau. This is so much harder when I know what he's doing, whereas with Jim I could imagine him comfortable in a bunk somewhere, or meeting people in hotels. I had no idea how dangerous intelligence work is. I'm terrified, but they need to be ready.*' She looked up. 'When was D-Day?'

He looked it up on his phone. 'Sixth of June, 1944.'

'This is the end of April,' she said, in a quiet voice, choked up. It felt like she knew these people – she had Georgie's teaspoon in her cutlery drawer, she'd seen the picture of her holding Betty as a baby. She had been real. She had sat in this space in front of the stove. 'She knew what could go wrong,' she murmured. 'She knew exactly what losing him would feel like.'

'Hm?' he said, walking over to her. 'You're getting all emotional over this, aren't you?' He leaned down to kiss her and she clung to him for a moment.

'It *is* emotional.' She brushed her hand over her wet eyes. 'I suppose she couldn't share these stories or publish them, not while it was top secret.'

'She probably could have done by the time she died,' he said, crouching down next to her, putting an arm around her.

'She'd signed the Official Secrets Act,' Amber said, looking at the first page. 'That's what this says – I was struggling with the dirt and mould, I couldn't read it at first. *An account of the events of the last year of the war, on Morwen, Atlantic Islands.*'

He crouched down beside her as she sat at the chair, a bit

numb. She could feel his warmth around her. He had the small book. 'This is a photo of Hugo. He looked a bit like a pirate, didn't he? Quite a looker.'

She took the page, staring at Hugo as he stared back down the camera, a little girl leaning against him, a pipe in the corner of his mouth, dark hair over piercing eyes.

'He was French,' she said, looking at the caption. 'This was a year after the end of the war, so we know he survived his mission. But Georgie didn't know that when she was writing. She knew he could have been killed. She could have been widowed again.'

'He could have been shot, as a spy,' Ben said softly. 'But he wasn't. He married the woman of his dreams, they had a baby and they lived happily ever after. Sometimes you just have to be prepared to take the risk. Take the chance.'

'Like us,' she said, turning to look into his eyes, taking his warm hand between both of hers. 'We will be happy, won't we?'

'I think so.' He pressed a kiss into her palm. 'I know so.'

He was speaking to her as if she was hurt, or frightened. Maybe she was, after her life had unravelled before. But Georgie had got on with life when her husband died, when her whole world changed, and she had built a new love, a new life.

Right now, Ben was the person Amber loved, and her future was filled with possibilities.

A LETTER FROM REBECCA

Dear Reader,

I'm so glad you found *The Girl in the Cottage by the Sea*. I hope you enjoyed Amber's journey to wholeness and love through the island of Morwen and music. I also loved following one of many thousands of war widows as Georgie reclaimed her power and future with her children. If you enjoyed their stories, you can keep in touch with other Island Cottage stories by following the link below. Your email will never be shared and you can unsubscribe at any time.

www.bookouture.com/rebecca-alexander

I think islands are magical. Small communities are changed by every birth, marriage or death. Even one new person can transform them, by bringing in new ideas and skills, other perspectives, other troubles. This whole series has been about the ripples that are created by people rediscovering themselves in an isolated place where the people depend on each other, where the bonds of love and friendship form.

My imaginary island of Morwen is based on the village where I live, and many wonderful islands all around the south-west of England, like Lundy, Guernsey, St George's and St Agnes. The cobbled alleys, narrow streets and tiny cottages all seemed to have their own stories – and histories. I urge you to find a favourite island of your own.

If you want to support me and the Island Cottage books, it's always helpful to write a review. This also helps me develop and polish future stories! You can contact me directly via my website or Twitter.

Thank you and happy reading,

Rebecca

www.rebecca-alexander.co.uk

 x.com/RebAlexander1

ACKNOWLEDGEMENTS

This book wouldn't be in your hands without a great deal of guidance and support from my wonderful editor, Rhianna Louise. I enjoyed writing *The Girl in the Cottage by the Sea*, and expert editing helped me make it into a stronger story, and allowed the characters speak louder and clearer.

Thank you also to the wonderful team at Bookouture, for continuing the process of refining the novel by copy editing and proofreading. They also produce the lovely covers and understand all the marketing business. I am truly grateful.

Much gratitude goes to my son Carey Bave, my first reader, who knows all my books. He keeps me writing, asks important questions, and advocates for the characters all the way.

And as always, much gratitude goes to my husband, Russell, who also loves island (and village) living and gives me space and solitude to write. His passion for music inspired me to create this book.

I want to give a shout out to every parent who has a sick child, whether like Kai or with a chronic illness. My daughter wrestled with a brain tumour, and taught me that any life, no matter how short, can be packed with laughter and love.

PUBLISHING TEAM

Turning a manuscript into a book requires the efforts of many people. The publishing team at Bookouture would like to acknowledge everyone who contributed to this publication.

Commercial
Lauren Morrissette
Hannah Richmond
Imogen Allport

Cover design
Debbie Clement

Data and analysis
Mark Alder
Mohamed Bussuri

Editorial
Rhianna Louise
Lizzie Brien

Copyeditor
Angela Snowden

Proofreader
Liz Hatherell

Printed in Great Britain
by Amazon